BROKEN FATE

BY

JENNIFER DERRICK

ISBN:978-1-63422-165-8
Cover Design by: Marya Heiman
Typography by: Courtney Nuckels
Editing by: Cynthia Shepp

For more information about our content disclosure, please
utilize the QR code above with your smart phone or visit
us at
www.CleanTeenPublishing.com.

For Jimmy. I may be a writer, but I can never put into words all that you mean to me.

And for Mom and Dad, you started me on the path and I am forever grateful.

CHAPTER 1

SNIP. DEAD GUY. SNIP, SNIP. **ANOTHER DEAD GUY AND HIS WIFE.** *Snip.* Along with their son. The dog's dying tonight, too, in the raging house fire that's killing his owners, but at least executing animals isn't my responsibility. My shears hover over the next lifeline and I pause for a moment, doing some quick math in my head. The son was my sixty-six billionth kill. I've reached another milestone in my career tonight.

I don't celebrate, though. *Snip.* While adding another billion to my total is impressive, I stopped celebrating after five-billion kills because it just seemed like spiking the ball in the end zone in front of the other team's players when the score was already eighty to nothing. It's rude. It's not like killing is difficult for me or that the humans can challenge me in any way. Snip, and you're dead. It's a job, not an accomplishment. *Snip, snip, snip.*

I'm the McDonald's of Death. I really should get a light-up sign for the front yard that says, *Billions and Billions Killed.* Just like McDonald's serves as many people as it can, as quickly as it can, my job is to put 'em on the assembly line, kill 'em, and serve 'em up to Hades. The difference is that McDonald's pays their workers. I don't get anything except immortality, which,

1

when you consider the monotony of an infinite lifespan spent doing the same crappy job, isn't anything to get excited about.

It's been an unusually busy day for me, and I'm up to my calves in lifeline pieces. There's a war going on in the Middle East, a train derailment in Japan, a bomb in a hotel in Germany, and a cruise ship sinking off the coast of Florida. Not to mention all the humans simply dropping dead from natural causes and accidents. I chop through a fistful of lines and wonder what possessed my sister, Lacey, also known as Lachesis, to mark this many humans for death on this one day. She knows this kind of carnage forces me to create horrible disasters so I can kill the most humans in the least amount of time. I don't enjoy it, but killing hundreds at one time is the only way I can keep up on days like this. She was either seriously pissed off at the human race or at me the day she drew up this schedule. Knowing Lacey, I'm betting it's the latter.

I'm finally nearing the end of this miserable day. I have one person left to kill, and she's the one I've been dreading the most. Amy Brickhouse, the most popular and cruel girl in school, is going to die tonight when she wraps her car around a tree. I'm not dreading it because I care about the girl, but because her death is going to make my life a living hell at school for a few days and I don't need any more drama in my life.

I glance at the digital clock hanging next to the door. The large red numbers read 01:33:45 AM. Amy is scheduled to die in a little over five minutes. Once I kill her, I can finally go to bed. While I wait, I sweep up some lifelines and put them into an oak box with a picture of my shears burned into the lid. I haul the box to the back of the room where I pile it with about a hundred others just like it, mentally reminding myself to put them in the chute and send them to Thanatos before I go to bed. He needs to start picking these souls up tonight and escorting them to the Underworld. Otherwise, there are going to be a lot of ghosts terrorizing the humans tomorrow.

That's what ghosts are, you know. They are souls that haven't yet been escorted to the Underworld. Thanatos usually does a good job of keeping the ghost population down, but sometimes he gets behind. Or lazy. Those souls left behind wander around, looking for the remnants of their old lives. They're just lost, but the humans freak out and scream about being haunted. We who run the death business try to keep the freak outs to a minimum, but we're not perfect. Sometimes, Thanatos likes to mess with the humans and leave a few ghosts around intentionally. When you do the same monotonous job for thousands of years, you start to do strange things.

Walking back to the front of the room, I check the clock again. *One minute.* I pick my shears up off the table and snip them twice in my hand, trying to work out the growing cramp brought on by overwork. It's a wonder I don't have carpal tunnel syndrome by now.

Amy's lifeline whizzes into place before me, thanks to the computerized racks that are programmed to bring each lifeline to the front of the room when it's time for me to cut it. I move my shears into position over her line and watch the clock. Three. Two. One.

Snip.

Amy's line falls to the floor, landing on the heap of lines already there. Reaching up, I unclip the other half of her line from the rack and drop it onto the floor, too. I'm done for the night. Sweeping the remaining lifelines into piles, I check under the desk and in the corners to make sure I don't miss any. I transfer each pile into a box and lug the boxes to the back of the room.

Dropping the boxes I'm carrying atop the closest pile, I thread my way through to the back of the room where a small, metal door is set into the wall. I open the door, place two boxes into the opening, shut the door, and push the green button on the wall. A loud whoosh sounds, and the boxes are on their way to Thanatos.

I repeat this process until there are no boxes left. Finally, I can head to bed. Placing my shears carefully in their protective box, I lock it in the bottom drawer of my desk. I open the door

3

to my workroom, stepping into the larger workspace that Lacey and my other sister, Chloe, also known as Clotho, share. It swings shut behind me, and I turn to make certain the security panel blinks red, indicating the lock is engaged.

It's a long walk, the equivalent of two city blocks, from my workroom to the stairs that lead up into our house, and I massage my aching hand as I walk. I trudge up the stairs and into our kitchen. The fridge is right in front of me. I think about getting something to eat but decide I want my bed more than food.

I tiptoe past my sisters' rooms to the bathroom and dry swallow two aspirin, hoping they will ease the aches in my hand and head. Crossing the hall to my bedroom, I flop onto the bed, still fully dressed. Morning will come soon, and, with it, the fallout from Amy's death. I need rest before I can deal with either.

When I pull into the parking lot at school the next morning, I see that my fellow students haven't wasted any time in creating a shrine to Amy. The early spring sunshine bounces off the flowers and Mylar balloons that are already taking over her parking space. It's bright, festive, and totally out of place. Death isn't festive. Well, it can be in a select few cases, but I'm not supposed to admit that.

I pull my midnight-blue, 1959 Thunderbird into my assigned space, but I don't get out of the car until my sisters are parked on either side of me. The kids at school always wonder why we don't carpool. We laugh it off as an inability to settle on one radio station, but the truth is that Creation, Destiny, and Death operate on very different schedules. We rarely leave or arrive at school together. Today is a rare exception.

The three of us push through the mass of grieving students loitering outside the front doors, show our IDs to the security guard, and head inside the school. On every hall, kids are crying, talking in whispers, and hugging each other. Some kids are even physically supporting others who are about to collapse under the weight of shock and grief. I shake my head. The over-the-top human response to death always disgusts me. Death is a fact of life, so why all the drama? Just accept it and move on.

"Well, it's going to be one of those days," Lacey says. "Better glum up. Look sad, blend in."

"I know," Chloe says. "It'll be hard, though. She wasn't a nice person."

"No, she wasn't," I add. "She accomplished nothing in her seventeen years except to make other people's lives miserable."

"Well, just try not to act like you enjoyed ending her life too much," Lacey reminds me.

I smile at her. "Do I ever? At least in public?"

"Nope, and that's what makes you great," Chloe says, leading the way to our lockers.

Even as I snipped her line last night, I knew the mourning for Amy would be extreme. Death doesn't happen often in high school. When it does, it's a big deal, although it's a bigger deal when the dead person was popular. Everyone mourns, even if they didn't care about or even know the deceased. Each person has to grieve harder than the one before, just to prove their own life matters.

I grab my books out of my locker and sigh as the herd of kids flows past me, talking of nothing but Amy.

"I've known her since the fifth grade," says one boy to another as they pass my locker.

"Yeah, well, I helped her with her physics homework last week," says the other boy, as if that forms a greater bond than six years' acquaintance. As if either of these two dorky kids were ever more important than a gnat to Amy.

I know this one-upmanship of grief will play out in the halls and even in the teachers' lounge in the coming days. Everyone, even the people who hated Amy, will try to grab some of her star power through imagined and exaggerated dealings with her. She will become a hero even though she doesn't deserve to be.

5

Sickening behavior, but it's typical of the human reaction to death.

Slamming my locker shut, I heft my backpack onto one shoulder. I arrange my face and posture into what I hope is a grieving, pained look. It probably looks more like constipation, but it's the best I can do.

I say goodbye to my sisters and walk toward my first class, keeping my head down and shoulders hunched so no one will see that I'm not quite sad enough. Perhaps they'll just think that I'm bowed with grief.

I bump into someone and look up to see Sarah Moore, co-captain of the cheerleaders, in front of me.

"It's just terrible, isn't it?" she says, and then heaves a big sigh. "At least Amy is an angel now." She drops her face into her hands and sobs.

"Yeah, terrible," I mutter as I push past Sarah. I have to get away before I burst out laughing at the thought of awful Amy as an angel. Besides, I'm pretty sure that since Sarah will now inherit Amy's kingdom of popularity, she's not exactly as broken up about her death as she wants everyone to believe.

Even with some extra dawdling in the halls and reading the announcement board twice, I'm early to English class. Without looking at the other kids, I slide into my seat and pull out my copy of *Anna Karenina*, opening it to a random page. I hunch over my book, trying to look like I'm hurrying to finish the assigned reading before class begins. Never mind that I've read this book fifteen times for fifteen different English classes and practically have it memorized. I just don't want to be drawn into fake reminiscences by kids who think that grief should be a shared experience.

As the students filter into the classroom, they gather in clumps to talk about the horrible news. A few minutes before class starts, though, the hum of conversation shifts from whispered remembrance to speculation. I look up from my book to see what could possibly distract the kids from their grief.

A new kid stands in the classroom doorway. His thick, sandy-brown hair hangs just past his chin, curling a bit where it brushes the collar of his polo shirt. His lower lip protrudes in a slight pout. The smallness of his upper lip accentuates the problem. On anyone else, that mouth would look ridiculous. Fortunately for him, his straight nose and square jaw are proportioned just right to negate the flaw and make him cute, if not stunning. The kid's attractive, but he's certainly not model perfect.

Cocking his head, he looks around the room, seeking a vacant seat. He doesn't seem uncomfortable, even though everyone is staring at him. Instead, he stares back, seeming completely at ease, as though he's known these kids all his life. Most kids would just slink into the nearest seat and pretend to be oblivious to the whispers and stares, even as their faces turned bright red.

Not this kid. He walks confidently into the room, drops his new student form on Mrs. Lapp's desk, and slides into the empty seat next to mine. After setting out his pen and notebook, he turns in his seat to face me.

"Hi, I'm Alex Martin," he says, holding out his hand for me to shake. He smiles as he speaks and the pout disappears, leaving an open, friendly face. Up close, his eyes are a strange greenish-blue with a hint of brown mixed in. It's like looking into a shallow ocean where you can see the sand through the water.

"Sophie. Sophie Moraine," I answer, taking his hand. Who shakes hands these days, especially among kids? I don't think a boy has shaken my hand since the nineteenth century. Someone has obviously drilled some manners into this boy, and I'm charmed in spite of myself.

He rests his elbow on the back of his chair and stretches his legs out in front of him, looking for all the world like he's been in this school forever.

"So, Sophie, is this school always so depressed? The lines to see the guidance counselors are backed up down the hallway with crying kids. I had to cut in line to get my paperwork so I wouldn't be late to class. Nearly started a riot. I hope my starting school here hasn't brought everyone to tears," he jokes.

7

"Ha. You're a funny guy," I say. "Seriously, though. The most popular girl in school died last night. She crashed her car into a tree."

His face instantly changes into the typical expression of sadness. "That's sad. You don't seem bothered, though," Alex says. "Did you know her at all?"

I lean in closer to him so I can whisper my answer. When I do, I catch a faint whiff of his cologne. It's clean and pleasant. Not the stinky, overbearing stuff that most of the boys wear.

"I knew her. She was mean, spiteful, and vindictive, and she was doing a hundred-and-two miles an hour, drunk, on a curvy road in the rain. She kind of asked for it, don't you think?"

"Maybe so, but someone's still dead. It's a sad thing when a life ends. You should show more respect."

I bristle at his subtle rebuke. What does this boy know of death?

"I see too much death every day to worry about the death of one mean little girl," I say, and then I immediately want to take it back. I've said too much to this stranger.

"What do you mean?" Alex asks.

I'm saved from a lie or evasion when Mrs. Lapp calls the class to order. I turn toward the front, but Alex keeps his body angled toward mine. He watches me the whole period. I keep my head turned away from him or stare down at my notebook, but I can feel him watching me whenever Mrs. Lapp's attention is elsewhere. It makes me itch to get away from him.

Great. Curiosity about me is something I can't afford to encourage. I avoid talking to my classmates for just this reason. It's not always that I don't want to get involved... I just can't. Getting involved leads to questions I can't possibly answer and attention I cannot repay.

When class is over, Alex follows me out into the hallway. I try to hustle on down the hall and away from him, but the slow-moving traffic keeps me pinned close to him.

"What did you mean earlier? That you see too much death?" he asks.

"Nothing. It was just a comment."

"I don't think so. That kind of statement has to be explained. Do you work in a morgue or something?" His tone is light, joking, but I know there's a serious question in there, and he wants an answer.

"No. Look, it just came out wrong. All I meant was that people die. It happens. I'm not going to get worked up about it, particularly when the dead person was a horrible human being." I lower my voice so those around us won't hear my betrayal of Amy's sainted memory.

He shakes his head. "That's harsh."

I shrug. "You get your arm slammed in a locker because some popular girl thinks she's a gift to the gods and you might feel differently," I say.

Alex looks down at me as we walk, and I can tell he doesn't believe I misspoke earlier. I'm not a good liar, and I know it. My poker face would lose me millions in a casino. At least he has the good manners to drop it.

"So, can you tell me how to get to the gym?" he asks.

I don't want to be a complete asshole to the kid, so I choke back my first response, which is to tell him to find it himself. Instead, I try to be polite.

"You go down this hall to the end and turn right, then take the next left. Go down the stairs at the end of that hall, and you'll end up in front of the locker room. Oh, and don't let anyone tell you to take the elevator. There isn't one you're allowed to use," I add, and then curse myself for being friendly.

I'm off my groove today, I think. The stupid behavior of my classmates must be getting to me. Usually, I wouldn't even speak to a human kid like Alex. Yet, here I am, helping him. I must be desperate to find someone else who isn't flogging themselves over Amy's death.

Alex watches me, probably trying to figure out what's wrong with me, too. I look away from him, instead watching the kids crossing the quad outside the windows. I hope he'll just walk away.

He touches my arm and says, "Thanks. See you later."

Watching his back as he walks down the hall, I hold my hand over the place on my arm that he touched. I know it's in my head, but it feels warmer than the rest of me. When he turns the corner, I exhale. Hopefully, he'll forget my comment by tomorrow. Most likely, he'll find other kids more appealing as the day goes on and he'll forget about me. Humans don't have long attention spans. That should work in my favor.

I push Alex Martin out of my mind and suffer through the rest of my morning classes. Even the teachers are sniffling through their lessons, and it makes me want to toss a chair through a window or pull a fire alarm. Anything to get them to stop and focus on something that's actually important.

At lunch I sit at my usual table, alone, as I prefer. Chloe and Lacey have the next lunch period, so I usually put my nose in a book and try to ignore the chaos around me. In the fall and late spring, I can escape to the yard outside, but though it's early March and spring is coming, it isn't here yet and it's too cool to sit outside.

Today is actually a decent day to be stuck in the cafeteria because all the kids are quiet, slumped into despair. Other than the occasional wailing sob, it's easy to read since I don't have to deal with the usual clatter and chatter from the other kids.

Lost in my copy of *The Eye of the World*, I don't notice anyone else until a blue cafeteria tray appears in my field of vision. I look up to see Alex Martin standing in front of me.

"Can I join you?" he asks.

"No," I say, immediately seeing the hurt on his face. I feel like I've kicked a puppy.

He turns and starts looking for another table with an empty seat. It's sad to watch him size up and dismiss the other tables. Jocks? *Nope.* Geeks? *Nope.* Burn-outs? *Nope.* Cheerleaders? *Absolutely not.* Being a mid-year transfer, he's as much of an outcast as I am. The other kids glance at him before quickly looking away. No one offers him a chair. I need to get rid of this boy, but I don't have to be cruel. I'm not like Amy.

"Oh, all right. Just be quiet," I say, pushing my own tray out of the way so he can put his down.

Relief and gratitude spread across his face. He sits down across from me and eats his pizza. I go back to my book, making it clear, I hope, that I don't want conversation.

After a few minutes, Alex pulls out his schedule, reads over it, and says, "I have Mr. Sturdivant for history next period. Anything I should know?"

I huff and slap my book shut, pushing it off to the side. Obviously, Alex is one of those people who is uncomfortable with silence and ignores the requests of others to be quiet. I can forget reading. Alex is likely to babble to himself if necessary to keep the silence from engulfing him.

"Do you like history?" I ask, folding my arms on the table and leaning forward.

"It's my favorite subject," he says.

"Then you'll like Mr. Sturdivant. He actually talks about why events happened instead of just making you memorize a bunch of names and dates. His exams are all essay, though, so most kids hate him."

"Sounds like my kind of teacher," he says. "I prefer to think."

I wait, knowing there will be more questions. With extroverts like Alex, there always are. I don't have to wait long.

"Have you lived here all your life?" he asks.

I chuckle. If only he knew exactly how long that was. Asheville, North Carolina didn't exist when my life began.

"No," I say. "We moved here a few years ago. We move around a lot."

"Military brat?"

"No. My mother gets restless. She doesn't like to stay in one place for long."

It's as good an explanation as anything else, and somewhat true. My mother does tend to get restless if left in one place too long. That isn't the real reason we move around so much, of course, but I'm prohibited from telling Alex any truth about myself.

"I've lived in Asheville my whole life," he says. "I only transferred here because there was an incident at my old school. I used to go to Saint Luke's."

"The boarding school. What kind of incident? Smoking? Drinking? Drugs? Vandalism? Did you get a girl pregnant?" I ask, running down the usual *incidents* that get kids transferred. "Were you the resident bad boy?"

"Depends on your interpretation of events," he says. "I drove a car through the headmaster's office one night."

Interested, I lift my head to look at him. He doesn't seem upset about his actions, merely indifferent.

"Well, that's a new one," I say.

He shrugs.

"Were you hurt?" I ask, and then follow it up with, "Why would you do something like that?"

"Not seriously, and I did it because I felt like it. I got some bad news and couldn't deal with it. I flipped out. I was kind of hoping I might die, but that didn't work out."

"So you tried to kill yourself?"

"Well, suicide wasn't my primary goal, but I wouldn't have been upset if it had happened. Of course, now I realize it was stupid, but at the time—" He trails off.

I could tell him that suicide is usually a waste of time. For it to work, I have to choose suicide as the person's manner of death and the attempt has to occur on their assigned death date. Unless those two conditions are met, the best someone can hope for is to avoid seriously injuring themselves. The worst case is that the attempt fails, and the person ends up on life support for the rest of their life. But I don't try to explain that to Alex.

"Amazing you didn't end up in jail," I say instead.

"Well, that's where the school wanted to send me. But I passed all the toxicology screenings and mental evaluations, so they settled for expulsion on the DA's recommendation."

"Huh. You probably know my mother, then. Thelma Moraine. She's the DA," I say.

"Ms. Moraine. Yeah, I know her. I thought your last name

sounded familiar. Your mom's cool. Tell her thanks for me. She really could have screwed me over, but she didn't."

"She'll appreciate that. But what was so bad that you felt the need to drive a car through a building?" I ask.

I've seen a lot of things in my three-thousand-plus years, but the picture of this seemingly normal, polite, somewhat preppy kid driving a car through a school building isn't coming together for me.

"Lots of stuff that I don't want to talk about," he says.

"That's fine. I'm not into forcing people to talk about themselves."

"Thanks. Maybe I'll tell you sometime."

I nod and reach for my book, but I stop when he starts to speak again. *For Zeus' sake, shut up,* I think.

"So, what's your story?" he asks, mimicking my posture by folding his arms on the table and leaning toward me.

"I don't have one," I say, moving away from him.

"You must. I've only been here half a day, and I've already heard rumors that you're depressed, crazy, possibly schizophrenic or, at best, simply rude. There's got to be a story behind that."

"Then why are you sitting with me?" I challenge. "If I'm so defective, you're going to get a reputation for consorting with the crazy girl. You don't want that kind of rep on your first day here. You don't seem shy. Go make friends with the cool kids."

"I don't care because I don't think you're any of those things. A little rude maybe," he amends with a smile. "It's my experience that people who are judged to be crazy are simply different from the rest of the herd. I like different, though, and I despise normal. If no one here thinks you're normal, then that makes you interesting to me."

So he thinks I'm some kind of interesting specimen who needs careful observation. That's not good. I can't have him watching me too closely. Best to end it right here. I give him what I hope is my most dismissive look.

"So I can add abnormal and interesting to, what was it? Oh, yeah. Rude, crazy, and depressed," I say, and I am gratified to

13

see him flinch from the coldness in my voice.

"Well, not in a bad way," he says. "I just meant——"

"I know what you meant," I snap. "I'm definitely not normal, but let's just say I find people intolerable and I have a lot going on that doesn't leave me time for the petty bullshit that is high school, or the narrow-minded kids who populate it. Especially kids who are stupid enough to try to commit suicide by driving through school buildings."

"I'm not intolerable," he says. "Or narrow-minded. Or stupid. Maybe you'll find that out if you can get past your condescension long enough to spend some time with a lowly worm like me. I might teach you a few things. I dare you," he adds with a wicked smile so impish that I almost smile back.

I sigh. Is he mentally challenged? A glutton for punishment? This kid isn't getting the message. How mean do I have to be to get rid of him? I can't explain to him that his very humanity, with all of its frailties and inconsistencies, makes him intolerable to me.

"Look, Alex, I'm sure you're a nice guy and all, but you have to understand I can't be your friend, so just get that through your head."

"Can't or won't?" he asks.

I pinch the bridge of my nose to tamp down the insulting reply that comes to mind. "Just leave me alone. I'm not unhappy, and I don't need to be fixed."

He holds up both hands to ward off my next attack. "Who said anything about fixing you? I don't think there's anything wrong with you."

"You haven't known me long enough to make that judgement," I say. "And it would be a mistake to think that I'm someone you want to hang out with."

"Then it's my mistake to make. I think you and I might be more similar than you think."

"I doubt that."

We sit in silence for a few moments, watching each other across the table. I'm waiting for him to realize that he doesn't

14

want to be near me, get up, and leave. He doesn't.

Instead, he picks up my discarded book. "I just finished this series," he says, leafing through it. "You'll love the ending."

"Don't spoil it. And don't lose my place," I say, grabbing for the book before my bookmark falls out.

"I won't. Just pointing out that we at least have similar tastes in reading material. Who knows what other interests we might share?"

He hands the book to me across the table. I snatch it from him and roll my eyes. *Please*. As if I have the time or inclination to share anything with this boy.

"Tell me something," he says when I don't immediately begin searching for our similarities.

"What?"

"How'd you know Amy was drunk?"

"Drunk?" I ask.

"Yeah. This morning, you told me she was drunk when she hit the tree. But you seem to be the only person in possession of that bit of knowledge. I've heard the story from probably two dozen people today, and they were all shocked to hear that. Said it hasn't been in the news reports."

Well, crap. I let slip the one detail that wasn't public knowledge. I knew yesterday was too much work. It made me careless, my brain melted by exhaustion.

"Uh, Mom told me," I say, scrambling for cover. "She got the police reports this morning and mentioned it over breakfast."

"Uh-huh," Alex says. "Must be a damn fast medical examiner in this town." His eyes bore into mine, and I know he doesn't believe me. Again.

"I guess," I mutter. *Crap, crap, crap*, I think. Two mistakes in one morning. I'm losing my edge.

Before he can start tearing my story apart, my phone vibrates in my pocket, notifying me of a calendar reminder. Alex raises his eyebrows. Students aren't allowed to have cell phones in school. My sisters and I are exempt from that rule, but Alex doesn't know that. To him, I'm now probably some

15

kind of troublemaker, as well as crazy and depressed. *If only that would make him go away*, I think.

Pulling out my phone, I check the screen. The reminder reads, *112, New York to London, 12:30*. I look at the current time displayed in the corner of the screen. It's now noon. I have to get home.

"Gotta go," I say to Alex as I put on my coat, gather my backpack and trash, and speed walk toward the cafeteria doors. I dump my trash in the can without slowing down.

"Is everything okay?" he asks as he trots behind me.

"Yeah, I just have some things to take care of at home."

"Don't you have to get a note from the office or something? You can't just leave school," he protests when I don't stop.

"Sure I can. I walk out the door, get in my car, and leave. I have a standing arrangement with the school," I add when his jaw drops at my brazenness. "It's fine. This happens a lot, and they give me some slack."

"What happens a lot?" he asks, but I'm already pulling my pass out of my pocket and waving it at the security guard standing by the front door. The guard waves me on.

I run to my car, glad to be away from Alex, his relentless questions, and his strange eyes that see too much. As I pull out of the lot, though, I can't resist. I glance in my rearview mirror and see him still standing in the doorway, watching me.

2

WHEN I GET HOME, I JUMP OUT OF MY CAR AND RUN FOR THE front door, banging it open in my haste. Mom is sitting at the dining room table, surrounded by legal paperwork and client files.

"Slow down," she says absently as I race through the living and dining rooms, dropping my coat and backpack as I go.

"Right," I call back from the kitchen where I'm already punching the unlock code into the keypad on the basement door.

I throw open the door and hop down the stairs, taking them two at a time. At the bottom, I flick on the light switch. The overhead fluorescent tubes flicker and then hold, illuminating the vast underground space where my sisters and I manage the fate of humanity.

I run toward my workroom, passing Chloe's spinning wheel and Lacey's shelves crammed full of measuring tapes, scales, and astrological charts. Spools of gold thread fill the shelves on one wall, all waiting to be spun into lifelines. Against another wall, our server farm hums away, processing all of humanity's records.

All of my work is conducted behind the ten-foot tall, eight-inch thick oak door at the end of the room. In the center of the door is a carving of me as I looked when I lived on Mount Olympus. My hair curls down to the middle of my back, and I'm wearing a one-shoulder gown that I remember as being made of white satin. Holding my shears in my left hand, I grasp a human lifeline, poised for cutting, in my right. I look like the goddess that I am.

The day I posed for that carving was pretty much the last time I looked that way, though. We left Olympus not long after the door was made, trading life among the gods for life among the mortals. I happily traded the gowns for the most casual fashions I could get away with.

The long hair is gone now, too, replaced by a short, swingy bob that hangs just past my chin and is easy to care for. Mom is constantly badgering me to grow it back, but I refuse. I compromised with her, and I keep it my natural auburn color instead of streaking it with lavender which, for some reason, is something I really want to do.

At the top of the door, inscribed in gold leaf, are the words, "θάνατος περιμένει όλους." It's my motto in Greek which means, "Death waits for all." The rest of the door is filled with elaborate carvings of animals, people, insects, and plants. They're supposed to symbolize life, to remind me that it continues endlessly. Whether I find that thought inspiring or depressing depends on what kind of day I've had.

Although I could have left the door on Mount Olympus, I haul it with me every time we move. Zeus presented it to me when he made me the Death Fate. For that reason alone, it is unique. Zeus gave me exactly two things—the door and my shears. Other than that, he's been an absentee father, only troubling to involve himself in my life when he needs something from me. Which isn't often.

Entering my code into the keypad on the door, I place my finger on the fingerprint scanner. I wait while it verifies my identity, and then I haul open the door once I'm cleared. A blast of perfectly dry and climate-controlled air hits me in the face. I pull the door shut behind me and lock it for privacy.

The cavernous space is illuminated by only a few soft lights. Harsh lighting has always seemed too clinical to me. This room may be a killing zone, but it doesn't need to look like a morgue. Billions of thin, gold filaments hang from racks mounted to the ceiling. Each filament is a human lifeline, spun by Chloe. They shimmer in the soft light like tinsel on a Christmas tree, blown by the slight breeze coming from the overhead vents.

No question, Chloe has the best job of the three of us. She determines who is born and when, and then her job ends before those lives turn problematic. She creates, never destroys. Must be nice. Occasionally, a human will say, "I wish I'd never been born," and curse Chloe, but far more people curse Lacey and me.

When Chloe finishes spinning a lifeline, she hands it over to Lacey. Lacey determines the length of each life and doles out the positive and negatives for that life. Win big at the casino? Thank Lacey. Blow all that money and end up homeless? Blame Lacey. She also assigns each person's date of death. Once assigned, it can never be changed. Not even Zeus can alter a human's fate once Lacey has recorded it in her files.

My job is to carry out the final act of every human life. I decide how each human will die, and then I cut their lifelines at the appointed time. My real name is Atropos, also known as, *The one who cannot be avoided*. No one escapes me—not the great, not the powerful, and not the wealthy.

I turn to my desk and punch the play button on my iPod dock. Pavarotti's voice belts out Puccini's "Nessun Dorma." I pull my box out of my desk drawer, lay it on my desk, and pop the clasp. My shears rest on the blue velvet inside.

Mythology refers to them as the "abhorred shears," but there is nothing abhorrent about them to me. No matter how many billions of times I've used these shears, they never fail to impress me. About a foot long, with handles encrusted with alternating rubies and emeralds, they are sharp enough to cut through any material. Hephaestus enchanted them and made them self-sharpening, which is wonderful since I lack the patience and time to do it.

If a human touches the blades, their life and fate are instantly forfeit. Zeus added that feature to protect against any humans who might try to steal my shears and control death. The idea of death falling into human hands scares Zeus. For that matter, anything that takes control away from the gods scares Zeus.

Technically I don't even have to cut the lifelines. I could just travel the world, touching humans with my shears and killing them. That's too time consuming, though. I'm not Santa Claus. I don't have super-speed reindeer, so I can't travel around the world in one night handing out death. Besides, a woman running around touching people with scissors and then having them drop dead is too conspicuous. Instead, I work here, keeping the killing private and easy.

I check the clock on the wall. There is only five minutes left before Flight 112 crashes into the Atlantic Ocean. I pull up the accident file on my computer and print off the schedule, showing who will die and when. Above me, the racks of lifelines begin to spin, like the automated system at a dry cleaner's, bringing all the ones for this accident to the front. They arrive already sorted chronologically. All I have to do is reference the schedule and snip each line at the right time.

Computers are a boon to my job. Before them, I manually recorded dates and manners of death, cross referenced and cataloged everything with Lacey's handwritten records, manually pulled every line to cut on a given day, and then I still had to do the cutting. As Earth's population grew, I rarely slept and free time was nonexistent. Having everything automated except the cutting gives me a little time to relax each day.

One-hundred and six lifelines hang before me now. Most are fifteen to twenty-five feet in length, indicating adults aged twenty to sixty. Longer lines represent the elderly, and the shorter lines are children. I sigh when I see three lines no more than a foot long in the group. *Babies.* I hate this part of the job, but there's nothing I can do about it. That was Lacey's call, not mine.

I move to the first group of lifelines and watch the clock. The seconds tick down. Three. Two. One. At 12:30:43, the plane crashes into the ocean. I gather the first sixty-eight lines in my fist and cut them with my shears. Those people are dead on impact. There's a one-minute pause, and then I snip eight more lines. I wait a beat. Then five more, and then ten more. Three more minutes. Two more lines. The cuts are happening less frequently now that the initial impact is over. These people are burning, bleeding out, or drowning. One cut, a five-minute pause, and then another cut. Only eleven people remain. I wait.

My schedule lists, "Drowning of people inside when fuselage sinks: 12:44:41." When the clock shows the right time, I cut ten of the final eleven lines. The one remaining line is incredibly short. I know it's a baby, probably not more than eight months old. Likely his carrier seat is bobbing in the water for now, perhaps stuck on a piece of wreckage. I sigh. The poor kid has minutes left. His parents are already dead. I guess that's a blessing.

I stare at that single line waving in the breeze from the vents and wish, yet again, for a way to change the outcome. I'd love to give everyone an easy death, but I'm not allowed to do that. Zeus has a master plan for the humans, and I'm bound to honor it. Part of that plan is that sometimes people need to die horrible deaths. It reminds the humans about the fragility of life and the specialness of the gift. Humans tend to forget just how lucky they are to be alive. Death is a good reminder. Random, unjust, and cruel deaths are even better reminders.

The clock ticks down, and I snip the baby's line. The tiny filament falls to the floor, landing on top of the other one-hundred and five lines. I stand a moment, silently respectful of the dead, and wipe away the tear that drips down my chin. It's my job. Only a job. Maybe one day, reminding myself of that will help.

After I've boxed up the lines and sent them to Thanatos for pick up, I glance at my clock. It's not yet one o'clock, which means I have to go back to school. Mom worked hard to make it so that we can attend school as our schedules dictate, but we aren't allowed to abuse the privilege.

Truthfully, she didn't work that hard, but I'm willing to give her the credit. She simply abused her power a bit. As Themis, the goddess of law and order, she has the ability to compel people to comply with rules and laws, so she "encouraged" the administration to accept the crazy excuses she crafted for us. Obi-Wan Kenobi used a similar power in *Star Wars* to get the storm troopers to leave Luke alone. George Lucas totally stole that from Mom. I'm supposed to be the only caregiver for a sick relative, Lacey is an elite swimmer training for the Olympics, and Chloe has some weird disease that requires treatment at odd hours. It's all lies, but Mom forged a ton of paperwork to support everything and then persuaded the administration to buy every bit of it. You've got to respect that level of trickery.

Regardless, there's too much time left in the day, so I have to go back to school. There's no point in arguing about it, either, because Mom won't bend the rule no matter how tired I am. It doesn't matter that we're all immortal and well past grounding age. What Themis says is law, and we don't disobey her. Not often, anyway.

I lock up my shears and head upstairs where I gather up my discarded bomber jacket and book bag. Mom calls to me from the dining room as I'm searching the floor for my car keys.

"Everything taken care of?"

"Yeah. Another hundred or so people dead and on their way to Thanatos. Chloe'll have them replaced by sundown," I say as I scoop my keys out from under the coffee table.

"I wish you wouldn't talk like that. It's not very respectful."

I wander into the dining room and take a seat at the table across from her. "Sorry. I'm just tired. Lacey's got humans dying by the truckload this week, and I'm just trying to keep up. It's one of those weeks that I swear she's trying to punish me for something."

"I know. But you know Zeus chose you and your sisters for

this work because he knew you could handle it," she says.

"It just gets old. Billions of kills and trillions more to go, unless Zeus decides to end the world early."

"Why don't you have some fun, then? You spend all your time alone when you're not working. You're either out walking or you have your nose buried in a book. You girls are in school again. You could join some clubs like Lachesis, or play sports like Clotho. They do just fine in the mortal world."

"And how many times have I broken their hearts when I've killed someone they loved or were friends with?" I ask. "Why would I subject myself to that sort of misery? Lacey still mourns that guy, Charlie, she loved, and that was over a hundred years ago."

"I know it's hard," Mom says, reaching across the table to take my hand. "You see all the misery and death in the world, and you're the architect of some of that suffering. But that doesn't mean you should lock yourself away. You're missing out on life, Atropos, and it worries me. It worries your father, too."

I snort at that. "Not likely. Zeus quit worrying about me a long time ago."

"He does. He just doesn't show it."

I shrug. "Whatever. Humans are just too much trouble, anyway."

"Then hang out with other gods. I know Apollo's interested. Or what about calling Persephone? You two always got along well."

"I've tried the god thing," I say, rolling my eyes. "Twice. Didn't work out so great either time, if you'll recall. And as for Persephone, you know how much Hades hates to let her out of the Underworld. She and I can't be all buddy-buddy as long as he keeps that leash so tight. And I certainly don't have time to go down there and visit her. I'm too busy killing people."

"I'm just saying that I think you're missing out on some great things by not opening yourself up to love and friendship."

"This from the woman who's still hung up on Zeus, even though he's been with how many other women? He only beds

23

you every few hundred years when he's bored with everyone else, and he still chooses Hera as his queen over you. Have you ever considered getting over him and seeing someone else?" I ask. "Maybe a human?"

"I have and I've rejected the idea. Your father remains the love of my life, even if he is a cheating asshole."

"Then don't tell me what I'm missing when you're just as dysfunctional." I pull my hand back and stand to leave.

Mom stands, too, and comes around the table to stand in front of me. "The problem is, Atropos, that you don't love anyone. You don't have relationships, functional or not. You don't love any of the gods, nor the humans. Sometimes I wonder if you really love me or your sisters."

That stings, and I lash back. "When do I have time to love anyone? Between the farce of going to school every day and killing thousands of people every week, when do I have time for anyone, even if I wanted them?"

"You'd make the time, if it were important to you," Mom says.

"Yeah, well, I guess it's just not that important to me," I say, swallowing the rising anger. We've had this conversation before, and it always ends the same way—with me pissed off and Mom hurt. I try to cut it off before things get worse.

"I've got to get back to school," I say, pushing past her. "There are still two hours left in the day, and I don't have to kill anyone again until three. I wouldn't want to break any rules," I say.

"Atropos—" Themis begins, reaching out to touch my arm.

I twist away from her and stomp out the door, giving it a good slam on my way out. I'll catch hell for that later, but I really don't care.

I climb in the Thunderbird, slam that door, too, and rev the engine as I back out of the driveway and turn toward school. Having Mom lecture me on love and loss is annoying. It isn't like I'm some teenager who needs lessons on the matter. Even though I'm trapped in the body of a seventeen year-old, I've lived for well over three thousand years. I certainly know my way around affairs of the heart. And I know enough to stay clear of the carnage.

Ares, the god of war, was the first god I dated and the only man I've ever loved. Right up until he dumped me with no explanation and broke both my heart and my spirit. I haven't loved anyone since.

I tried dating just one other time. Thanatos and I tried to date in the sixteen hundreds, but it ended before it ever began. We never even kissed. He was too arrogant for me, and I was too closed off for him. I also didn't trust him. He always seemed more interested in my job than in me. I gave up on the gods after that.

As for humans? I've avoided *any* romantic entanglements with them. Dating humans isn't forbidden, and my sisters certainly date their share. It's easier for them, I think, since they aren't the ones who have to kill their lovers.

I don't want to get involved with someone who I have to kill. Even if the man lives to be a hundred and fifty, he's still going to die… and I'm always going to be the one responsible. I'll be left behind with the guilt and a broken heart. That's just too much baggage for even a goddess to deal with.

It's also impossible for me to have a long-term relationship without raising questions. I don't age. At some point, the human is going to wonder what's up, and I'll have no choice but to end the relationship and vanish out of sight. Telling the truth—that I'm a goddess of fate—is forbidden. As if anyone would believe me, anyway. One-night stands don't appeal to me, either, so I keep to myself.

I pull back into my parking space at school. The shrine to Amy has grown and is now lopping over into the adjacent handicap space. If anyone needs the space, they're going to have to shovel a pathway in. I shake my head at the folly of humans and trudge to my fifth-period class. Advanced calculus

25

is not my favorite subject by far, even though I'm good at it.

I'm late, but Mr. Myers is used to it and no longer asks for a pass. He doesn't even stop lecturing. He just glances my way and nods as I creep toward my seat in the back of the class.

As I make my way down the aisle, I glance at the desk in front of mine. It's been empty since October when the previous occupant moved away. Now Alex Martin is sitting in it. Of course. When I get close to his desk, he smiles at me.

Okay? he mouths.

Nodding at him as I pass, I slump into my chair. I can't get away from this guy. I pull out my supplies and start doodling, only half listening to the lecture. I've heard it all before. After drawing for a few minutes, I'm shocked to see that I've drawn Alex as he looked at the lunch table. I quickly rip out the page and crumple it into a ball, drawing an annoyed glance from Mr. Myers.

What is wrong with me? I haven't spoken to the boy for more than thirty minutes total. He's probably a complete loser. After all, he *is* human. But something about him strikes me as different.

He's smart, I'll give him that. During class, he volunteers the answers more than any other student… and he's always right. Refreshingly, he's not obnoxious about it, either. He doesn't wave his hand in the air, grunting, "Ooh, ooh, ooh," like the brainiacs do. Mr. Myers asks, and Alex answers, as if it's just the two of them having a private conversation.

I can't get Alex's comments about me at the lunch table out of my mind, either. He isn't scared off by my reputation, one I've cultivated for the express purpose of keeping the humans away from me. The ruder and meaner I am, the farther away they get, which means no messy entanglements for me.

Alex is different. He's already figured out my attitude is pasted on, and he wants to know why. I'll have to be doubly unpleasant. That thought just makes me tired. Dropping my chin into my hand, I doze.

I'm jolted awake when a wad of paper hits me on the head.

Mr. Myers has turned to write some problems on the board, and someone has chucked a note onto my desk. I unfold it, laying it flat among my notes.

Wake up! Meet me by the front doors after school.

Alex

I don't hesitate. I scribble No on the paper, refold it, and toss it over Alex's shoulder onto his desk.

After he unfolds the note, his shoulders shake with silent laughter. He shakes his head, writes something else on the paper, and hands it back to me over his shoulder.

You know you want to... the note reads.

I snort before covering it with a cough. This is stupid and childish. I can't stop myself from smiling a little at Alex's silliness, though, as I write back.

I don't want to meet you after school. If you think I do, you're delusional.

I toss the paper over his shoulder again and then settle back in my seat as Mr. Myers turns back toward the class. Alex doesn't get a chance to open the note for another ten minutes. Mr. Myers finally turns back to the board, and I see Alex quickly read the note. He shakes his head, and I hear him snicker.

A normal response would be to get offended or pissed off. A normal person would stop with the foolishness right now. But Alex is amused that I'm being rude to him, and that reaction puzzles me.

I'm not being funny. I'm serious, and I think he knows that. I decide there must be something wrong with the kid. Some sort of impairment that makes it impossible for him to recognize "get lost" signals. Maybe he hit his head when he drove that car through the headmaster's office. I shake my head and return my attention to the problem on the blackboard.

Alex has the answer before the rest of us, and he and Mr. Myers spend the rest of the period discussing higher derivatives. The bell finally rings. Jumping up, I run for the door. In my haste to put some distance between myself and Alex, I trip over Juliet Jackson's backpack, nearly spraining my ankle. I'm fast, but not fast enough. Alex catches me just outside the classroom door and grabs my arm.

"Delusional, am I?" he asks with a smile. "That would explain the pink panda I keep seeing roaming the halls."

I try to yank my arm out of his grip. He doesn't let go.

"Joke," he says when I don't respond.

"One would hope," I say, injecting some frost into my voice as I keep jerking my arm. "Let me go."

"I'm not letting go because the second I do, you're going to bolt again. I won't let go until you let me talk."

"Fine, talk," I say, letting my arm go limp. He lets go but keeps his hand in the air, ready to make a grab. I stand my ground.

"Look, all I'm asking is for you to meet me after school. I've got something I want to show you."

"Not a good idea," I say.

"Why not?"

"You don't know anything about me, nor do I, you."

"Which is why spending some time together is a good idea," he says.

"Trust me. You should take your cue from the rest of the kids. Just assume I'm crazy and depressed and stay away from me. I'm not someone you want to know more about."

"Will you stop telling me who I should and shouldn't want to know? I have a mind of my own, and I can use it. I just want to get to know you better. It's not a crime."

"It should be," I mutter, looking at the floor.

"What?"

"Nothing," I say.

"Please? Meet me after school. Just once."

I ignore him and start walking down the hall. To my relief, he doesn't follow. He does call out after me.

"You just look like you've had a rough day, and I happen to know of something that might lift your spirits a little. It's not like I'm asking you to marry me and have my babies. If you change your mind, I'll wait at the doors until 3:15."

28

He's so loud that people turn to stare in our direction. I'm not embarrassed, just a little pissed at Alex for making such a big deal out of this and drawing attention to me. The boy is clueless.

It doesn't matter anyway. Since I have to kill someone at three, I know I'll never make it home and back to school by fifteen after. I'm safe. I throw a dismissive wave over my shoulder at Alex as I walk away. Maybe he'll get the hint and stay away after I stand him up.

SCHOOL LETS OUT AT 2:45. I HURRY TO THE PARKING LOT, JUMP in my car, and speed home to kill my latest victim. I can't remember anything about this guy other than he needs to die at three o'clock. In my defense, the humans tend to run together after a while. His thread is already waiting for me when I enter my workroom. One quick snip and the deed is done.

I sit down at my desk to check my schedule. It's going to be another busy night, although the afternoon is slow. A tornado outbreak will plow through the Midwest, and a skyscraper hotel in Dubai is going to catch fire. Thousands dead. *Yippee.*

I double check to make sure I've entered everything into the computer so it will pull and sort all the lines I'll need to cut tonight. Everything is correct, and I can rest until seven thirty. I should just stay down here and work on my homework but since I'll be here all night, I want to get out for a while. At least that's the lie I tell myself.

I glance at the clock on my desk. It's ten past three. I have time to get back to the school and meet Alex—if I want to. Part of me wants to see whatever it is he wants to show me. The other part of me knows that encouraging him in any way is insanity. I can't even be friends with him without putting both of us in an awkward position. Staying away is the right thing to do.

I lean back in my chair and study the lines hanging around the room. Mom said I'm missing out on life. Maybe so, but my life isn't like the ones that hang on my racks. I'm immortal, and that makes things different. I don't know what it's like to have limited time—for things to really matter. Every day is the same to me, and nothing matters beyond getting the job done. Indifference is the only way to stay sane. It's best to let the lives of the humans pass me by like a never-ending circus parade.

What if I had a little fun… just once? Would it kill me? Of course not. Nothing can kill me. It can make me miserable, but it can't kill me. And I'm already pretty damn miserable, so what would really change?

I think about Alex. He wants to spend time with me in spite of my nastiness, and he's excited about showing me something. I could go with him today, see whatever he wants to show me, and then forget him. Chances are that he'll turn out to be an idiot like the rest of the humans are, and it won't go any further than one outing. I could satisfy my curiosity about him, maybe have a little fun, and no harm would be done. As a bonus, I could show Mom a good faith effort to get out more and get her off my back for a while.

I get up and pace the room for a few minutes, thinking this through. Alarms in my head are screaming, *Bad idea*, but there's a small part of me saying, *It's just one afternoon. Go.* I battle the voices, trying to force the smart, sane one to win, but I lose the war.

I look at the clock. It's now 3:17. Well, that's good. The decision has been made for me. Alex has probably already left school. I procrastinated long enough. Disaster averted.

I feel smug for about a minute, and then I do the stupidest thing I've done in three thousand years. I yank open my workroom door and slam it shut behind me, not even checking to make sure the locks are engaged. Running upstairs, I dash out the front door and leap into my car, gunning it down the driveway. I take the corner at the end of my street practically on two wheels, and I run the two red lights between my house and the school. At the second one, I dodge an elderly man crossing the intersection on his scooter. Not that it matters. I can't kill him if he's not supposed to die today, but it's the principle of the thing. Mowing people down is just bad form.

The turn into the school parking lot is a sweeping right-hander with a posted speed limit of twenty-five miles per hour. I hit it at forty-three. A couple of teachers are talking on the sidewalk, and they shoot me dirty looks as I fly past.

When I reach the front of the school, Alex isn't there. I'm nearly ten minutes late, and it's just as well. My moment of insanity has passed, and it's better that nothing came of it. Rather than linger, I drive toward the exit on the other side of the lot. Maybe I'll swing by the bookstore and pick up some new releases. That's a sane, safe activity.

As I'm waiting to turn left, I glance to my right to check traffic and see Alex on the sidewalk, walking away from the school. He's hunched over under the weight of an overstuffed backpack.

I can turn and go home, and he'll never see me. He'll never know I came looking for him. That's the sensible choice. Or I can continue with my stupidity and honk the horn. Again, I choose stupidity. Alex turns in my direction, and I wave. He hurries to the passenger side of the car. I roll down the window, and he leans in.

"You came," he says.

"Well, yeah," I say, unwilling to reveal my personal struggles. "I was curious."

Alex lifts one eyebrow. "Curious about what I have to show you, or about me?" he asks.

"Don't flatter yourself," I say. "I'm only interested in whatever you have to show me. You were right. I've had a bad day, and I've got a bad night coming up. I could use something interesting to take my mind off things for a while."

"Okay," he says, a little smirk playing on his mouth. I can tell he doesn't believe me, but no way am I going to admit I'm even a little bit interested in him as a person. I've gone too far with this lunacy already.

"Get in," I say, reaching over and lifting the lock.

"Nice car," he says as he slides into the passenger seat. "What is this, a '58 Thunderbird?"

"'59," I correct.

"Wow. Who did the restoration?"

Telling him the truth, that I bought the car new in 1959, isn't an option. So I lie. "I did." This is sort of the truth. I rebuilt the engine about fifteen years ago, and I perform all the maintenance on the car myself because I don't trust anyone else with my baby.

Alex looks at me, respect in his eyes. "No offense, but I wouldn't have thought—" He trails off.

I wave a hand in his direction. "I get it. There's no right way to tell a girl that you're shocked she can restore a car."

"I didn't mean—"

"Yes, you did. But it's okay," I say. "It is unexpected. Anyway, what do you want to show me?" I ask, changing the subject and bailing him out.

"It's not so much a 'what' as a 'where.'"

"Tell me where to go, then," I say as I pull out of the parking lot. "I just have to be home by seven thirty."

Alex gives me directions that take us out of Asheville and onto the Blue Ridge Parkway. I know the road well, and I soon realize he is directing me toward Mount Mitchell. I'm uncomfortable with the idea, but I don't say anything.

The reason my family lives in Asheville is because of its proximity to Mount Mitchell. Near the top of the mountain, off the main roads and hiking trails, well hidden among the rocks, is a gateway to Mount Olympus.

Mount Olympus is a real mountain in Greece, but the part of Olympus that the gods use is shielded from human view. Humans can trek all over the mountain, but everything they see and experience is a hologram, crafted and maintained by Zeus. Every year, he adjusts it just a bit to make it look a bit more weathered and decrepit. Ruins, after all, are constantly deteriorating, and if there were never any changes, people would get suspicious. The real mountain beneath this hologram contains our palaces and homes, which look just as beautiful as they did three thousand years ago when we first built them.

Almost every mountain on Earth has a gateway to Olympus. Zeus built the gateways when he allowed the gods and goddesses to live in the human world. His only restriction on our freedom is that we always live close to a gateway so we can get home quickly if we need to. The day Zeus said we could leave, Mom had us packed and off Olympus in a matter of hours. She left partly to get away from Zeus and partly to get away from the petty politics and jealousies that make up life among the gods. We lived in Tibet, near Everest, first. Since then, we've made the rounds of all the mountains on Earth. We've lived on or near most of them more than once. I'd love to live at the beach, just once, but it's never going to happen. Sand dunes aren't mountains, and they can't have gateways.

If Alex wants to show me something on Mount Mitchell, I'm going to come up with some excuse to go home. While I don't think we'll run into any gods and the gateway is well hidden, I still don't want Alex up there. I don't want him near anything that has to do with who and what I really am.

Alex interrupts my thoughts as I'm trying to come up with a good excuse to go back home.

"The turnoff is coming up soon, so you might want to slow down."

"I know this road pretty well, and I don't think there's a turnoff here. Are you sure you're not thinking of someplace else?"

"I'm sure. Slow down and it's on your right."

I hit the brakes to humor him and, sure enough, there's a tiny clearing in the trees just wide enough for a car. After I turn, we bump down a rocky road completely covered by trees. Even though it's still daylight and the trees haven't fully leafed out, the canopy makes it so dark that I have to flick on the headlights.

"Huh," I say. "All the times I've been up here and I never noticed this road."

"Few people do. I only know about it because one of the guys at St. Luke's told me about it."

"We won't meet any oncoming traffic, will we? There's not enough room for two cars in here," I say.

"Not likely. There's a place to pull over just ahead. We'll pull off there and then walk the rest of the way. It's way too steep for this car, and I don't want to scratch your paint job," Alex says.

"Smart man."

I find the spot where the road widens just a bit, pulling the car off the road. We get out and start walking. The incline increases quickly and we hike in silence, both of us concentrating on our footing too carefully to talk.

"Is it far?" I ask after we've been hiking for twenty minutes. Thank the gods I'm in good shape. Alex, I notice, is a bit pale and panting, but he's not laboring so I don't worry about it.

"Another quarter mile," he says. "It's worth it. Trust me."

We continue hiking and what was a road becomes nothing more than a pathway up the mountain. It's nearly overgrown in places, and it's hard for me to see the trail, but Alex obviously knows where he's going.

In addition to the steep climb, we're battling small trees and big plants that slap and scrape at us. Just as I'm about to tell Alex to forget it, that I'm not this much of a nature girl, we climb one particularly rough patch and heave ourselves over a rocky ledge.

I lie there panting, not willing to go any farther.

"We're here," Alex says. He's sprawled beside me on the grass, breathing harder than I am.

"Great. Where is 'here,' exactly? What was worth nearly having a heart attack to see?"

"Get up and see," he says.

I stand and look around. We're on a flat, open spot near the top of the mountain. It can't be more than two acres of land. Three sides of it are open to the view of the valley below and the neighboring mountains. In front of me looms a sheer rock face that falls down from the top of the mountain. Against this wall is what Alex wants to show me. At least, I assume it is.

"It's a church," I whisper.

"Well, it was," Alex says, sitting up on the grass. I extend a hand down to him and help him up. He sways a bit on his feet before he stabilizes.

"Are you okay?" I ask him. "You're really pale."

"Fine. Just not used to that kind of exertion," he says. "Been a while since I've been up here."

I wander toward the church. Alex is right. "Was" is the best term for the building. The wooden roof of the stone structure fell in years ago, and the windows are long gone. The stone steeple still stands, attached to the front wall of the church rather than the roof as is common today. Surrounded by the tiny wildflowers of early spring, the church is beautiful, even if it's broken.

I head for the hole in the wall where the front door used to be and enter the sanctuary. It's a small church; there are only four rows of pews on either side of the center aisle. Running my hand over the polished stone of the pew on my left, I marvel at the beauty. Although they are worn, moss covered, and pitted with weather damage, I can tell they were once works of art.

The end of each pew is carved with scenes from the Bible and the backs are inscribed with dates and names. Probably the names and birth/death dates of influential members of the church. Some of the names have small birds or other animals carved next to them.

There is no choir stall or baptismal area here. A small stone altar is all that graces the front of the church. While I'll never understand the human obsession with religion, this sweet, simple church speaks of more than hell and damnation. It was once the heart of a community of friends and families. Another aspect of human life I don't understand, but that I wish I did.

I glance behind me and see that Alex hasn't come in. He's leaning against the doorframe, hands stuffed in the pockets of his jeans, grinning.

"It's beautiful," I say.

"I thought you'd like it. I come up here when I need some peace."

"I can see why," I say as I move around the altar and gaze up at the round hole in the back wall that used to be a window. Sunlight streams through into the church, and the occasional bird flies in to rest among the few remaining rafters.

I walk back up the aisle to Alex. "Do you know how old it is?" I ask.

"Come on," he says, indicating I should follow him outside.

He leads the way to the front left corner and points down. There I see the cornerstone of the building. It reads, *Dedicated April 12, 1773.*

That's relatively young, to me anyway. I think of things as old only when they reach thousands of years of age. Even Westminster Abbey isn't old to me, and parts of that church date from 1245 A.D. This is impressive for this part of the world, however. So many buildings in America tend to be destroyed well before they reach even this modest age.

"Its isolation is what's kept it safe," I say.

"That and, well, what else would you do with the land?" Alex asks. "You can't get up here easily, and I doubt you could get a better road in here. Besides, no one else can build here."

"Why not?"

"I haven't shown you the best part, yet," Alex teases. "The thing I really wanted you to see."

I can't imagine that it gets better than this picturesque little ruin, but I follow Alex around to the other side of the church. I gasp when we round the corner. In front of me is an old cemetery, complete with crumbling headstones, overgrown pathways, and out-of-control moss growing on every surface. It's perfect.

"Sacred ground," Alex says, finishing his earlier thought. "No one can build here, even if they want to."

The cemetery is surrounded by a low stone wall. I climb over it, so eager to walk among the dead, the people I put here, that I can't be bothered to find the gate. As I wander among the graves, I'm on the lookout for any snakes lounging in the weak spring sunshine.

The oldest graves are in the front of the cemetery. The majority of the headstones here are broken or so badly worn that I can't read the names or dates. The one date I can make out is 1775, but the name is long gone. I have no idea if the person here is male or female, or how old they were when they died.

Farther back in the cemetery, I find the graves of a few Confederate soldiers. These headstones are in better shape than the markers in the front and most list names, ranks, and dates of birth and death. Squatting down, I clear away the weeds from one grave, and I am surprised to see the name of an individual I actually remember. Sergeant Tommy Andrews, killed at Gettysburg.

I never met him, but I remember killing him, even though most of the three days of fighting at Gettysburg remain one long blur of line cutting and exhaustion in my mind. He died July 2, 1863 on Culp's Hill. Only sixteen, he wasn't cut down by random cannon fire. That would have been too easy. He was killed by his older brother, James, who fought for the Union. I hated forcing one brother to kill another, but I needed to make a point about the evils of war. Not that it stuck in the human psyche. They're all still far too willing to shoot each other for no good reason. Tommy's parents are buried on either side of him, but James' grave isn't here. I can't remember when or where he died, but evidently, he wasn't welcomed back here. Not surprising, really.

I rest my hand on Tommy's grave. "I'm sorry," I whisper. "I had to."

I stand and move on, looking at other graves but seeing no one else I know. I'm still lost in the past when Alex says, "I take it you like it."

I turn to find him sitting on top of an above-ground burial vault. The plaque reads, *Amos Winton, 1872 - 1924.* This looks to be the most recent in the cemetery. Either the church was still in use as late as 1924, or someone deliberately brought old Amos here after the church disbanded.

"I wonder where the people who used this church all went?" I ask, looking around at the abandoned ruins, once clearly the heart of a community.

He shrugs. "Who knows? Wherever their settlement was, it looks like it's long gone. I've hiked around here, trying to find the remains of the houses, but I haven't found anything. Probably one of those cases where the young people moved away for jobs and marriages and the old people just died out. I'm not the sentimental sort, but it's kind of sad that a whole community just disappeared. But I guess everything dies eventually."

How right he is.

Alex pats the space next to him, and I hoist myself up beside him on top of old Amos.

"Thank you for showing me this," I say.

We sit quietly for a few minutes, enjoying the birdsong and the sunshine.

"It doesn't creep you out, does it?" Alex asks after a while.

"No. Should it?"

"I don't know. Most people get creeped out by death, but you don't seem to mind. After your comments about Amy this morning, I figured you could appreciate this place for what it is, and not see it as depressing or morbid."

I smile, thinking about just how little death "creeps me out." Sure, there are some deaths that stay with me and seem unjust, as Tommy's does, but for the most part, it's easy for me to view death as a fact of human life.

I don't have the emotional reaction to death that humans do. Since I'm never going to die, I don't view someone else's death as a warning of my own mortality. Death is an abstract concept to me, more like how I imagine a human feels about the death of a star in the heavens. Interesting to watch and maybe a little sad, but not personally relevant.

"Do you worry about death?" I ask him. It's rare for me to talk to humans about death since most of them will do anything to avoid the topic. But I sense that this is something Alex isn't afraid to discuss and maybe even needs to talk about. Maybe it's why he brought me here.

"All the time," he answers. "That's part of why I like to come up here. Being here reminds me that death happens to everyone, has always happened to everyone, and there's no escaping it no matter how much I want to."

"That's pretty deep," I say, impressed by his acceptance of the inevitable. Most humans think they can somehow avoid me, that if they just do the right things or make enough money, I won't come for them.

"And mature. There are a lot of people five times your age who can't accept the inevitability of death," I say.

"It's silly, I guess, but coming here actually makes me worry about it less. You'd think it would be the opposite," Alex says.

"No, I can see that. When you know what's coming and you can look it in the face, it's easier to deal with than when you hide from it. Regardless, you have plenty of time before you have to worry about it."

He shrugs. "I guess."

He goes silent, and I wait. He's swinging his legs and kicking his heels against the side of the tomb, head down in thought. I can tell he's grappling with something, so I let him work it out. Finally, he lifts his head and looks at me.

"You asked earlier why I drove my car through the headmaster's office."

I nod. "But I stand by what I said. You don't have to tell me."

"I want to. I've wanted to tell someone for a long time and you seem, I don't know, nonjudgmental."

I shrug. "I try to be."

"My mom died from breast cancer a year ago," he says. "I couldn't handle it. I got stuck in the angry phase of grief and lashed out at everyone. Then I got some more bad news, and I lost it. That's when I drove through the office.

"While I was in the hospital, a friend at St. Luke's told me about this place. He said it helped him to deal with his grandmother's death. That seeing something so old helped him put it in perspective. He was right, and I've been coming here ever since."

I don't know what to say, so I wait to see if he'll go on.

"Hey, I'm sorry to dump this on you. I barely know you, and here I am telling you about my horrible past."

"It's okay," I say. And I'm surprised to find that it is. For the first time in decades, I haven't minded listening to a human talk about their life. Weird.

"It's just that I can't talk to my dad. He's worse off than I am. And my friends from St. Luke's cut me loose when I got expelled." He looks down at his lap, and I can see the rejection still hurts.

"I understand. Really. I know what it's like to want to talk about things but have no one who you can talk to." That sums up my entire existence. If I want to talk about the pain my job causes me, I'm out of luck. Mom and my sisters don't want to hear it, and Zeus just tells me to quit whining.

"I didn't mean to bring it up. I guess starting school on the same day someone died just dragged it all up again. All those depressed kids."

I snort, and he glares at me.

"Sorry. It's just I know that very few of those kids are really depressed or grieving. Most of them are simply having their first brush with mortality and finding they don't like it. They don't know death the way you do. You're entitled to your grief."

"Thanks, I think. You have a strange outlook on death and grief, you know?"

"I've been told," I say. "I'm sorry about your mom. What was her name?"

"Helen. She was thirty-eight years old. It wasn't fair."

"No, it wasn't."

Helen Martin. I think hard, but I can't remember her. I hate that I'm responsible for Alex's pain. Well, technically, Lacey's responsible since she decreed that Helen's life would be so short. That she added cancer to Helen's fate just gave me a convenient cause of death. I could have chosen something else, but Helen still would have died young. It doesn't matter how I choose to kill someone. It always comes back to the same thing—I am the monster who actually ends a life. It's hard not to feel guilty, even though I never have a choice.

I think of what I might say to ease the grief I see etched so plainly on Alex's face. Tears have welled up in his eyes and I can see he's breathing deeply, trying not to let them fall. Coming here might be soothing on the whole, but talking about Helen clearly upsets him.

I lay my hand on his arm. "It wasn't fair, but maybe it was necessary," I venture.

He turns to me and I see the fury in his eyes, along with raw grief unhealed by a year's passage. I realize too late that I chose the wrong words.

"Necessary? It was necessary to take a young mother from a family that needed her? That still needs her? My sister was only twelve. She still needs her mother. My father needs his wife. Don't talk to me about necessity."

Pushing my hand away, he slides off the vault. He starts pacing the cemetery.

"I shouldn't have brought you here. I should have known you wouldn't understand. You're just like the rest who say, 'Get over it, it'll be okay.'"

"Hey," I shout at him. "I do understand. Maybe more than you think. Let me ask you something," I say, sliding off the vault and walking over to him. I grip his arm to hold him still. "Do you believe in fate, or a divine plan, or anything like that?"

"I used to, until it seemed too cruel. I was raised in church. We were taught that God has a master plan, but His plan sucks if that's true."

Wrong church, wrong god, I think. But at least he understands the principle.

"Okay, then. If you believe that things happen for a reason, then your mother's death was necessary and had a purpose. That doesn't make it any easier to take, I know, but maybe you can find solace in knowing that it was preordained and that there was nothing you could do about it."

"But it wasn't fair."

"No one has a fair life," I say. "Name one human who doesn't face the death of a loved one, an illness, an injury, or some other horrible, life-altering event."

"I can't do that," he says.

"I know, and that's my point. Everyone suffers. You're just suffering at a younger age than some. But if you believe that there is some sort of master plan to the universe, then you have to believe that suffering has a purpose, too. Yours and hers," I add.

"And what is the purpose of losing a mother so young?" he asks.

I think for a moment. There are lots of purposes, and Lacey and I have used them all over the years. "Maybe you needed to learn how to handle grief. Maybe you and your sister needed help in growing up. Maybe your father needed to learn to stand alone. Maybe your mother had completed her life's work and it was time for her to go. Maybe the population needed balancing.

"I don't know what the purpose was, and you'll never know either. Somehow, you have to learn to be okay with that or it will eat you up inside. It already is," I say.

Alex stares at me. His eyes are intense, and the color reminds me of the ocean just before the storm rages. I drop my hand from his arm and step back, afraid that I've made him angrier. I've said too much, gotten too involved, and probably hurt him more than I've helped. But something about him kept me talking well beyond the point when I should have simply shut up.

"I'm sorry. I shouldn't have said anything. It's not my business. Let's go. I'll drive you home."

"No, wait," he says, running a hand over his face and walking toward the back of the cemetery.

Sensing that he doesn't want me to follow, I walk back toward the church and go inside, giving him a moment to calm himself. Sitting in one of the pews, I think. I can look in the computer at home and find the exact reason why Helen died so young. For one crazy second, I think about looking up Helen's file and giving Alex the answer he so obviously wants.

I shake my head. That is definitely forbidden. I am not permitted to discuss fate with a mortal. If I tell Alex anything about his mother, I will be punished. Besides, knowing why his mother had to die won't make it okay for him. Dead is dead, and the reasons don't matter.

I look up at the open hole behind the altar and see that the rocks beyond are no longer brightly lit by the sun. It's getting late, and I need to get home. If Alex doesn't come back soon, I'll have to drag him off this mountain.

After a few minutes, I hear footsteps behind me, but I don't turn around. Alex comes down the aisle and sits down beside me.

"Sorry," he says, bumping my shoulder playfully with his. "I brought you up here to cheer you up, and I ruined it."

"You didn't ruin it. You did take my mind off my problems," I say.

That gets a rueful smile from him.

"Do you want to walk around some more?" he asks. "Talk about lighter things?"

"I would, but I have to get home."

I'm surprised that I am sorry I can't spend more time up here with Alex. He's complicated and dark, but with a lighter side that cares deeply about other people. Not so different from myself. And this place is calming. Even with the recent drama, I feel better than I have in a while.

"Yeah, you mentioned you have a bad night ahead of you. Homework?" he asks.

"Something like that." It's as good an evasion as anything else.

"We could study together, if you want," he offers, and I hear the hope in his voice.

"No, thanks. I don't work well with others. I'll get everything done much faster on my own."

"Okay. Will you come up here with me some other time, though?" he asks. "If I promise not to drag you down with my problems?"

"I'd like that," I say. And I mean it.

We head back down the mountain to the car, and I drive Alex home. With Van Morrison's "Into the Mystic" cycling on repeat in the background, we spend the hour talking about the books we've read and what's in our *To Be Read* piles. He's read almost as much obscure stuff as I have, and he hasn't had thousands of years to do it. He's the first human I've met who can match my reading ability and taste. I'm impressed.

When he gives me directions to his house, I realize he lives less than a mile from my house. That's disquieting in some respects and comforting in others. We say goodnight and I drive home, thinking about how a day that started out so badly could end up so well. I find myself looking forward to school tomorrow for the first time ever.

CHAPTER 4

THE NIGHT IS ANOTHER LONG ONE, AND CHLOE KEEPS ME company through most of it. Rarely do I let anyone into my workroom, but I'm so unsettled by my afternoon with Alex that I crave Chloe's calming, optimistic presence.

"So, who's the new kid in your grade?" she asks from her perch on the stool in the corner. "He's kind of cute. All the girls in school are talking about him."

"His name's Alex Martin. He's in my English and calculus classes. He's decent," I say as I snip the lines of the Dubai hotel fire victims.

"Wow. That's high praise from you."

Shrugging, I think about telling her about our trip up the mountain, but I refrain. The fact that I willingly spent time with a human will set her antennae quivering, and she won't leave me alone until she hears every detail. Since I'm not even sure what I'm feeling, I don't want to talk about it.

"Do you think he has a girlfriend?" Chloe asks.

I shrug again. "I don't know. He didn't say. But since he's from the area, it's possible I guess."

"Rats," she says. "Everyone's hoping he's single so they can make a play for him. Prom's coming up soon, you know."

I cringe when I think about that. Alex's social life certainly isn't my business, but I find I don't like the idea of every girl in school panting after him, hoping for an invite to prom. And that makes me nervous. I shouldn't care. He's a human, after all. An intolerable one who can shack up with however many girls he wants.

I shake my head and tune into Chloe's chatter about school and softball practice. Anything to distract me from thoughts of Alex and a hundred girls.

Chloe stays with me until the last line is boxed and on its way to Thanatos. She opens the door and steps out, walking quickly across the room. I don't follow her. Instead, I stop at my desk. Halfway to the stairs, she looks back at me.

"Aren't you coming up to bed?" she calls.

"In a minute. I've got a few things to take care of to get ready for tomorrow. You go on," I tell her as I sit down in my chair and pull it up to my computer.

"I can stay," she offers, but I can see the fatigue in her eyes. Her job isn't nearly as tiring as mine, and she isn't used to the lack of sleep I deal with every day.

"No. You're about to fall over as it is. Go on up."

"Okay. Goodnight," she calls as she heads upstairs.

I lean back in my chair and let the quiet envelop me. It's three-thirty in the morning. Everyone else is asleep. Down here, I can't even hear any noise from the street above. I inhale and exhale consciously, letting the stress of the day dissolve.

I turn to my computer and double-check tomorrow's schedule. It's blessedly light. No major disasters and not that many people dying in general. Maybe I'll have a chance to do some much-needed cleaning down here. *Or*, I think guiltily, *catch up on my homework.*

I hate the ruse of going to school, but it's necessary for us. My sisters and I will always look like teenagers, and school helps us blend in. It wasn't a problem until the middle of the twentieth century. Girls didn't always receive formal education, so three girls staying home with their mother all day wasn't considered odd. I miss those days. Now that school is mandatory in much of the world, my sisters and I have to go when we live in a civilized country.

Well, we don't *have* to go… We experimented with homeschool exactly once. It lasted until Mom found out she would have to keep records and adhere to government rules. In other words, she had to put forth consistent effort and didn't like it. We were back in traditional school within a month.

Besides, Mom thinks it's good for us to get out of the house. That's mostly my fault. My sisters enjoy going out, but I won't leave the house unless forced. Over the centuries, Mom begged me to get out more, but since I don't find anything fun about hanging out with people I'm going to kill, I refused. When governments started mandating education for everyone, she seized the opportunity to throw us—meaning mostly me—into school. Looking back, I should have gone out more. I just never believed Mom would go so far to make me socialize. Her heart is in the right place, but I'm not sure where her head is.

I've pleaded with her to stop the torture and promised to go out more, but she knows I wouldn't. Her only concession has been to alternately move us to third-world countries where school isn't required. She also let me try college, but the loose schedule didn't meet her requirements for social interaction. I can't live in the dorms or sorority houses, after all, so I pretty much showed up for class and went straight home. I thought it was great, but Mom wanted more. The prison-like confinement of high school forces me to be around people for several hours each day. Mom hopes I'll eventually learn to play well with others. Not likely.

I do try to look on the bright side. Living on Earth, even with school, is better than being under Zeus' direct control. Most of the time, that makes it tolerable. But there are days like today where it's all too much.

I turn off my desk lamp and computer, starting to get up, but then sit back down. My curiosity about Alex has been building all day. I've tried to tamp it down, to forget him, but I can't. Even Chloe's chatter couldn't take him out of my thoughts. I boot the computer back up and give in to temptation.

I search for Alex's record in our database. What I'm doing isn't forbidden, but I rarely bother to check on the humans once I assign their manner of death. I forget them until I see them again on their date of death. However, tonight, I want to see what kind of fate Lacey devised for him and refresh my memory about how and when he'll die.

I find his file but just as I'm about to double click and open it, I pull back. Do I really want to know what Lacey has planned for him? He's already faced grief and loss. What if his fate gets worse than that? Do I want that knowledge?

I think for a few moments and decide it doesn't really matter either way. He and I aren't going to become friends. I enjoyed our afternoon together, but that has to be the end of it. If his fate is bad, I can live with it. He is, after all, just another human. Easy come, easy go.

I double click on the file. His entire past and future lies before me. I scroll down to the end of the document, looking for the relevant part, the date of death. I don't have to scroll far.

May fifteenth of this year.

I read the page again. The date doesn't change. May fifteenth is a little less than two months from now. I quickly scroll back up, looking for the details on how he will die. I'm furious when I find them.

Lacey has given him a brain tumor. It wasn't enough to give his mother cancer; she had to give it to him, too. Reading quickly, I see he received some treatment and the tumor receded, but it returned a couple of months ago. Now, it is spreading rapidly, and there are no more treatments to be tried.

I read my notes in the file. The tumor will kill him. I didn't assign him a merciful, quick death from an accident or anything like that. Oh, no. I, in my infinite wisdom, decided he should die from complications brought on by the tumor. I could have shown him mercy and killed him in some less painful way, but

I did not. He was just another human who came to me from Lacey with a short expiration date and a handy cause of death built in. Just like his mother. I wish I could have a do over on his file.

The return of the tumor must have been the bad news that prompted him to drive his car through St. Luke's. I can see why. The death of his mother, the diagnosis of his own cancer, the treatment, the elation at thinking he beat the disease, and then the reality that it was back and deadly would be enough to drive anyone over the edge. Or through the wall. The tumor also explains his panting and paleness up on the mountain today. He shouldn't have been up there at all in his condition.

I scroll through his file, looking for any bright spots. There are none. I go back to the root directory. There is another file with Alex's name on it but when I click it, the computer informs me that it's password protected.

That's not unusual. Lacey often restricts access to files that contain controversial plans or ideas that she knows Chloe and I won't approve of. Nothing she does is ever against Zeus' master plan, but there are some decisions and judgments that she keeps private. Normally, I don't mind, but today, I do. What about Alex prompted her to protect this document?

I try a few likely password combinations, hoping to get lucky, but the file remains locked. With no way to crack the password, I'll have to confront her and risk pissing her off.

Whatever. Alex has less than two months to live and, from what I can tell, he knows it. No wonder he spends so much time thinking about death. His own is approaching fast, and he's trying to make sense of it. I feel pity for him, which is something I've never felt for a human.

I lean back in the chair. *Well, crap.* I silently curse my mother for goading me into spending time with Alex. If it wasn't for her little pep talk today and her relentless insistence that I socialize, I wouldn't have gone to meet him and I wouldn't be feeling bad about having to kill him. Now, I'm feeling protective of him and I don't like it.

Well, I can fix that. I'll go back to my original plan and freeze him out. I'll be the biggest bitch in the world to him until he gives up, decides I really am crazy, and leaves me alone. I'll forget about our afternoon on the mountain and how much I liked spending time with him. I can and will end this before it goes any further. Turning out my desk lamp again, I head upstairs for bed. I have a feeling that sleep isn't going to come easily.

I'm still awake when the alarm beeps in the morning, having spent the night alternately swearing to drive Alex away and then deciding I shouldn't be that cruel. The only good news is I'm tired, crabby, and primed to be a total bitch to Alex and everyone else. I won't have to act crazy. I probably *will* be crazy.

My attitude goes to waste because Alex isn't in school. I look for him in English, at lunch, and in calculus, but he never appears. I only have to deal with the grieving kids in the hallways, and they already know I'm a bitch. For once, I don't even have to fake looking upset because I actually am a little sad over Alex's fate. And I'm mad at myself for even caring. I'm sure it makes me look, if not grief-stricken, at least unhappy.

After school, I walk with Lacey to our cars. Chloe has softball practice today, so Lacey and I are alone. I decide to find out what she's hiding in that password-protected document and to find out why she cursed Alex.

"So," I begin, "what's the deal with Alex Martin?"

"Who?" she asks. Lacey looks confused, but I can tell she's faking ignorance. I play along because I know it's easier than calling her out on her childish behavior.

"The new kid in school. He's in a couple of my classes, so I got curious last night and pulled up his file. You've got him dying from a brain tumor in two months."

"Oh, him," she says too casually. "Yeah, I know who you're talking about."

She doesn't say anything else, so I press her. "What'd he do to deserve that kind of fate? First you kill his mother, and then you give him terminal brain cancer. That's kind of harsh."

"Why do you care?" Lacey challenges, swinging her long, brown braid back over her shoulder. "You never show this kind of interest in a human. I've handed out far worse, and you've never complained."

"I've talked to him a few times in class and at lunch," I say. "He seems like a decent guy. Plus, Chloe and all the other girls are going crazy over him. They think he's some kind of catch, but he's not. He's dying, and I just wonder why you gave him such a raw deal. Is he being punished for something?"

"No, I'm not punishing him. And before you ask, I'm not punishing anyone else, either," she says, cutting off my next question.

"Why then? Is that what's in the password-protected document?"

Lacey narrows her green eyes at me, and I can tell she's angry. She doesn't like being questioned. Red blotches are creeping up her neck. I wait for the explosion.

"You shouldn't be nosing around in my stuff, Atropos," she says.

"Why not? It's not forbidden. And it's not *your* stuff. It's our stuff."

"True, but you know there are decisions I make that you and Chloe don't get to know about. Only Zeus knows certain things."

It chafes me when she gets all superior on me. I am, after all, the eldest sister. "So you aren't going to tell me?" I ask.

"No. But Alex's fate does serve a very special purpose." Her smile when she says that gives me the creeps, and I know this purpose can't be good.

"I'm sure he'll find that comforting on his deathbed," I say as I climb in my car.

"I find it interesting that you care," she retorts with a smirk as she gets into her own car.

I curse her under my breath and resist the urge to get back out of my car and smack that smirk right off her face. She always acts like her work is more important than mine or Chloe's. The power to manipulate destiny went to her head a long time ago.

What she doesn't get is that without Chloe, she'd be unemployed, and, without me, she'd have a lot more work to do. Managing an infinite destiny for every human would get time consuming. As it is, I kill people and let her off the hook.

I drive by Alex's house on the way home, but it doesn't look like anyone is home. There are no cars in the driveway, and all the blinds are down and closed.

When I get home, there's plenty of work to keep my mind off Alex. I don't finish until late and when I'm done, I'm too tired to dwell on Alex's fate or whereabouts.

Alex isn't in school the following day, either, and I find myself relieved. His absence makes it much easier for me to stick to my plan of freezing him out. Out of sight, out of mind, and I don't even have to try to be rude. It's also easier to tell myself I can forget our afternoon on the mountain and that I had no fun whatsoever up there with him.

School lets out, and I head toward the parking lot. A blonde girl I don't recognize is standing by the doors, studying each student as they exit the school. She's younger than the kids in the high school, probably middle-school aged. She's obviously looking for someone.

I come abreast of her, and she jogs to get in front of me.

"Are you Sophie?" she asks, walking backward so she can face me.

"Yeah."

She lets out a breath. "Thank goodness. I was so afraid I wouldn't recognize you, but he said I wouldn't be able to miss your red hair and leather jacket. But it's kind of warm, and I was afraid you wouldn't be wearing the jacket."

She inhales to continue, but I hold up a hand to stop her. "Who said? And who are you?" I ask.

"Oh, sorry. My name's Emily Martin. Alex sent me. I'm

Alex's sister?" The last is a question, as if I might not know who Alex is.

"Oh, hi. He mentioned he has a sister."

"Huh. That's surprising. Usually, he tries to forget about me. Says I'm too annoying."

I can't help but smile at the girl. She sure is peppy. "What can I do for you?" I ask.

"Alex hasn't been in school for a couple of days, and he sent me to see if you could get his assignments. He said you have two classes together, and that maybe you could get the rest? He said you're the only person he knows here, and he hopes you'll help him out."

Done delivering her message, Emily stops and waits for my verdict. I'm trying to figure out why a dying kid cares about homework. He isn't going to finish school, so why does it matter? If I were in his shoes, I'd say, "Screw school," and go do something fun with the time I had left. Anyone else would probably do the same thing. But that's what makes Alex interesting. He isn't like me, and he isn't like other humans.

"Why don't you get them for him?" I ask. "It would be easier."

"Oh, I don't go here. I go to St. Margaret's School for Girls. Security doesn't allow kids who aren't students in there," she says, pointing toward the doors where the guard is checking the IDs of everyone going into the school.

"Oh. Right. Well, I guess I can do it. Do you have his schedule?"

Emily thrusts a piece of paper into my hand.

"Thank you, thank you," she says. "Can you bring it by the house later? Alex said you know where we live."

"Yeah, sure."

Emily runs off to the bike rack and hops onto a pink-flowered contraption. She pedals off, throwing a wave over her shoulder in my direction.

I go back inside to hunt down Alex's other teachers. After an hour, I have all of his assignments and I can finally go home. I figure I'll go by Alex's house after dinner because I have my own

54

chores to take care of, first.

When I finally get home, I kill a few people and set up tomorrow's work before going upstairs for dinner. We're eating together as a family tonight, which is rare. Usually at least one of us is missing from the table. I eat in the basement a lot, grabbing bites in between line cuttings. Tonight, I'm free, but I still bolt down my food and quickly excuse myself.

"Where are you going?" Mom asks.

"I have to take some assignments to a classmate who's out of school for a few days."

"Since when do you volunteer?" asks Lacey.

"I didn't volunteer. His sister asked for my help."

"Who is it?" Chloe asks.

"Alex Martin."

"Ooh. Can I go with you?" she asks.

"No. I think he's sick. He doesn't need you drooling all over him or pumping him for information about a girlfriend. I'm just going to drop off the work, answer any questions he has, and come home."

"Don't rush. Stay as long as you can," Mom says with a wink in my direction.

I roll my eyes. "It's nothing like that. I'm just the only person he knows at school."

Lacey snickers into her salmon.

"What's with you?" I ask her.

"Nothing. I just think it's funny how you spend a lot of time justifying your interactions with Alex."

Chloe looks at Lacey, and then at me. "What'd I miss?" she asks.

"Nothing," I say, shooting Lacey a look that dares her to mention what we talked about in the parking lot yesterday. "And I'm not justifying anything."

"Okay. I just can't remember you ever being so nice to a human. Makes me wonder what's up," Lacey says.

"Nothing's up. Good grief," I say as I grab my coat and the folder with Alex's assignments off the hall rack, slamming the door shut behind me.

It's chilly but not cold outside, so I decide to walk to Alex's house. The sun is setting. I'm grateful Alex's house is to the west so I can appreciate the reds and golds in the sky as I walk. I don't spend as much time outside as I would like, so sunsets like this one are a rare treat for me. Taking my time, I tell myself I'm enjoying the view when the truth is I'm stalling.

Emily didn't say Alex was sick, but that's the only reason I can think of for him missing two days of school. Unless he's in trouble with the law again, but I don't think it's that.

I wonder how bad his illness is. I know he isn't dying yet, but whatever's keeping him from school is likely the beginning of the end. I mentally brace myself for whatever I'll find when I get there.

The sun is fully down by the time I reach his house, the sky a deep purple. After ringing the bell, I glance around the small, shabby yard illuminated by the porch lights. With all the illness and grief in this family, I'm sure no one has time for yard care and it shows. One brave plot of daffodils by the porch steps adds a little color, but weeds are nearly choking out the flowers. I bend over and pluck the largest weed. It helps, but not enough.

I hear light footsteps coming toward the door, and I straighten. The door opens, and Emily greets me with a big grin.

"I knew you'd come," she says.

"If Alex is asleep, you can just give these to him later," I say, holding up the folder of assignments.

"No, he's up. Come on. I'll take you to his room."

"Is that okay? I mean, I don't want your dad to get the wrong idea or anything."

"Get the wrong idea about what?" asks a booming voice.

A man built like a linebacker comes around the corner into the foyer. He looks like a bigger, older version of Alex, down to the perpetually pouting mouth. The only difference is that this man is blond like Emily, whereas Alex's hair is dark. That must be his mom's influence.

"Are you Mr. Martin?" I ask to be polite, but I already know the answer.

"I am. And you are?"

"Sophie Moraine. I'm in classes with Alex, and I'm just bringing by his assignments. I can just leave these," I say again, waving the folder at him, "if you'd rather I not stay."

"Damn waste of time for the boy to be studying, but he insists. You can go on back. Do him some good to have some company, I expect. Let me take your coat," he adds, reaching for my jacket, which I hand over. He hangs it on the coatrack by the door before disappearing into the living room, where I can hear a ballgame playing on TV.

"Come on," Emily says, grabbing my hand and towing me down the hall.

The hallway is lined with family photos, but most go by in a blur because we're moving too fast. The only one I see clearly is a large wedding photo of Alex's parents. I'd guessed correctly that Alex inherited his mother's dark coloring, but beyond that, very little of her is visible in him.

Emily drags me to a closed door with a *Keep Out* sign on it. Ignoring the sign, she throws open the door and lets it bang against the wall. I turn my head away. Since Emily didn't knock, I don't know if Alex is decent, and I don't want to embarrass him if he needs to get himself together.

"Geez, Em, Don't you know how to knock?" Alex asks.

"Sure, but why bother? Sophie's here," Emily says.

"Great. Send her in. And shut the door on your way out," he adds, clearly dismissing her.

I slide into the room around Emily, who sticks her tongue out at her brother and slams the door behind her.

"She's real mature," he says to me.

I walk further into the room, clutching the folder to my chest. It's a typical human boy's bedroom. There's a desk with a computer sitting on it in one corner. The closet door is ajar because of all the clothes and sports equipment spilling out onto the floor. The blue carpet has seen better days. Alex's bed

57

is pushed up against the far wall and when I dare to look in that direction, I'm pleasantly surprised.

Floor-to-ceiling bookshelves bookend the twin bed. More shelves stretch lengthwise across the bed, leaving just enough room for Alex to sit up beneath them. Every shelf is crammed tight with books and the shelves above him bow alarmingly under their loads. If I didn't already know how Alex will die, I would guess death by books when those shelves collapse one day.

Alex watches me examine his room. I wander to the bookshelf on my right and scan the titles. Despite the disorder in the rest of the room, the books are organized by genre and author, the sign of someone who respects their collection. He has everything from classics including, *A Tale of Two Cities*, to *Marvel* comic books. There are more than a few children's books, too. I smile when I see the complete collection of Frank Baum's *Oz* books.

"Those are some of my favorites, too," I say, running my hand over the spines.

"You can borrow anything you want," Alex offers.

"Thanks," I answer, finally turning to him. "I envy your collection. We move so much that I don't keep many books on hand. I mostly use the library, although I did get an e-reader last year. That's allowed me to keep a few more books, at least."

"I'd love to have one of those. It would make taking books to all my doctor's appointments so much easier. But since I had to give up my part-time job a couple of months ago, funds are low."

I glance at the table beside his bed. It's covered in a fleet of prescription medicine bottles, a dosing cup, and several varieties of vitamin supplements. A glass of water, half empty, sits there, too.

I look at him closely for the first time since entering the room. He's wearing his pajamas, but he doesn't look that bad. He's a little pale and there are shadows under his eyes, but I can't tell he's dying just by looking at him. He looks like he could simply have a cold, or maybe he stayed up too late for a few nights.

He meets my gaze squarely, as if daring me to look away.

"Go ahead and ask," he says.

"Ask what?"

"What's wrong with me."

"It's not my business. If you don't want to tell me, you don't have to."

"Brain tumor," he says, tapping his forehead. His tone indicates total acceptance of his condition, but anger that it's there at all.

"Some days are better than others," he continues. "The day I took you up the mountain was a great day, but those are getting rare. And when they do happen, they usually end up costing me. I overdid it that day, and so these last couple of days have been bad. Constant headaches and nausea." He shrugs.

"I'm sorry," I say, having no idea what else to say.

"Not your fault. It is what it is."

"Is it—" I start to ask if it's fatal, since that's the expected question and I'm not supposed to know the answer already.

"The doctors say I'm dying," he flatly says. "The treatments don't work anymore, so all they can do is make me comfortable. Like that's really possible."

I'm silent for a moment. "I'm sorry," I say again, but this time, it comes from my heart. I am sorry that Lacey and I have laid this on him, and even sorrier that none of it can be undone.

He shrugs, resigned. Trite apologies mean nothing.

"If you're dying, why bother with school?" I ask, handing over the assignment folder.

"Because there's always a chance I might beat this, and, if I do, I'm not repeating a grade."

I turn back to the bookshelves to hide my emotion. I can tell him fighting is just a waste of energy, that he might as well enjoy himself because the date is set, but I'm forbidden from doing that, so I sigh instead.

"Come sit down," he says, patting the edge of his bed. "You're pacing, and it's making me tired to watch you. Talk to me for a while. I don't get many visitors."

I perch on the edge of the bed, facing Alex, who is propped

against the headboard. I don't know what to talk about. I'm not good at small talk, with humans or gods, under the best of circumstances. Making small talk with someone I have to kill in a few weeks is beyond uncomfortable.

"Do you have any questions about the assignments?" I lamely ask.

He flips through the folder. "No. It's pretty clear."

We lapse into silence again.

"It's a buzz kill, isn't it?" he asks.

"What?"

"Me dying. Makes it hard to talk to me now, doesn't it? The other day, you had no trouble telling me off, and now you can't come up with a single word. Happens all the time. People find out I'm dying, and they don't know what to say.

"It's okay, though. You can say anything you would have said to me before you knew. You can even tell me to get lost some more."

I smile. He's right, of course. But I don't think I'll tell him to get lost. "What are you reading now?" I ask, leaning over to see the cover of the book lying beside him on the bed.

"*A Game of Thrones*. I saw a kid reading it during a chemo treatment and wondered what the hype was about."

"Do you like it?"

"So far, yeah."

I reach over him and pick up the book, opening to the page he's bookmarked. I nod, seeing he's at the part where Eddard leaves home to become the new Hand of the King. "I remember this one," I say. "Read it a couple of years ago. I've read all the ones that are out so far."

I don't tell Alex he'll never see the end of the series, but I know he won't. Hell, he probably won't make it past this first book. Alex will never find out how it all ends. I wonder why he's even starting it, but I guess it's for the same reason he's still in school. He has to believe he might live.

Somehow, that thought depresses me more than anything else. That an avid reader such as Alex should start a series with no hope of reaching the end is just sad. I stare at the wall on the other side of the room so he won't see the sadness on my face. He doesn't need pity, especially over something as silly as a book.

"Will you read to me?" he asks.

His request snaps my attention back to him. It seems like an awfully intimate thing to ask of someone he hardly knows. But then I remember that he's really just a kid. He's scared, alone, and sick. Don't all kids like to hear stories when they're ill?

"You have a soothing voice," he says.

"That's the first time anyone's ever told me that. My sisters tell me it's too annoying. Of course, I'm usually giving them orders," I say with a little laugh.

He raises an eyebrow at my offhand remark, but he doesn't say anything. Thank goodness. I have to stop slipping around him. Normal people don't give their sisters orders, do they?

"Well, I think it's comforting. Please," he says when I try to hand the book back to him. He pushes it back at me. "The tumor makes my vision a little blurry, and it's hard to read such small print."

I can't resist the plea in his voice or the blatant need for companionship. Or the need to read. "All right."

I open the book and begin to read. Alex watches me, and I'm self-conscious at first. I'm aware that he sees me push my hair out of my face and scratch my nose. Eventually, he relaxes back against the pillows and lets the story envelop him.

I get lost in the book, too, and read close to eighty pages before I realize how late it is.

"Oh, crap," I say when my phone buzzes in my pocket. I have a line cutting in twenty minutes. Even running home at top speed, I'll be cutting it close.

I slap the book shut. "Sorry, but I've got to go. I'm late for something."

"You're always running off," Alex says.

"I have obligations."

I don't want to just leave him. He looks hurt that I'm so eager to get out of his house. I glance again at his bookshelves and make a snap decision I hope I won't regret later.

"Are you allowed out of the house?"

"Maybe next week. I'll have to see how it goes. Why?"

"That part's a surprise. Let me know when you're well enough to go out. If you want to," I add, scribbling my cell number on the assignment folder and tossing it onto the bed.

I run out of the house, grabbing my coat as I dash past a startled Emily in the foyer.

I run hard all the way home. Thankfully, I'm in good enough shape that I can run a six-minute mile. I make it down the stairs and into my workroom with three minutes to spare. I cut the lines and then drop into my desk chair to rest for a minute. I glance at my calendar for the coming weeks. I should be able to carve out some free time when Alex is well enough to go out.

Just before I shut down the computer, I have another idea. I order a Kindle from Amazon and instruct them to send it directly to Alex's house. While I'm at it, I throw in a gift card so he can buy a bunch of books. He'll be able to carry the e-reader to his doctor's appointments and adjust the font size so he can read even when his vision isn't that great. Kindness isn't my forte, but it feels like the least I can do for him.

CHAPTER 5

A WEEK GOES BY AND ALEX DOESN'T CALL OR COME TO SCHOOL.
I resist the urge to stop by his house, partly because I don't feel
like I know him well enough to drop in unannounced, but also
because I feel like it's not my turn to make contact. I left him my
number. He'll call when he's ready. Or not. Either way, I'm not
going to press him. I have my pride, and I'm certainly not going
to go panting after some human boy. I'm not Chloe.

I do see Emily. She comes to the high school on Wednesday
and asks me to get some more assignments for Alex. I get them
and I'm a little excited to have an excuse to go by his house,
but this time when I emerge from the school, she's still there,
waiting for me. *Well, damn.* I hand over the folder, but I stop her
before she pedals off on her bike.

"How is he?" I ask, forgetting I shouldn't care.

"He's doing better. He should be back in school next week.
They've found some new combination of drugs that's helping.
At least for now."

"That's good. Tell him hello for me."

She starts to pedal away, but then jams on the brakes and
turns back to me.

"Listen," Emily begins. "I promised I wouldn't say anything but I'm going to, so don't let him know I told you. He's picked up the phone about fifty times to call you, but he keeps putting it back down. I don't know why. He won't talk about it, just tells me to butt out. But maybe you could call him?"

I smile at her. "No. I made my offer. He either will or won't call. That's up to him."

"But don't you want him to call you?" she asks.

I shrug. "Only if he wants to. He's got enough to worry about. If he doesn't want to call, I don't blame him."

Emily shakes her head. "You're as stupid as he is. I think you two would be good for each other. He seems happier when you're around, when he talks about you."

I laugh at the certainty of a thirteen-year-old. In her world, you either like someone or you don't. They either like you back or they don't. She doesn't see the problems inherent in a relationship between the living and the dying, between a mortal and an immortal. She can't grasp the complications of Alex having too little time and me having far too much. The chasm between death and an infinite fate cannot be crossed.

"We'll see," is all I say.

She huffs, gets on her bike, and channels her frustration into furious pedaling. "Just call him," she hollers into the wind before she turns the corner and disappears.

I don't call. The decision has to be his.

It's Friday afternoon when my phone rings and the tone indicates something other than an appointment with death. I check the screen and see that it's Alex. I let it ring a couple of more times, thinking fast. If I pick it up and he wants to hang out, I'll be trapped. I invited him, and now I'll have to go through with it. I begin to think my offer wasn't such a great idea, after all. Maybe it would be better to let it go to voicemail and ignore him, like I should have done all along.

I sigh. And maybe I'm just a big idiot. I answer the phone.

"So, you said I should call you when I'm ready to get out of the house," Alex says when I answer.

"I did. I take it you're ready?"

"More than."

"Okay. One question. I want to take you somewhere, but you need to be able to walk a little to enjoy it. And it'll take most of the day to get there, see it, and get back. Are you up for all of that?"

"Yeah. I get tired, but if I sit down and rest for a minute, I'll be okay."

"If you're sure. Is Sunday okay?" I ask.

"Fine."

"All right. I'll pick you up around nine on Sunday morning. Wear comfortable, outdoor clothes," I say.

"Sure. And thanks for the Kindle. It came a few days ago. I love it, but are you sure it's not too much? I don't want to keep it if it put you out."

"You're welcome and, no, it wasn't too much. Don't worry about that. We readers need to stick together. I know how much easier it will make things for you."

"Okay," he says, uncertainty in his tone. "If you're sure. Where are you taking me, anyway?"

"That's a surprise. You'll have to wait."

"That's mean."

"See you Sunday," I say.

"See you."

Now I know Alex can go out, I have to get everything ready so I can spend the day away from my work. Since death never stops, it's almost impossible for me to take a whole day off. Thankfully, Zeus gave me a way to take some time off now and then. Twice a year, I am allowed to put death off for one day. Everyone who's currently scheduled to die on Sunday will simply die on Monday instead. It means doubling up on Monday, but since neither day is overwhelmingly busy, it's doable.

I've used this power only twice before, most recently when World War II ended. I was so tired after that war I had no choice. It was take a day off or have a nervous breakdown. I don't use the perk more often because I can't just take a day off. I have to visit Mount Olympus and ask Zeus for permission. And he always asks why. By the time I've done that, my mom, my sisters, and most of the gods all know my business. I'd rather work than answer questions about my personal life or mental state. When they find out I want to spend a day with a human, they're going to talk about me for weeks. I shudder just thinking about it. The humiliation is almost enough to make me abandon this plan altogether. Almost.

There's no use putting it off, so I grab my jacket and head for the car. It's a beautiful day and the drive to Mount Mitchell is pleasant. Windows down and radio blasting some vintage Rod Stewart, I allow myself to enjoy the moment and try not to focus on the upcoming encounter with Zeus.

When I reach Mount Mitchell, I park in the far corner of the visitor's lot. It's getting late in the day, so there aren't many other cars here. This is a relief. On crowded days, it's much more difficult to get to the gateway without a human seeing me go off the trail and reporting me to a park ranger. Sitting in the park jail until they decide to release me isn't fun. I know because it's happened fairly often. I miss the days when the big mountains were just lawless wilderness.

I get out of the car and grab my hiking boots from the trunk. Leaning on the bumper, I slip off my sneakers and lace up my boots. The gateway to Mount Olympus isn't far, but I have to hike some rough country to get there.

Properly shod, I toss my sneakers into the trunk, slam the lid, and head for the hiking trails. The temperature is cool but not cold, and the sunshine filters through the trees, decorating the trail with an ever-shifting pattern of light and shadow. The trees are just beginning to leaf out, and everything is a brilliant, light green. Insects buzz over the few early blooming flowers, and the birds are chirping. I'd love to slow down and enjoy the view, but I have a mission so I walk quickly.

At first, I follow the Mount Mitchell Trail, but after half a mile, I veer off onto the Old Mitchell Trail. After a mile or so of easy hiking, I come to a maple tree with a divided trunk. This is where I leave the trail. I stop walking and wait, listening for any approaching hikers.

I hear voices further down the trail so I stay put, pull a map out of my pocket, and pretend to read it. A young couple emerges from the woods, holding hands and laughing. They're heading back toward the visitor's center. I nod at them as they pass. After they're gone, I wait a bit longer, but I don't see or hear anyone else. I step off the trail and quickly move deeper into the woods.

The incline is steeper here, but it's not unmanageable. After another mile, I reach a creek. The winter was dry and the water isn't running high enough to even reach my ankles. This is good. The last time I came up here, I had to wade through knee-deep water. Today, it's a dry crossing. Once I'm across, the land slopes sharply upward and the hiking gets harder.

I head ever higher up the mountain, picking my way over rocks and fallen trees. Finally, the trees thin and the rocky face of the mountain becomes more visible as I climb above the tree line. I scrabble over piles of rocks until I reach one that is a bit different from the others. It's about the size of a dishwasher, and it doesn't quite follow the natural contours of the others. A casual passerby likely wouldn't notice the difference, much less notice it's fake, but those of us who know what we're looking for can easily spot it.

It's lighter than it looks, and I pull it away from the others to reveal a low, narrow opening. The only way to get in is to get down on my belly and shimmy through. Once inside, I reach back out of the opening and pull the fake rock until it's almost back in place over the hole. I leave enough space so that a thin beam of light still filters through, but otherwise, the opening is obscured.

I turn, slide down a dusty incline, and land on the floor below. There's room to stand, so I get up and brush off my jeans. Except for the tiny beam of light coming from above, it's pitch black in here. I grope around at the base of the slide for one of the flashlights that's always kept nearby. Finding one, I flick it on.

Three tunnels lead out of the cave, and I take the one on the left. I follow it until it forks, and I take the right this time. It's cool and damp down here, and moisture drips from the walls, making for slippery footing. I slow my pace because I don't need to bust my butt in a fall.

Eventually, the tunnel opens into a small room. The walls here are a strange blue, phosphorescent rock that is, as far as I know, only found in this cave. The room glows with a soft blue light, bright enough that I can turn off my flashlight. Stalactites hang from the ceiling, dripping water into the shallow pool that fills the center of the room. They glow almost green, their natural yellowish color mixing with the blue light emanating from the walls.

The pool is ringed by stalagmites, some worn down to nubs from thousands of years of gods and goddesses using them as seats, shelves, and coatracks. The bottom of the pool glows purple, thanks to a thick, phosphorescent moss that covers the bottom. The whole place looks like a 70's acid trip.

I sit down on a stumpy stalagmite near the edge of the water and remove my boots and socks, arranging them neatly beside the rock for my return. Another pair of boots lies on the floor next to the adjacent stalagmite. These were carelessly kicked off and now lie on their sides with their tongues hanging out and their laces knotted.

Picking up one boot, I turn it on its side. A sword and shield are burned into the leather on the heel. I know that logo. My heart jumps once, and then settles back into a normal rhythm. These are Ares' boots. I remember Chloe mentioning once a few weeks ago that he was rumored to be hanging around these mountains. I dismissed it at the time, thinking he'd have no business here, without any wars going on in Asheville. Unfortunately, it looks like Chloe was right.

I drop the boot next to its mate as if it is a dangerous animal. Even though our relationship ended centuries ago, I don't want to run into Ares, either here or on Olympus. I talk a good game, telling everyone I'm over him and it never mattered much, but the truth is very different. Everything about Ares mattered to me once, and, in my quiet moments when I can be honest with myself, still matters. I'm no longer crazy or deluded enough to act on any feelings I might have, but it's safer for me to avoid him altogether.

I think about not going to Olympus and giving up on spending the day with Alex. If I leave the cave now, I won't run into Ares. But that's the coward's way out, and I refuse to take it. It isn't fair to punish Alex for the fact that Ares dumped me for Aphrodite—that he threw every intimacy and kindness I gave him back in my face and all but laughed at me for being naïve enough to think he loved me. Alex deserves the day out, and I'll give it to him, crazy ex-boyfriend or not.

Rolling up my pants, I wade into the pool. The moss is spongy and squeezes up through my toes. The water is freezing. I curse under my breath. Some gods are lucky enough to be able to teleport at will. I call it poofing. They don't have to hike through the damn wilderness and wade in a cold pool. Heck, they don't even have to use cars when on Earth. They just poof around.

My sisters and I are not so fortunate. We're what Zeus calls, "grounded goddesses." We can't poof on our own. To get to Olympus, we either have to use this portal or be touching a god who can poof. To get around on Earth, we have to use conventional transportation. It's a pain in the butt and one of my biggest gripes with Zeus.

I wait for the pool to recognize me. The moss is a living thing, and it knows all the gods and goddesses. If someone other than a god ever tries to use this pool, they'll only have the thrill of standing calf-deep in freezing water.

I feel a tug on my legs, as though someone is trying to pull me under the water. That's just the warm-up act. The pull grows stronger until I feel like my legs are going to pop out of my hip sockets. Suddenly, there's one quick yank and I'm flying through space.

I used these portals for years before I was willing to open my eyes on the journey. When I finally mustered the courage to look around, I saw crazy fractal patterns everywhere, like some sort of cosmic kaleidoscope exploded and sent shards flying into space. Zeus says that each god sees different patterns and colors, but I've never asked anyone else what they see. For all I know, they're not looking, either.

I pass through a particularly pretty pink and yellow pattern and then I see blue sky, clouds, and, below me, Mount Olympus. There are tourists climbing all over the ruins of Zeus' palace and the other monuments. I'm looking at the hologram that protects our mountain. As I fly closer to the ground, the landscape starts to pixelate and get staticky, like a TV station that won't quite tune in. Then, just when it seems like I'm going to crash into the mountain, I'm through the hologram and hovering over Zeus' real palace on Mount Olympus. In the forecourt of the palace is a pool identical to the one I just left. It pulls me to it, and I touch down in the water with a tiny splash.

Zeus' palace looms before me. It's a massive, marble structure surrounded by one-hundred and four columns. A red carpet trails from the main doors, down the steps, and right up to the pool. I think it looks like a big, red tongue hanging out of an open mouth, kind of like the cover of a Rolling Stones album. Absolutely ridiculous. Restraint is not Zeus' strong suit.

I step out of the pool and into one of the pairs of sandals that are always kept here for visiting gods. It wouldn't do to track up the red carpet with wet, mossy feet, after all. The sandals are too big for me, and they make alternating flapping and squishing sounds as I follow the carpet up the steps.

The marble doors are open, and I enter the palace. The sheer size and opulence are supposed to make me tremble at Zeus' might, but all I ever think when I come here is that my father is full of crap.

Mount Olympus is a strange combination of the ancient and the modern. The buildings are all ancient, majestic marble structures. However, what goes on inside looks like what goes on

70

in any home in modern suburbia. Those of us who live among the mortals sometimes bring things to Mount Olympus that we know the others will enjoy, resulting in life that looks less like a royal court and more like a YMCA rec room. Over the years, it's become downright ridiculous.

I shake my head as I walk past the gods and goddesses. Hera, Zeus' current wife, is listening to an iPod that Chloe gave her. Nyx is reading the latest Stephen King novel. Poseidon and Apollo are gathered around a laptop, watching *Star Wars*. Some of the lesser gods are playing *Halo* on an Xbox. The disconnect between what gods should be doing with their time and what they really do gets larger every time I come back here. They spend less time ruling the world and more time fooling around, not seeming to care that the human world is falling into chaos.

Zeus is sitting on his throne at the end of the hall, bobbing his head in time to the music pouring through his headphones. He looks ridiculous, his mane of white hair smashed down by the headband. I approach the throne and wait for him to acknowledge me.

"Daughter," he finally says, sliding the headphones down around his neck. "What brings you here?"

"I need Sunday off," I say, skipping the pleasantries. I just want to get this done and get home.

"Hmm. That's odd. You haven't asked for a day off in, what, seventy years or more?"

"Then it shouldn't be a problem, should it?" I ask, more snark in my voice than I intend.

Zeus raises an eyebrow but he doesn't say anything. He turns to his assistant, Ganymede, who is perched on a small ottoman next to the throne. Ganymede looks like a thirteen-year-old boy, and a pretty one at that. Zeus chose him to be his cup-bearer a few millennia ago, and he gradually turned him into his personal gofer.

"When was her last day off?" he asks Ganymede.

"Nineteen-forty-five."

"Good grief, girl, what are you trying to do? Kill yourself

71

through work?"

Like that's possible for an immortal. As it is, I simply say, "Not really. It's not like taking the whopping two days per year that I'm allotted makes much difference in my stamina level."

"Don't get smart," he cautions, turning back to me.

I shrug. "Just stating the truth," I say, stuffing my hands in the pockets of my jeans. Seeing my balled fists will just provoke him further.

"Sunday, you say? Why?" he asks.

This is the part I hoped to avoid but knew I could not. I'm allowed to take time off for any reason, but Zeus always wants to know why. I think it's some misguided fatherly instinct that makes him want to know if I'm okay, but at times like this, I wish he would just remain the absentee father.

"I want to spend some time with a friend."

"This friend is human?"

"Yes, he's human," I say, rolling my eyes. "He's sick, and I want to show him something special."

"Hmm." Zeus leans back on his throne and thinks for a moment. I wait. "You never spend time with the humans. Is this boy special to you?"

"No. Geez, Zeus." I feel the flush creeping up my neck and I breathe deeply, trying to keep it from becoming noticeable to him. I fail, feeling my cheeks heat.

Zeus just raises his eyebrow at me. I squirm under his glare. Damn. *Just leave it alone*, I beg him silently.

"Good for you," he bellows, making the others in the hall turn our way. *Great.* More attention. "About time. Bring me the hourglass," he directs Ganymede.

Ganymede jumps up and retrieves a large hourglass from a table on the other side of the great hall. It's carved with the same animals and insects that adorn the door to my workroom and filled with black sand. Each grain of sand represents one human life. The grains move through the hourglass very slowly. When a grain enters the bottom chamber, it means I've done my job and the life is over.

For me to have time off, Zeus has to stop the flow of sand through the hourglass. Only he has the power to manipulate the hourglass, to literally stop the passage of time for one day. I can stop it for a few minutes—or however long it takes for Zeus to notice the sand isn't moving—by not doing my job, but if I do so without permission, Zeus will punish me so fast and thoroughly that there's absolutely no incentive to try.

Zeus waves his hand over the hourglass, and small sparks strike the glass. "At 12:01 AM on Sunday, the sands will stop. You will have until midnight on Sunday off. Those scheduled to die will live one more day. You are prepared to double up your work on Monday?" he asks.

"I am. I know the rules," I remind him.

"Then your request is granted."

"Thank you." I turn to go.

"I would be remiss if I didn't tell you it pleases me that you've found someone to spend time with. I worry about you being so alone."

"I'm not alone. I have Mom and my sisters," I say, turning back to face him.

"So you do. But it's not the same as having someone special."

Says the man who has about a hundred "someone specials." I roll my eyes. "He's not special in that way, Zeus. He's a guy who happens to be tolerable and shares some of my interests. That's it. He's dying, and I'm trying to be nice."

"So be it. But it thrills me to see you opening up a little. At times, I've feared I made some mistake when I created you and that maybe you are defective somehow."

"Defective?" I cry. "Maybe I'm not the most well-adjusted god in the pantheon, but I'm not defective. You try dealing with nothing but death for a few thousand years and see how you turn out. Defective," I say again under my breath.

"What is it with you and Mom this week? I got the same lecture from her last week," I continue.

"We want you to be happy and enjoy your life."

"What keeps me happy is not having to deal with emotional

bullshit, either of the human or god variety."

Zeus' eyebrows come together, and I realize I've gone a tad too far.

I retreat. "I'm just saying that my job makes it hard to be with anyone, god or human, and I don't need you and Mom trying to fix me up. All I want to do is give this guy one enjoyable day before I kill him."

Zeus sighs. "It's progress," he says. "It's taken three thousand years, but it's progress. Go on, then," he says, waving a hand in dismissal.

I back away from the throne, resisting the urge to turn and run, as I know that would make me look weak. I'd probably just trip over the too-large flip flops and land on my face, adding to my humiliation. Once I'm a respectable distance away from him, I turn and walk toward the exit.

"But remember," Zeus calls to my back, "this boy may be dying, but you are forbidden from telling him anything about who you really are."

"Like I could forget," I mutter under my breath. "No worries. It's not like I want him to know I'll be killing him in a few weeks," I call back to Zeus as I stride to the door.

I'm almost outside when Ares slips out from behind a pillar and grabs my arm. *Crap.* I feel every eye in the place boring into my back, watching to see what will come of this encounter between the former sweethearts. *Barf.*

Ares moves to stand in front of me, but he doesn't let go of my arm. Probably figures that I'll run if he does. He's not wrong. Gods, he's easy to look at, something I conveniently manage to forget sometimes. He has short, curly brown hair that tends to flop over his forehead so that you want to brush it back. Round, innocent-looking eyes as deep green as a virgin forest stare back at me. When he smiles, you can't help but smile back, even if you hate his guts.

He's tall and broad, which can be scary or comforting, depending on the situation. I remember how, when we were together, he delighted in resting his elbows on my head. I'm so much smaller than he is that he actually has to bend down a little to make it possible. The discrepancy in our heights is so great that he started calling me, "Little Atropos," in private. I loved it. Once. I shake my head and return my thoughts to the present.

"What?" I snap at him.

"I heard that you want some time off to spend with a human boy. Is that wise?" he asks.

"It's not your business, is it?"

"No, but I worry about you. A human? Really? Isn't that something you always swore to avoid? For good reason, I might add."

"You don't get to worry about me," I say. "And you don't get to question my judgment. You gave up those rights eons ago when you dumped me." I wish I could shout at Ares, but I'm keeping my voice to a whisper to cheat my audience out of its gossip.

"You're right. And that's not really what I meant to talk to you about," he says, shaking his head. "I just got distracted."

"Then what is it? I've got to get home before dark, so spit it out."

"I want to apologize for how I treated you all those years ago. I shouldn't have been so callous. There were better ways to end our relationship than just dumping you after we'd been making out for an hour."

I can't help but laugh. "Yeah, like about a hundred. But seriously? It's been a couple of thousand years. Don't you think it's a bit late?"

"Well, I've wanted to for a while, but you hardly ever come up here. When you're on Earth, it's hard to get you alone."

"Is that why you've been skulking around Asheville? Chloe said you were," I add when he looks surprised I know.

"Partly, yes. And partly, well, because I like to look out for you." He drops his head as though this thought embarrasses him.

"Good grief. I don't need your help. And what's brought this

75

on, anyway? It's not like you've ever cared before. Oh, wait, I get it. The latest floozy dumped you and now you're lonely, am I right?"

He doesn't say anything, but his cheeks get red, and I know I've hit a nerve. "Well, let me save you the trouble. I'm not someone you can dump and then pick back up when you need to fill a void in your life."

He opens his mouth to speak, but I cut him off. "Save it. I've got to go. Don't hang around Asheville, don't look for me, and don't worry about me." I push past him and run down the steps to the courtyard. Slipping out of the borrowed flip flops, I step into the pool and let it take me back to the cave on Mount Mitchell. I see Ares running down the steps after me, but I'm gone before he reaches me. Unnerved, I shake the whole way back to the car.

It's almost dark by the time I leave the cave, so I try to hurry back to my car. The fading light makes things difficult, and I stumble over roots and rocks in my haste. After tripping over a particularly large root and landing face-first in a pile of leaves, I force myself to slow down. It might be dark, but I know the way and there is no point in breaking a bone just to get there two minutes faster.

I'm almost back to the Old Mitchell Trail when the young man steps out from behind a grove of trees and blocks my path. I brace myself for a fight or a good lie about why I'm off the trail, but I relax when I recognize him.

"Thanatos," I say. "You scared the crap out of me."

"Sorry," he says, but his smirk indicates that he's really not. "I just came to say hello, Atropos. Or is it Sophie you prefer these days?"

"Either," I say. "What brings you out here?"

I rarely see Thanatos in person, for all that we are coworkers in the business of death. He has more contempt for humans than even I do, and he outright hates most of the gods, so he only journeys from the Underworld when he has no choice.

He hasn't changed since the last time I saw him. He still looks like a seventeen-year-old kid with green eyes and blond hair. Like most of the male gods, he's ripped and sports a full six pack. He wears nothing more than a loincloth and sandals, his usual outfit, but he doesn't appear bothered by the evening chill.

"I've come to give you a warning from my sisters," he begins.

"Oh, gods. What is this? Crazy ex-boyfriend day?"

"What?"

"Never mind. Go on." I'm not about to tell him about my meeting with Ares or Zeus.

"I'm sure you know how much they admire your power," he says.

I snort. I can't help it. Admire isn't the right word. Covet is more accurate. "*Lust after*" would be another appropriate expression. Thanatos' sisters are the Keres—disgusting, parasitic women who feed on the blood of those who die violently. Wherever there's a war, a bomb, or a plague, you'll find the Keres in the middle of it, lapping up the blood. The more violent the death, the sweeter the blood. To them, anyway. Can't say I ever tried it.

They're cruel, too. Rather than peacefully escorting a soul from an already-dead body to the Underworld as Thanatos does, the Keres rip the soul from a dying person and cast it off while they feast on the body. Eventually, Thanatos tracks down the soul and takes it to the Underworld, but not before the body has been desecrated and the soul has wandered the Earth, alone and confused, sometimes for weeks. It's the ultimate form of disrespect for the dead, and I despise everything about the Keres.

The feeling is mutual. The Keres' ultimate goal is to control the manner of death, as I do, so they can feed their appetites. In their opinion, humans should always be dying from some horrible plague or war wounds. Peaceful death does nothing for them, and they can't stand the fact that I don't make every death a horrible one.

77

If anything, I deliberately create fewer violent deaths just to make them uncomfortable. Since there are hundreds of thousands of them, they need a lot of blood to keep the troops fed. I get perverse satisfaction from denying them. Even Lacey can't stand the Keres. The advances in medicine, warfare, and safety that she has allowed have happened, in part, to help starve the Keres. There are far fewer pandemics and wars today than there used to be, which means less food for the Keres despite the increase in population. Sucks to be them.

"So what's the message?" I ask Thanatos, humoring him.

"That they are starving. If you don't start crafting more violent deaths, they will take your job. And when they do, they will not be lenient with the humans. You coddle them too much. My sisters will not be as kind."

"And they wonder why I don't like them?" I mutter.

Thanatos glares at me. "I've come to present a compromise. If you hand over your shears now, my sisters will still allow many humans to die peacefully. They'll limit the bloody deaths to a fair number. Enough to satisfy their needs, but not so many that the humans feel persecuted. You can retire and live however you please. However, if you resist, every human will die violently with no mercy for anyone."

"Seriously? That's your big compromise? Quit my job or the humans will all violently die? What makes you think I'll go for this?"

"I know you have, we'll call them, 'mixed feelings,' about your job. You told me once you wished you didn't have to be the Death Fate. This is your chance to get out of it."

"Okay, I'll give you that one. My job doesn't thrill me. But I'll never give it up, at least not to the Keres. I may not love my job, but I do it well and respectfully. Your sisters are just flying killing machines with no respect for Zeus' master plan or the humans."

"Since when do you care about the humans?" Thanatos asks.

"I don't, but there's a difference between not caring and total disrespect."

Thanatos is silent. He's good at it. Finally, because it's almost dark and I need to get out of the woods, I press him. "You've passed on this threat several times over the centuries," I remind him. "And it's never come to anything. In fact, every time they've tried to take my shears, your sisters have gotten their asses kicked. What makes any of you think this time will be different?"

"They have powerful allies this time. More than that, the Oracle at Delphi has finally foretold your downfall."

"The Oracle, huh? You do know she's bat-poop crazy and that most of her prophecies are just the words of a psychotic, not a psychic?"

"Perhaps," Thanatos says. "But you might not want to wait to find out. Surrender your shears now, and you can spare humanity my sisters' retribution. And avoid your own punishment," he adds.

"Let me think," I say, pretending to do just that. "Um, no. Not a chance in Hades. Either your sisters are bluffing or the Oracle is nuts. Either way, I'm thinking I'll be just fine."

"I guess that's the risk you'll take then."

I nod. "I guess so. Go tell your sisters they'd better learn to like Spam, because they won't be getting any extra human flesh and blood any time soon."

Before I can say anything else, Thanatos steps back behind the trees and vanishes.

"Asshole," I mutter.

I continue walking back toward the visitor's center, thinking over the encounter as I go. As uncomfortable as Thanatos' warning makes me, I don't think I'm in any real danger. Even if he's telling the truth about the Oracle prophesying my doom, her prophecies are so unreliable and vague as to be laughable. There's even a good chance the Oracle isn't really an oracle at all. It's possible she's just high on some gas that leaks out of the Earth's core at her location.

I'll tell my mom and sisters about it when I get home, but I can't see any weakness that will allow the Keres to steal my shears or defeat me. My shears are safely locked up in my workroom in a secure area below a house that the Keres cannot enter. There's no way for them to get my shears without me handing them over. And that isn't going to happen.

I get back to the parking lot to find the park ranger looking at my car, jotting down the plate number. I jog up to him. "Sorry," I say. "I got distracted by the view, and it got dark faster than I thought it would." It's always best to play the ditzy tourist when in danger of getting caught.

"Okay. I was getting ready to lock the gate for the night, but I wanted to make sure no one was left in the woods. I was getting ready to go looking for you."

"I'm fine," I say, getting in the car. "Sorry if you had to wait for me."

"Be more aware next time," he says as I drive off. I give him a wave as I exit the lot and head for home.

When we sit down to dinner, I tell my mother and sisters about Thanatos' warning, but I don't mention the encounter with Ares. I don't need them knowing he's still interested in me. We all agree that Thanatos is likely bluffing and that even if the Oracle has foretold my downfall, it's probably just psychotic ravings. To be safe, however, my mom feels we should increase our vigilance.

"I know you girls don't always lock the door to the basement, but from now on, it gets locked."

I groan. "But it's such a pain to have to enter the code every time one of us needs something down there."

"I know, but you're the most vulnerable when you're down there. You sometimes take your shears out of your workroom. If the Keres somehow accessed the basement, they could steal them. Keep your shears inside your workroom and keep that door locked, too. This may be all bluster, but a little extra caution on our part can't hurt."

"I promise," I say.

"And I'll increase the protection spell on the outside of the house. They shouldn't be able to get beyond that," Mom says.

I think this is all overkill, but I see her point. I've had enough fights with the Keres over the years to know I don't want to find them anywhere in this house.

After our strategy session, I go downstairs to work. The death show always goes on, even amidst threats and broken romances. After cutting a few hundred lines, I emerge from my workroom to find Lacey hunched over a table loaded with astrological charts. I watch as she reads one chart and then turns to her scale. A newly spun lifeline rests in one scalepan. Into the other, she places blobs of green goo that she scoops from a jar on her desk. She keeps adding and removing goo until the scale balances evenly. After that, she removes just a tiny bit more until the lifeline overbalances the goo.

The green goo represents this person's financial health. Lacey is setting this person up to never have quite enough money. They won't live in poverty, but neither will they be comfortable. Her job fascinates me, probably because it is more about creation than destruction. I'd like to create something once instead of always destroying.

I let her finish her task before approaching her desk. "What do you really think?" I ask her. "Do you think the Keres have anything to use against me?"

She keeps her back to me, still messing with the scale. "No. But that doesn't mean they aren't looking. They could get lucky one of these days."

"You're probably right," I say. With those words, I remember the whole reason I'd been in the woods today. "Crap," I say.

"What?"

"I'm supposed to take Alex somewhere on Sunday. That was why I was in the forest when Thanatos showed up. I went to see Zeus." "Maybe you just shouldn't go," Lacey says. "Put it off for a few weeks until the Keres back off again."

"I don't know when I'll have another chance. He's getting

81

sicker."

She shrugs. "Where are you going?"

"I wanted to take him up to the ruins of the old Oz theme park. He has all the books, so I know it's something he'd like."

Lacey leans back in her chair and stares at me. She tilts her head, considering. I brace myself for some cutting remark or joke about my involvement with a lowly human.

"I know I gave you crap about him the other day, but you really feel something for him, don't you?"

I'm surprised. Lacey and I don't really discuss personal things. Our relationship has always been coolly professional, even distant. Her showing some concern for me throws me off.

"I don't know. I've only known him a few days. I've barely talked to him." I don't mention the day on the mountain. Lacey doesn't know about that, and I want to keep it that way.

"Sometimes things just aren't rational. You, me, and Chloe know that better than anyone."

"They are with me. I make them that way."

Lacey laughs. "You think you do," she says. "But control is an illusion."

"Whatever. Look, I can't afford to like this guy or any other human. My job is killing them, not liking them."

"Who said it has to be one or the other?" she asks. "Ever since Ares, you've acted as though there's some law that says you can't have feelings for anyone. Maybe it's just time to give that up and try loving someone. It might be a positive experience."

"Humph," I grunt, plopping my hip down on the side of her desk. "Now you sound like Mom. I've watched enough humans and gods suffer through love and loss to know that very few people find the experience to be positive. Gut wrenching, painful, stressful, and scary, sure. Positive? Not so much."

"So, back to the original question," I say, eager to change the subject. "Do you think it'll be safe to take him to the park?"

She shrugs. "Should be. Hardly anyone knows those remains are even up there. Besides, you won't have your shears with you and those are what the Keres really want."

"You're right. We're being paranoid for nothing," I say. "This won't come to anything, although I'll take my weapons just to be safe."

"Of course I'm right," she says. "I'm always right."

There's not a hint of teasing in her voice. She's serious.

"And there's my sister," I say.

She just smirks at me. The sisterly bonding moment is over, and we're back on familiar ground again.

CHAPTER 6

SINCE I DON'T HAVE TO PICK UP ALEX UNTIL NINE ON SUNDAY
morning, I wake up extra early just to revel in a day off. Making
a pot of coffee, I drink a cup on the back deck while I watch the
sunrise. I take my time reading the paper, as it's always fun to
see my handiwork show up as *news*. I even make some cinnamon
rolls and leave them out for my mom and sisters. Okay, so the
rolls are out of a can, but it's the thought that counts.

Then, feeling like I should do something productive, I head
downstairs and clean up my workspace. I prop the door to my
workroom open to let out some dust while I sweep. I'm already
breaking the promise I made to Mom by not keeping my
workroom door closed, but it does get kind of grungy in here.
I'm organizing some files when Chloe comes downstairs, still
in her pajamas, clutching a cup of coffee and a cinnamon roll.

"Oh," she says, catching sight of me. "Thanks for the rolls
and coffee, but I figured you'd sleep in since you've got the day
off."

"Nope. I wanted to enjoy it, but I felt like I should do one
productive thing, so I came down here."

"I've got to get an early start today, too," she says as she sits down at her spinning wheel and places the coffee cup on her desk. "I've fallen a little behind."

"Behind?" I ask. "Aren't you running about five years into the future right now?"

"Yeah, but Lacey took the lines I gave her the other day and assigned them their destinies. Almost every one of them is going to have multiple children. I've got to get busy."

I just shake my head. "Please. You're so far ahead, you make the rest of us look like total slackers."

She giggles. "Well, it's better to be ahead than behind. Besides, I might want a little time off, soon, too."

"What for? Oh—" I start, seeing the familiar look on her face. "You're in love again."

"Well, heavy like, anyway. He's on the baseball team."

"I hope he's not scheduled to die soon. I can't deal with any more broken hearts right now. Lacey's still mourning Charlie, you know."

"He's not. I checked. He's going to live to an old eighty-four. Of course, I'll be long gone by then, but it'll be fun while it lasts."

I stuff some files into an already-overstuffed drawer. "I don't know how you do it."

"Do what?"

"How you deal with humans so philosophically. You love them and, when it's over, it's over. You don't seem to suffer. I admire that about you."

She shrugs. "I don't know. I guess I just go into it knowing it's a limited-time deal. Keeping that in mind makes it easier. But I do hurt, Atropos. I'm not some tramp who just uses guys and then lets them go."

I wince at the hurt in her voice, hurt caused by my casual assumption she can easily love 'em and leave 'em. "Gods, I'm an asshole," I say. "I didn't mean it like that."

"I know. I just wanted you to know that it's not all fun and games with me. I love them and I hurt when it's over, whether it ends through death or a breakup. But my life has to go on, too."

She picks up her thread and starts turning the wheel. I

watch her for a minute, wondering how the softest, most fragile of the three of us can be the strongest. Moved, I walk to her end of the room and lightly kiss her blonde curls.

"What's that for?" she asks.

"You're too good for the rest of us," I say.

I wander back to my area. The clock on my desk reads 8:45. Time to get going. Shutting down my computer, I close and lock the door to my workroom.

"I'm off to go get Alex," I tell Chloe as I pass by her spinning wheel.

"Have fun. Seriously," she adds when I roll my eyes. "Just enjoy the day for what it is."

When I get upstairs, I grab my keys and jacket off the sofa and head out. I stop on the sidewalk, surprised by the weather. Not that it's bad—it's actually great. The sun is shining and the temperature, although still chilly from the night, holds the promise of warming up nicely. It's strange because last night the forecasters were calling for cool rain all day. Zeus must have changed the weather for my benefit. I'm not sure whether to thank him later or resent yet more interference in my life.

I'm still puzzling over that when I pull into Alex's driveway. He is already waiting on the porch steps.

"You said to be ready," he says as he climbs in the car. "I didn't want to make you wait. Or make you deal with my father and sister." I see Emily peeking at us from behind the living room curtains, and I give her a little wave.

Glancing over at Alex, I try to see if he looks ill. I don't want him to overdo it if he isn't well. This trip isn't that important.

"I'm fine," he says.

"What?" I ask, feigning innocence.

"I see you checking me out, looking to see if I'm okay. Don't worry about it. It's a good day. And the weather! I was worried last night when I saw the forecast."

I say nothing about the likely intervention of my father on that front.

"So, where are you taking me?" he asks.

"It's a surprise."

"How long till we get there?"

"Two hours, give or take."

He settles back in the seat, idly caressing the leather with his fingertips. I smile. Boys and their cars.

"Tell me something," he says as I drive. "What do you want to do after you graduate?"

"Why do you want to talk about that?" I ask.

"I'm fascinated by people who will live to see the end of high school. I'm curious about what dreams and plans they have."

"I haven't given it much thought," I say, which is a lie. I've spent centuries thinking about what I'd like to do. But I'll never get the chance to do any of it. I'm not dying like Alex is, but I don't get to have any dreams, either. My life will remain the same for an infinite number of years.

"Don't you have any dreams?" he asks when I don't elaborate on my nonexistent plans. "Anything I can vicariously enjoy?"

"Sorry, no," I say.

This isn't totally the truth. I do have one dream, but I never speak of it because it's pointless to wish for something I'll never have. I want to be mortal. I want a life where I can have any job I want, where I can love freely, and not have to keep everyone at arm's length all the time just to preserve my sanity. *Freedom.* That's my dream.

I glance over and see that Alex is watching my face. No doubt he can see I'm hiding something from him, so I decide to share my minor dream with him. The one that is slightly more realistic, if still unlikely.

"Well, just one," I amend.

"Tell."

"I want to live by the ocean."

"That's it?" he asks, clearly disappointed.

"Well, I've lived around mountains all my life. I've never gotten to live at the beach. In fact, I've only been to the ocean once."

"Not very ambitious," he says. "Seems like someone as smart

87

as you would have bigger dreams than that."

I shrug. "Best I have. What do you want to do?" I ask him.

"What *did* I want to do, you mean," he corrects me.

"Okay, what did you want to do before you got cancer?"

"I wanted to be a veterinarian. I love animals."

"That would be fun."

"Yeah. Our dog died last year. I wanted to get another one, but Dad said no. He doesn't want to take care of it after I'm gone."

"That sucks. Wouldn't Emily take care of it?" I ask.

"She would, but she'll be off to college in a few years. Dogs live longer than that."

I think for a moment. Taking another step closer to the abyss of emotions created by caring for a human, I take a deep breath before saying, "What if I agreed to take it?"

"You'd do that?" he asks.

"Sure. My sisters and mom love animals, too."

This is true. We've had a succession of pets over the centuries. My fondest memory is of the farmhouse in Wyoming, near the Big Horn Mountains, that we lived in during the late eighteen hundreds. We had dogs, rabbits, chickens, and horses. I miss that lifestyle. We haven't had a dog in at least twenty years. Now that I think about it, I'm not sure why. I guess we just got so busy, we sort of forgot to get one.

"We're currently pet-less," I say, but I know no one would object to a dog in the house. You could keep it until—" I wave a hand in the air, not wanting to say it.

"I'm dead," he finishes for me.

"Yeah. Then I'll take care of it. You can name it, and I promise not to change it."

"Wow," Alex says, and I see a little-boy glint in his eye. "I'll ask my dad, but I bet he'll go for it. Thanks."

"No problem. I'll get something out of it, too."

We lapse into silence again. I'm sure he's already picking out dog names. He leans his head against the window. Soon, his breathing evens out and I know he's asleep. I turn the radio on low, find a classic rock station, and drive on toward Beech Mountain.

When we get there, I follow the Beech Mountain Parkway, turning back and forth along the switchbacks up the mountain, then veer off onto Oz Road, which is relatively new. When Oz was open, you either had to get up here by ski lift or take a shuttle bus up from the town below. Recently, someone got the bright idea to build houses up here and built the road, but then the development went bust, leaving just a road to an abandoned theme park.

At the end of the road, a rusting traffic gate hangs over the driveway that leads into the park. That's okay. I don't need to drive beyond it. We'll walk from here.

I pull the car off the road and park it behind some large rocks and overgrown shrubs, hiding it from casual passersby. If anyone comes up here, they'll have no trouble finding the car, but anyone simply driving by will likely miss it. I'm not expecting company because Lacey's right. Very few people know this old park is even up here.

I turn off the engine, gently shaking Alex's shoulder. "We're here," I say when he opens his eyes.

He looks around at the unmarked driveway and the nothingness surrounding us, and then looks at me like I'm nuts.

"Well, we have to walk a bit," I amend.

We get out of the car, duck under the gate, and start walking up the driveway. I have to slow my usual pace a bit to allow Alex to keep up.

"Where are we?" he asks.

"It's a surprise."

"So you keep saying," he mutters.

The driveway is cracked and weedy beyond the gate. The park's been closed for more than thirty years. Much of it has been lost to vandalism and nature but what remains is special, in a creepy sort of way. Something about abandoned places always attracts my interest. Hanging out in them is like listening to voices from the past whispering their stories to me.

We walk until we come to a crumbling concrete platform next to a small house. It is falling in, and nature has reclaimed most of the area around it. The only way in would be via machete. Metal ski lift towers rise above us, their wires and gondolas long gone.

"What is this place?" Alex asks.

"Well, this specifically is the old museum and gondola house. The only way up here used to be by ski lift or bus. This was the drop-off point for both. The road we came in on is a recent addition."

"Okay. But a museum for what?" Alex asks, waving his hand at the small cottage.

"Keep walking," is all I say.

The paved road ends just past the gondola house, and now we walk on a dirt path that is slowly being overtaken by plant life. It used to be a brick path, but the bricks were stolen long ago.

The path ends at a stone wall with two wooden, emerald green doors set into it. The paint is peeling and faded but still bright enough to be pretty. The doors and wall are twice as tall as either of us. Painted on one door is a massive, yellow letter, "O," and on the other is the letter, "Z."

"Oz?" Alex asks, clearly confused.

The doors are equipped for a padlock, but there isn't one. There used to be, but I guess over the years, the landowners gave up replacing it every time someone cut it off. We're still technically trespassing, but an unlocked door makes it easier.

I push on the door with the, "O" on it, and it groans open on rusty hinges. It doesn't give easily, and I only manage to open it wide enough for Alex and me to slip through. It's very different from the days when it would be opened with a flourish by a costumed Emerald City guard who would announce all visitors. We step inside, and I push the door shut behind us.

"Welcome to the Land of Oz," I say, waving Alex in with my own little flourish.

"You're kidding, right?"

"Nope. This used to be the Land of Oz theme park."

Alex looks at the ground beneath us. "The Yellow Brick Road?" he asks.

"What's left of it," I say, noting that only a few yellow bricks remain here and there, and most of those are broken. "Most were stolen by souvenir hunters, I think."

We follow the Yellow Brick Road until we come to the ruin of Auntie Em and Uncle Henry's farm. The remains of gardens and animal pens look sad among the detritus of ruined buildings. Here and there, a Mason jar from Auntie Em's house or a tool from Henry's barn lies scattered among the weeds.

We circle Dorothy's house. I want to go inside, but there's so much overgrowth that I can't find a clear path in. The last time I was here, I was able to get inside, but nature has closed in on the house since then. An identical house can be seen around a curve in the path, except it is mangled and tilted.

"Why two houses?" Alex asks.

"That's the house after the tornado," I explain, pointing to the damaged house. "When visitors went through the first house, they'd hear sirens and wind effects to indicate that the tornado was coming. An employee would direct them to the storm cellar, which was really an underground corridor that linked the two houses. The tourists would see a film of stuff flying through the air and have to navigate a maze that simulated the confusion of a storm. When the 'storm' was over, they'd come back upstairs and exit into the second house, which was made to look wrecked. Keep in mind this was in the days before CGI and high-tech rides."

"How do you know all of this?"

"I found this place a few years ago, and I became interested in its history. The funny thing is that people who live around here often don't know this is even here. It only lasted ten years before it went under, so I guess it never made a deep impression in the community psyche. You've got to find some serious old-timers if you want information."

"You're right about that. I never knew this was here, and I've lived here my whole life."

We walk on, passing all the relevant landmarks. Scarecrow's house, the Tin Man's house, and Lion's den. Alex looks at everything intently, peering into windows where the weeds allow it and circling all the ruins. Having seen it all before, I'm content to stand on the path and watch him have some fun.

"I wish I'd brought a camera," he says.

"If you want pictures, I have some at home from the first time I was up here. I've even got some that were taken inside a few of the buildings."

"I'd love to see them," he says.

Farther on down the Yellow Brick Road, we come to a rock formation that, were it not for some idiot vandal who chipped off the tip of the nose long ago, looks like the Wicked Witch of the West in profile.

"This wasn't carved for the park," I say, happy to play tour guide. "It's a natural formation. The developer of the park once said that this was what sold him on this as the place for his park."

"I guess if you've got a rock that looks like a witch, you have to take that as a sign," Alex says.

There's an old wooden bench here, and I dust it off before testing it with my weight. It sags but holds and I sit down, leaning my back against the rock. The witch's nose is above me. Alex sits beside me.

"Do you like it so far?" I ask.

"Yeah," Alex says, looking around. "I do."

"I thought you might. I saw all the Oz books on your bookshelves the other day and figured you'd get a kick out of this place. I was just afraid you'd been here before, and it would wreck my surprise."

He leans back against the rock and tips his face toward the sun. "Wonder why it closed?"

"Times changed. There were no real rides here, and it lost out to parks that had roller coasters and big thrills. This was really nothing more than a themed hike through the woods. Cute and fun, but not something kids would get excited about."

"It's a shame," Alex says. "Everything dies eventually." I don't respond to that, knowing he's thinking of more than amusement parks.

In front of us are the remains of an aviary. The screens are all torn down, but a few birdhouses still remain on the higher branches of the adjacent tree. Some are still even in use. As we watch, a mother bluebird flies in and out of one house, probably building a nest for the spring hatching.

"Life always goes on, even among the ruins," I say.

He nods. "It just sucks that we can't remain part of it forever."

I say nothing. He won't always be part of it, but I will. We sit in silence for a few moments, watching the birds. Alex reaches over and takes my hand, gently holding it. I'm startled, but I don't pull my hand back. Instead, I curl my fingers over his.

"You know why it took me so long to call you?" he finally asks.

"I assumed you'd come to your senses and decided not to hang out with someone who is—what was it? Oh, yeah. Crazy, depressed, possibly schizophrenic or, at best, simply rude," I parrot back to him from our first conversation, but I smile.

He laughs. "Well, the thought did occur to me, but I decided weeks ago to take my chances on that front."

"What then?" I ask.

"I wasn't sure I should drag you into my illness. Getting involved at this late date probably isn't good for either of us, but especially for you."

I nod, getting it. I had the same thoughts, only in reverse.

"I'm only going to get sicker. Days like this, where we can do anything fun are going to be rare. If you spend time with me, you're going to have to watch me go downhill. Hell, soon, I won't even be able to go to the bathroom by myself. And then, I'm going to die. Which is fine for me, but you'll be left behind. That's a lot of crap to dump on a friend, much less a potential girlfriend."

"I understand. Don't think I didn't think about all of that, too, because I did. But I've decided to deal with what comes when it comes. I can live on a day-to-day basis. I'm pretty strong," I say.

"I can see that," he says. "You're not like the rest of the kids in school, are you? There's something inside you that's different. I just can't figure out what it is."

"Don't look too hard," I say. "You're likely to end up disappointed."

"Doubt it."

I turn away from the busy birds to face him. He reaches up, gently cupping my face in his hand. I start to pull back, startled, but then I close my eyes and lean into his hand. I can barely remember the last time anyone touched me with such tenderness.

"There's not much love in your life, is there?" he asks, resting his forehead against mine. "You don't know gentleness."

Shaking my head, I keep my eyes closed. I am not going to cry in front of Alex, but he's breaking down my carefully erected defenses, simply by seeing through them.

I feel him tilt his head, and his lips touch mine. I resist the urge to run. His lips are soft and tentative, as though he's afraid I'm going to run away. Or smack him. When I do neither, he intensifies the kiss.

I reach up and place my free hand on the back of his neck, twining my fingers in the thick, soft hair at the base of his skull and pulling him closer. He moans softly against my mouth before pulling away. I'm simultaneously disappointed and relieved that he ended it.

"That was——" he begins.

"Yeah," I finish, letting out a whoosh of breath.

"I think there's something here that we can work with," he says, letting out a shaky laugh.

I just nod. Not since Ares have I welcomed the touch of any man. I was hoping that whatever is going on between Alex and I was just infatuation or flirtation, easily dismissed. There was something in that kiss that tells me what lies between us is more than simple infatuation. Damn it.

Alex stands up and pulls me up with him. "So, before I

commit an act of public indecency in front of these poor birds, why don't you show me the rest of this park?" he says.

We start walking, and he doesn't let go of my hand. The path leads to the witch's castle. It's darker here, the vegetation denser. It was all planted to add to the scare factor, but years of neglect have made it worse. Or better, if you're into horror films. Stone faces watch us from the trees. Usually, I just find them mildly creepy, but today, they seem to be taunting me, reminding me of the disaster that's about to befall me. Occasionally, I glance down at our joined hands and wonder how this happened. How did I fall for this boy? This *human*. This *dying* human. I've set myself up to experience exactly the pain I swore I'd never feel, and I can't quite figure out how or why it's happened.

After some more wandering, we make it to the remains of the Emerald City. A stage show once performed here, and Alex surprises me by climbing up on the stage and singing. His strong, tenor voice singing "Somewhere over the Rainbow" impresses me so much that I'm moved to applaud.

"Join me," he says, holding out his hand to help me on the stage.

I shake my head and back away. "No. If I sing, every bit of wildlife within sixty miles will either flee or drop dead from the horror," I say.

He shrugs and slides off the stage. "Okay. So I'll add 'not a singer' to the list of things I know about you."

It's still early, so we decide to walk back through the park rather than leaving from Emerald City as we would have done in the park's heyday. When we return to the witch's castle, Alex says he wants to explore it some more.

It looks less like the castle from the movie and more like a sandcastle carved out of rock. It's tiny compared to the movie set, having only a few towers and none of the big turrets featured in the film.

There's only one small room that visitors can enter, and the entrance is unblocked. While Alex climbs around on the towers, I cautiously poke my head into the small room, wary of any animals that might have moved in over the winter. It's empty, so I venture inside.

The cave-like room is supposed to simulate the one in which Dorothy was held captive, but there's really nothing here that looks like the film set. It's just sandstone walls and a dirt floor. At one time, a table placed in the center of the room held a large hourglass just like the one used in the movie, but the hourglass is gone, the table is overturned, and only one leg remains unbroken. The only other feature of the room is a barred window, designed to give the place that dungeon feel.

"Hey, Sophie," Alex calls from above me. "Come out here."

I go outside and look up at Alex. He's pointing toward the sky. "What's that?" he asks. I look where he's pointing, and I see a mass of something flying toward us. "Is there some kind of flying monkey effect that still works out here? Or are those some kind of birds?"

Squinting, I try to see the figures rushing toward us. I know there aren't any flying monkeys here. There never were. And the creatures coming toward us definitely aren't birds; they're too big. The leader comes closer, and I can finally see exactly what it is. The Keres.

"Crap, crap, crap," I mutter under my breath.

"Alex, listen to me," I shout to be heard over the increasing sound of rushing wings. "Get in the room below and do not come out, no matter what happens or what you see. Do you understand? I'll come for you when it's safe."

"Safe from what?" he asks. "They're just birds, right?"

"No time to explain. Just do it. Do not come out of there."

The Keres are descending rapidly now. Alex catches sight of the first one, and I see his face register the fact that these are no ordinary birds. Any argument he was going to make dries on his lips. He clambers down the castle's exterior and dashes into the room. I climb down behind him, but stop outside the door to the room and turn to face the oncoming threat.

The Keres are awful-looking creatures. Their wings are black and leathery, spanning roughly ten feet across. They have

96

talons instead of fingers and fangs instead of teeth. Despite those mutations, their bodies are human-like and female, but so stringy and wretched-looking that it's hard to call them human. Their skin is yellowed from age and exposure, hanging limply over their bones because they have almost no body fat.

Their clothes, which are really just pieces of fabric draped over their bodies, are stained with the blood of millions of kills. The fabric might have originally been white, but it's hard to tell, now. Pupil-less black eyes complete the picture of death.

"Are you crazy? Get in here!" Alex tugs my shirt, trying to pull me into the room as the Keres circle overhead, dropping lower and lower.

"I can't. This is my fight," I say, pulling away from his grasp. "Stay in there," I repeat when it looks like he might come out to join me.

Thank the gods I didn't come here unarmed. I reach up and unhook my necklace. The charm dangling from it is shaped like a tiny, gold sword, but it is more than a charm. I nick my palm with the point and run the blade through my blood. The charm grows, quickly becoming a Scottish claymore, the favored weapon of the Highland clans. Fully extended now, it weighs six pounds and is almost five-foot long.

Unlike the Scottish claymores, mine does not sport traditional decorations. The guards are tipped with stylized representations of Cerberus—Hades' three-headed dog— rather than quatrefoils, and the pommel features a large ruby on one side and an emerald on the other, mimicking the design of my shears.

The sword was a gift from Hades. Zeus didn't see a need for my sisters and me to have weapons, but after a few fights with the Keres over the centuries, Hades thought I should be able to defend myself. When I chose the claymore, he thought I was being ridiculous. Many grown men couldn't decently wield a claymore due to its weight and size. It proved to be no trouble for me, however. Unlike the weak Highlanders who used two hands to hold the sword in a fight, I fight mostly one-handed and am damn proud of it.

I hold my sword in front of me now and advance on Ker, leader of the Keres. She's hovering just a few feet above the ground, watching me with those soulless eyes.

"Give me the boy," she says.

CHAPTER 7

I SHIFT SO I'M STANDING BETWEEN KER AND THE CASTLE entrance. A quick glance behind me reveals Alex pressed up against the back wall of the room, jaw hanging open in shock. *Great.* This mess is exactly why I never get involved with humans. I lower my defenses, care for someone, have some nice moments, and now, it's all wasted. I'm going to have to flush his memory so that he won't remember any of this day. Our kiss and everything else will be lost. It's no more than I deserve for bringing a human into my world, but the thought only pisses me off even more.

"First Thanatos and now you," I say to Ker. "It's been a regular parade of death around here lately."

Ker doesn't even acknowledge my remark. "Give me the boy," she repeats.

"Nope."

"He's dying anyway. Let me have him now, and I can spare you the pain of becoming attached to him. I'll keep him safe until it's time for you to kill him."

"You can't touch him. Alex's death will be peaceful, and Thanatos will take him to Hades. It's already written in our

99

books."

Ker laughs. "You think so?" she asks, tilting her head and considering me with those black eyes. "You might be wrong about that. Books can be changed, can't they? Pages removed, words crossed out, that kind of thing?"

"I'm never wrong in matters of fate or death," I say. "What's written cannot be unwritten. Now, why don't you and your disgusting groupies go on your way? I don't want a fight here today."

"Nope," Ker mimics me. "I may not be able to kill your little toy, but I can take him from you. Who knows what you might give me to get him back. Your shears, perhaps?"

"Never. I wouldn't trade anything for a mere human, least of all my shears."

Her face changes from mockery to fury. "Then we have nothing more to discuss."

She raises into the air with a scream, and the rest of the Keres echo her. Their battle cry is worse than listening to five thousand fingernails being dragged down a chalkboard. There's nothing else to do except fight them. They're never going to let Alex leave that cave without snatching him, and I'm not leaving him.

I glance back at Alex one more time. Fear has replaced the shock, and now he's shaking. Backing up, I move closer to the castle's entrance, seeking cover for just a moment under the archway. I reach for the bracelet I always wear on my right wrist. It's a typical gold cuff with a large, oval opal set in the center, but when I press and slightly turn the opal, it springs open, revealing a small compartment. Inside is a glittering black powder. I take a pinch and cast it up into the spring breeze.

The wind whips up, dead leaves and pine straw blowing into my face. The strong wind pushes the Keres back just enough to give me the precious seconds I need to ready my defenses.

The wind condenses into a solid-looking column, and then collapses into a single spot on the ground. There's a moment of stillness before the wind is suddenly expelled upward as a rapidly growing black cloud. It quickly separates into four separate clouds. Each morphs into a single hell horse. They hover above the ground, waiting for instructions.

A hell horse is an awesome thing to behold, unless you are the poor soul on which it is about to be unleashed. Each horse is jet black with red eyes, leathery wings, and a flaming mane and tail. I can only tell them apart because I've known them for centuries and can recognize the subtle variations in the size and colors of their flames. These horses—Alastor, Abatos, Aeton, and Nonios—belong to Hades, and they usually only serve him. Fortunately, Hades is kind enough to lend them to me in times of extreme need. An attack by the Keres definitely qualifies.

I lift my arm to the sky. "Go," I scream at them. Three of the horses immediately engage the Keres. The Keres scream in outrage, and I smile. First point to my side. The remaining horse lowers himself to the ground and canters up to me. He bows low and I climb onto his back, grabbing the reins.

"Good to see you again, Aeton," I say, affectionately patting his neck. Aeton nods once, and we take off to join the fight. We've fought the Keres many times over the years, and we work well together.

"There's a human boy in that castle. We have to keep the Keres from taking him," I tell Aeton.

He whinnies loudly, shouting instructions to his brothers. I don't speak hell horse, but I know he's passing my message on to them because they instantly close formation and fly closer to the witch's castle.

To anyone watching from the ground, we would seem to be outnumbered. Four horses and a sword-wielding goddess shouldn't stand a chance against several thousand furious, taloned, and fanged Keres. But the simple fact is that we're better and smarter than they are. The Keres are fierce fighters, but tactics and strategy aren't their strong suit. We've never lost a battle, and I don't intend for today to be the first.

Aeton carries me higher into the center of the Keres' formation. I strike out with my sword, cutting down Keres by the handful. I can't kill them, unfortunately, since they are immortal like me, but I can hurt them badly enough to remove them from the fight. Aeton gets his share, too, shooting them down with the flames that spew from his mouth.

The other three horses repel the Keres that are trying to get to Alex. So far the horses aren't having much trouble keeping the Keres out of the castle, but I can see that Ker is sending more of her troops down there in an attempt to overpower them. Alex is watching the fight from the window, eyes wide with terror.

I'm too busy watching out for Alex, and I fail to see the Kere coming toward us until she lands behind me on Aeton's back. She sinks her talons deep into his unprotected rump. Aeton screams in pain but never falters. Years of practice lead me to lean well right as he brings his head around from the left and blows her off with a jet of flame.

"Good boy," I say, patting his neck in approval.

All the remaining Keres are now focused on the castle, leaving us with little to do up here. Aeton flies me down to rejoin the battle. I'm searching for Ker. If I can get to her and take her out, the rest of the Keres will give up. They are weak and directionless without their leader.

I spot her battling Alastor at the entrance to the cave. She's on his back, her talons sunk into his neck to keep him from turning his head and shooting her off with flame. She can't kill him because Hades' horses are as immortal as the rest of us, but just as I can wound her troops, she can hurt him.

Aeton and I fly downward, sword slashing and flames spewing as we cut a path to the ground, but we're too late. With a wicked twist of her arms, Ker breaks Alastor's neck. I cry out, and Aeton whinnies in rage. I know that Alastor will mend, but I also know he feels the pain of the break. He collapses to the ground. Ker jumps off his back, flying into the castle.

"Down," I scream at Aeton.

He dives to the ground and I dismount, ignoring the flips in my stomach caused by the rapid descent. Aeton flies back up to join his remaining brothers. I don't worry about them; the loss of their comrade will spur them on to a quick rout of the remaining Keres. Alex is now my concern.

I race into the castle, sword held high and ready to strike. Alex is sprawled in the far corner. His eyes are closed, but I can see the rise and fall of his chest. He's alive, but out cold. There's a bloodstain on the side of his head and a matching one on the wall behind him. Ker must have tackled him and whacked his head on the wall. Now she's sitting on his chest, her talons poised to rip into his body.

"Don't do it," I scream at her.

"You can't stop me." She laughs in triumph. "Come any closer and I'll make it harder on the boy than it has to be. You know he won't die. Not yet. I can't kill him, and I can't take his soul because his fate dictates that he must live a while longer. But I can wound him to the point where he will suffer in a hospital on life support for weeks until it's time for you to kill him. Unless you want to give me your shears, that is."

I lower my sword. My instinct to attack her, wound her, wars with the desire to keep Alex safe. If I go after Ker, she'll hurt him. But if I don't do something, she'll still hurt him. I hesitate, thinking. I need to buy a few moments to formulate a good plan.

"There's nowhere for you to go," I tell her. "Even if you hurt him, you can't get out of here without going by me. Your troops are being taken out as we speak, and there's no one else to help you. You can't get out of here without me and the hell horses taking you apart."

"So? You can't kill me. I can wound him... and your heart as well."

I shrug. "You could do that. You can wound him, and then I'll do the same to you in return. Or, I might tear you into so many pieces that it will take you a solid year to put yourself back together.

"Wanna risk it?" I ask her, lifting my sword in challenge.

Her eyes flash from me blocking the entrance to the barred window, and she shrieks in frustration. "The Oracle prophesied your downfall! You're supposed to willingly give me your shears to save the boy."

"That's what you get for believing a crazy woman. You kinda have to choose here. Getting out in lots of pieces versus me letting you go with just a slight injury. Hurt him, and it'll be the little pieces route."

"I'm not worried. A little time spent mending is nothing compared to watching you suffer. What I want most is to hurt you, and hurting this boy seems to be the best way to do that. Of course, I can be reasonable. If you give me your shears, I'll let the boy go without harm."

"Not gonna happen, so stop asking," I say. "I'm not stupid enough to trade my power for a human life. I'd like to save him, but he's not worth that. You can have him."

I watch as she tightens her talons a little more on Alex's chest, checking to see if I'm bluffing. She draws blood, but I don't react. I stand still, sword arm relaxed by my side, letting her believe that I don't care.

When she sees I'm not going to come after her, Ker turns hungry eyes to Alex, giving me the opening I need. I throw my sword side-arm style, sending it whirling like a propeller across the room, straight at Ker. She turns her head back toward me, but it's too late. My sword cleaves her neatly in two at the waist. Black goo splatters Alex and the wall behind him.

She lets loose one scream of pain before falling silent. I walk toward her and retrieve my sword.

"Didn't think that through, did you?" I taunt. "I don't know how you think you'll ever get my power if you can't even defeat me in a simple fight."

She's struggling to poof out of the castle. Poofing is more difficult when you're not all in one piece. "What's coming won't be a simple fight," half of her hisses. "I'll have your power, this boy, and any other human I want before it's over," she says. "It is foretold…"

"By a nutcase. Yeah, we covered that," I say.

Ker finally manages to get both halves of herself out of the room and off to whatever hellhole she'll use to recuperate. Alex is still breathing, but I need to make sure the fight is over before I tend to him.

Outside, I see that Aeton and the others have just about finished off the remaining Keres. As expected, most fled when Ker went down, but a few diehards are still fighting. I call Aeton down to me, mount up, and fly with him to finish off the others. A few sword strokes later and we're done. We return to the ground, and I slide off Aeton's back.

"Thanks," I say to him and the others. I pet each one on the nose. "Take care of Alastor."

Aeton whinnies his farewell to me, and the three horses turn to their fallen brother. Each places a hoof on Alastor's flank. Aeton lifts his head to the sky and lets out a cry. The others join in until the sound of whinnying is so loud that I have to cover my ears.

Hades responds to their call by turning them back into black clouds and pulling them down into the Underworld. They'll be as good as new after a few days, but Hades isn't going to be pleased that I let one of his horses get so badly hurt.

I wish I could be as certain that Alex will be okay after today. It's too late to do anything about it now, though. After scanning the sky to make sure no more danger is approaching, I turn and go back into the castle. I jam my sword into the ground near the door so that it stands hilt up, ready to grab if need be, and walk to where Alex lies.

I crouch down next to him and lift his shirt so I can examine the damage done by Ker's talons. The wounds aren't bad; she broke the skin, but he won't need stitches. Still, he needs a good dose of disinfectant. Who knows where Ker's talons have been. The head wound isn't serious, either. The bleeding has mostly stopped, but I use the edge of his shirt to wipe away the excess. He'll have a goose egg tomorrow, but he'll live.

There's nothing I can do for him now except wait for him to wake up. I sit and lean back against the wall, pulling Alex toward me. Resting his head on my lap, I stroke his hair until he begins to come around.

"It's okay," I murmur as he begins to move. "They're gone, and you're okay."

Finally, he opens his eyes and looks at me. I mentally cross my fingers and hope that he won't remember anything. Maybe I'll get lucky and the combination of his brain tumor and shock will have erased his memory.

I watch while he takes in our surroundings. Confusion comes first, followed by awareness, and finally, recollection. Damn. Today isn't my lucky day.

When he struggles to sit up, I help him. He looks down at the blood and goo splattered on his clothes and the wounds on his chest. Then he looks at me and takes in the blood splatters on my clothes. Finally, he looks toward the cave entrance and sees my sword standing at attention there. Turning to me again, he asks the only reasonable question.

"What the hell was that?"

He follows it with the only other reasonable question and the one I'm dreading more than any other.

"And *what* the hell are you?"

My heart breaks a little at the betrayal in his voice. I was a fool for thinking I could keep my true self a secret.

"I always knew you weren't normal," he says. "Always running off, missing school, never talking about yourself except in the most general terms, never mentioning your family. I knew there was something you were hiding. But I never dreamed it would be this, this—" He falters, unable to find the right word to describe what he's just witnessed.

"Disgusting? Frightening? Horrifying?" I try to finish for him, hanging my head in shame. "You're right. It's all of that and more."

He thinks for a moment, and I see the most amazing transformation pass over his face as he processes what just happened. He actually smiles at me.

"No, no. The word I'm looking for is badass. I had no idea. I mean you were so cool with that sword. And those horses! That was so awesome." His smile is huge now. He's thrilled by what he's seen, not scared.

I don't know whether to laugh or cry, so I end up giggling a little hysterically. Here I am expecting recriminations, fear, and hatred, and he's complimenting me? This guy is crazier than most of the gods. I force myself to stop laughing and to treat this mess with the seriousness it deserves.

"You're not traumatized? Scared? Afraid to be in the same room with me because I might do to you what I did to the Keres?"

"No. I'm a dead man anyway. Even if you intend to kill me, it doesn't matter, does it? But I would like to know what you really are and what that was about."

I hang my head. "I'm not supposed to tell you," I say, knowing the right course of action is to flush his memory immediately, not engage him in conversation.

"Hello," he says, motioning to the still-bleeding wounds on his chest. "I'm the one with holes in me, here. I deserve to know the truth, don't you think?"

He's right. Even if I can't let him remember it forever, in this moment, I owe him the truth.

"You're not going to like me when I'm finished," I warn.

"I'll judge that."

I inhale and decide to begin with the simplest yet hardest fact. The one that will turn his admiration of me into hate and fear.

"My real name isn't Sophie. It's Atropos."

When that doesn't get a reaction, I press on. "I am the third goddess of fate. I am the one who cuts human lifelines and ends your mortal lives."

"From Greek mythology, right?" Alex asks.

I nod.

"That stuff isn't real," he scoffs. "Greek gods don't roam the Earth. You've been reading too much Percy Jackson. What are you, really? An assassin of some sort?"

I shake my head. "All the gods are real. We just keep our

existence quiet. After Jesus Christ entered the picture, people didn't want us around. But we're all still here, still controlling your lives.

"Those things I was fighting? They're the Keres. Death spirits," I clarify when he looks blank. "The hell horses belong to my uncle, Hades. Zeus is my father. And I am, as I said, a goddess of fate."

He thinks about this for a moment. I watch him work through the denials in his mind. Ultimately, what he's just seen and survived has no other explanation, short of hallucinogenic drugs, and he knows it. He just has to come around to acceptance. I wait.

"You're supposed to be an old hag. We read about her. You," he clarifies, shaking his head, "in freshman lit. You're supposed to be old and wrinkled. But you're beautiful."

"Well, I am old, at least," I say. "I'm about three thousand years old."

"You don't look that old."

I shrug. "That's immortality for you. But thanks for the compliment," I say, rolling my eyes.

"You know what I mean," he says.

"I know. It's just amusing to me when I see these myths of me and my sisters as wrinkled old crones. I don't even know how or when that story got started.

"I think the humans started portraying us as old because it's easier to believe only old people have that much power over life and death. It's harder, I guess, to think of young women as the arbiters of fate. Young people, particularly women, aren't supposed to have that kind of control. Plus, it's easier to hate an ugly old hag than a pretty young woman. And everyone hates me," I say.

Alex shakes his head again as though trying to clear it of moths or something. "So if you're an immortal goddess, what are you doing in high school?"

"Blending in. Three women who look like kids but who aren't in school attract attention, something we avoid."

"So when you go running off, you're—" He stops and waves his hands in the air, unable to say it.

"Running home to kill people, yes," I say, completing his thought. I wait, knowing the worst part of this situation is about to dawn on him. I don't have to wait long.

"Ker said you would kill me, so you know when I will die."

I nod. "Yes. On the assigned day, I will cut your lifeline and end your life."

Alex is silent, and I let him think. I brace myself for his reaction. This is where my badass turns into betrayal.

"When will I die?" Alex finally asks.

"I won't tell you that. It doesn't really make a difference, does it? You're better off living each day as it comes without that knowledge. Trust me. You're not the first to ask, and you wouldn't be the first to regret the knowledge."

"Can you at least give me a general idea? Will I get to graduate? Will it be tomorrow? Do I get another couple of years?"

The desperation in his voice cuts me. I want so badly to ease his mind, but I know there is nothing I can say that will ease the knowledge of impending death. Tell him it's soon, and he'll become depressed. Tell him it's later, and he'll worry about it until then.

"Sorry, no," I shake my head. He must see something in my eyes because he jumps up and starts pacing the small room. There's a slight limp when he walks, which I assume is from Ker tackling him to the ground.

"Soon enough," he says.

I watch him pace, knowing there is nothing I can do for him. Comfort from Death is no comfort at all. He goes to the window and looks out at the Yellow Brick Road.

"So are you the one who gave me cancer?" he asks without turning to me.

"No, that was my sister. But I am the one who decided that you would die from it. Lacey stamped you with both cancer and an early death. Letting you die from it was the easy choice for me."

"Well, it's certainly not easy for me. And there's no way to change it? To something maybe less painful or quicker?"

"No."

He turns to face me. "Why me?" he asks. It's an age-old question, asked by every human who ever got a raw deal from the Fates.

"I don't know why you're dying young. I'm not privy to Lachesis' reasoning. I tried to find out, but she won't tell me. There is a purpose, though. Lachesis has to adhere to Zeus' master plan for the universe. Everything she does fits into that somehow," I say, as if that could possibly be of any comfort. It sounds noble to say that death has a purpose, but it doesn't matter to the dying. Dead is dead, no matter the reason.

"Up on the mountain, when we were talking about my mom, you could have told me who you were, and yet you didn't. You let me believe you were just a normal human who had nothing to do with it. But you killed her," he accuses.

"That's true," I say. No point in sugarcoating the truth. "I did snip her line, and I let her die from cancer, too. But it was her time, and I had no choice. That's the part you have to understand. I have no choice in who I kill and when. Only how, and that's not much choice at all.

"Even if I had known that I would meet you and become friends with you, or more than friends," I amend, "I still couldn't have done anything differently. Just like I can't change anything that will happen to you."

He remains silent, glaring at me. I should shut up, but I can't. I have to make him understand the incomprehensible.

"If I had told you then what I am, you wouldn't have believed me. And if you did, you would have hated me. Just as you're hating me now. Aside from being forbidden to discuss my immortal life with a human, I also know there is no way to make what I am and what I do acceptable to you.

"Humans hate and fear death, so they hate and fear me. I accept that. It's why I never get involved with humans. However, you were different somehow, and I wanted to spend time with you. I also wanted to keep you far away from my role as the Death Fate. I just wanted to be Sophie with you and forget that I am Atropos for a while."

I snort sarcastically after I say that. "What I wanted were two things that can never be. This is my fault," I say, waving a hand to encompass the mess in the room.

"Obviously," he says, looking again at the goo on the walls. He stands there, looking down at me, head cocked to the side as if studying a dangerous snake. I drop my head, unable to look at the hurt and confusion in his eyes. I don't expect him to understand or forgive me for anything, and I don't want to see his back when he walks away from me in disgust.

The minutes pass and he doesn't move. Neither do I. The next move has to be his. I stay hunkered down inside myself, braced for his rejection. Finally, he takes a deep breath and crouches down in front of me. He lifts my hand from my lap and cradles it between his.

"I don't hate you. What you are is not your fault. You didn't choose it, did you?"

I shake my head, but I still don't look at him. "On my seventeenth birthday, Zeus gave me my job. He didn't ask me. He didn't even ask my mother. He decreed it would be so and it was."

"Okay, then. The person I see is still the same Sophie that I met a few weeks ago. You don't kill for pleasure like those things that attacked us. You do a job that has to be done. You're right. I don't like your job. But I don't hate you."

I look up at him, unable to believe the words coming out of his mouth. "But I'll kill you. I killed your mother. Eventually, I'll kill everyone you love," I say. I don't think he understands the reality of the situation. "How can you accept that?"

He shrugs. "I've known for a long time that death is coming for me. I've dealt with that truth. That it should come packaged as a beautiful girl who I care about is an unexpected bonus. It's comforting to know that I'll be done in by someone who cares

111

for me, not some faceless grim reaper."

I smile up at him. "You're crazy, you know that?"

"It's been mentioned," he says.

"I'm sorry that I have to kill you. And I'm sorry you got dragged into this fight with the Keres."

"So what was that all about?" he asks. "I'm sure there's a good reason why I'm all bloody."

"Unfortunately, there's not. You got caught in the middle of an ancient feud that's recently kicked up again." I give him the condensed version of my ongoing fight with the Keres and how Thanatos recently delivered a warning from them.

"I'm sure they can't get my power, but I can't stop them from using people like you as leverage to get what they want. It's part of the reason I tried to stay away from you. I didn't want to make you a target."

"Well, I'm glad you didn't give them what they wanted," he says. "The thought of those things controlling death is definitely bad."

"Yeah, it is."

"They won't come for me when I die? I heard you mention Thanatos. He's not with them, is he?"

"No. The Keres only come to those who die violently. They feed on the blood. Zeus created them that way. Don't ask me why," I say with a shrug, anticipating his next question. "Thanatos comes for those who die quietly. He can be scary, but not violent. He'll escort you to the Underworld, and then leave you in the care of Hades."

"Well, that's something," Alex says. "Will you be with me when I die? Do you, like, come in through the window and kill me or something?"

"No, I'm not the Tooth Fairy. Your lifeline is stored at my house with all the others. I work there."

"Oh. But can you be with me?"

"Nope, sorry. That's against the rules. There's just too much chance of your family or friends being there. I can't be exposed that way."

"Even if I sent everyone else away?"

"Even if," I say.

"Will you think about it, though? Try to find some way? If I have to die, I'd rather you do it in front of me and not hide away in some room."

"I'll think about it," I say, knowing that I cannot and will not do what he asks. Not only because it's forbidden, but because I am too much of a coward to face him at the moment of death.

"So I suppose ever getting to see you work is out of the question, too?"

"Absolutely. That is really off-limits." I shudder at the thought. Who would want to watch one person kill other people, even if it's only by snipping their lifelines? It's not like I stab people or cut their hearts out or anything, but what I do is killing all the same.

The thought of Alex watching me grab a fistful of lifelines and chop through them all at once makes me ill. It's bad enough he knows about it without having him see the cold, mechanical way I deal out death. If I'm not a monster to him now, I would be then.

"We should get going," I say, standing up. "I don't think the Keres will be back today, but we should still get out of here. It's getting late."

Although it's just late afternoon when we emerge from the castle, I'm so weary that I'm surprised it's still light outside. It seems like it should be much later. The late day sunshine filters through the tiny spring leaves and twinkles on the remains of the Yellow Brick Road. The day has lost its magic for me regardless.

Alex leans heavily against one side of me as we walk, exhausted by the events and his injuries. I keep my sword fully extended in my other hand until we reach the car. Before we get inside, I slice my palm and rub the blade through the blood, shrinking the sword. I hang the pendant back around my neck. When I look up, I see Alex watching me.

"That's the most bizarre thing I've ever seen," he says.

I raise an eyebrow at him. "Seriously? After today?"

113

"Well, okay, one of the most bizarre," he amends. "Why do you have to do that?"

"I don't really know," I say, looking down at the blood dripping from my palm. I retrieve a tissue from my pocket and apply some pressure to stop the bleeding. "It was just one of the rules Zeus laid down when he allowed me to have a sword. When Zeus declares a rule, you don't argue."

"I can't believe that you're Zeus' daughter," Alex says. "The daughter of the most powerful god in the universe made out with me in Oz. It sounds like a weird dream."

I laugh. "Well, just remember that I'm one of Zeus' many daughters. It's nothing special, believe me."

"It's pretty cool to me," he says.

I unlock my door and then lean across the seat to unlock his. He slides in, fastening his seat belt. I stick the key in the ignition but rather than start it, I turn to him. "Before we go, there's one thing I have to ask you," I begin.

"What?"

"You are not supposed to know anything about what you've seen today and what I've told you. I'm supposed to flush your memory so that you remember nothing. But I don't want to do that," I hasten to add when his eyes widen in shock.

"Memory flush? I'm not too jazzed about the idea myself," he says.

"There are two reasons I'd rather not. Well, three," I amend, thinking of the selfish reason. "First, if I do it, you lose all memory of today."

"Including our kiss?"

"Including that."

"There's no way to keep that one memory? I might be okay losing the memory of the Keres, but that kiss is one I'd really like to keep."

"Nope. You'd always wonder what happened before or after that moment. I can't leave you with fragments because trying to find the missing pieces will make you crazy. It's an all-or-nothing deal."

"What are the other reasons?" he asks.

"Second, doing the memory flush sometimes takes out more than I intended. It's not usually a problem, but your brain is already compromised by the tumor so the results might be unpredictable. I don't want to deprive you of more than necessary, and it's a real possibility that I might."

"Thank god for the brain tumor, then," he says.

"Ha-ha," I say. "The last reason is purely selfish on my part. I think you deserve to know the truth."

"In other words, I'm a dead man, anyway, so I might as well know how it's going to happen?"

"No. Well, not entirely. If you're going to hang out with me, you deserve to know exactly who and what you're hanging out with. It's been bad enough these last few weeks trying to keep my secret. If we're going to have any sort of relationship, it needs to be based on honesty, not a pile of half-truths and lies.

"If you want to walk away after what you saw today and what you know I am, I'll flush your head and you'll remember nothing of today or the last few weeks. I'll just be one of the girls in your classes at school. That is what I would and should recommend. You don't want to be hanging out with death, after all."

He thinks for a moment. "What do you want?" he asks.

"What I want is often what I cannot have. If I were free to make any choice, I'd choose to be with you, openly and with full knowledge. But I'm not free and I'm supposed to abide by certain rules, the most important being that humans know nothing of my existence. I shouldn't even be having this conversation. I should just flush you and be done with it. I'm selfish, though, so I'm giving you the choice."

He is silent, mulling over what I've told him.

"I choose you," he finally says. "Even knowing who and what you are, I still choose you. So please don't flush me because I want to remember today. I want to be with you. Until I can't anymore."

I exhale the breath I'd been holding while waiting for his

answer. I'm flabbergasted that he's willing to stay with me, but I'm also happy. Sad. And worried. Alex has turned me into an emotional mess. It's an uncomfortable feeling, but wonderful at the same time. Like a shirt with a tag in it that annoys you to no end, but in which you know you look fantastic.

"Okay. In exchange for me leaving your brain unmolested, I need you to swear that you won't tell anyone about what you saw and heard today. You can't even tell Emily or your dad. I'm still just Sophie if anyone asks. That's as much for my safety as yours."

"I swear. Your secret will go with me to the grave. And that won't be long," he says.

"Don't joke. If you tell anyone, I will flush your head to the point where you won't even remember starting at Asheville High School."

"You can trust me."

"I know. That's why I'm giving you the choice when I've never done so for any other mortal."

I start the car and pull away from the Land of Oz. Alex looks tired, so I don't try to make conversation. Instead, I turn on the stereo and tune to my Native American flute music playlist. It's not long before he's asleep. *No wonder*, I think. He's had the kind of day that would wear out a healthy human, never mind one who's already terminally ill.

As I drive into the twilight, my thoughts turn to the choice I gave him and the fact that he chose me. I shouldn't have given him that choice. Not that I regret his decision, but it was wrong and selfish of me to allow him to choose.

Part of me secretly hoped he'd run away. No shame in that, after all. No one should be friendly with death. It's not natural. Instead, he chose me, which is wrong on so many levels, yet exactly what I wanted.

The honorable, right thing to do is to flush his head of all memory of me, to go back to the day he walked into my English class, and simply erase myself. I can do it right now while he sleeps so that the only question he'll be left with is why he's in the car with me, and a simple lie will take care of that. Flushing him would also return my life to its more comfortable and predictable routine. I could go back to being the cold, heartless bitch that everyone expects me to be and eliminate the nosy intrusions of my family.

By the time I pull into his driveway, I've talked myself into it. Doing the right thing sucks, but it's the right thing for a reason. Alex stirs when I cut the ignition. *Damn.* It's easier if he stays asleep.

"You're home," I say, not looking at him. I'm gripping the steering wheel so hard that my knuckles are white.

While he fully wakes, I close my eyes and enter the mental state necessary for a memory flush. It's like meditation but deeper, a loss of awareness of everything except my mind and his. If done correctly, he won't even know I'm in his brain.

I see his memories, little sparks of light shining on his neural pathways. Newer memories glow brighter, while older ones are duller. I look for the bright ones and I filter through them, looking for his first awareness of me. I flip through today's memories, and then go back further. I see the day he received the Kindle, and then our conversation in the cafeteria. Finally, I find that first English class.

Just as I'm about to start rearranging and removing memories, I feel his lips on mine. For a moment, I think I'm experiencing his memory of our first kiss and I wonder how I made such a mistake, but then I realize this kiss is happening in real time.

My eyes pop open and I pull away, severing the mental connection.

"I'm sorry," he says. "Was that not okay?"

"No, it's fine," I say, raising my fingers to my lips. "I was just surprised."

"Well, you looked like you were deep in thought. I just wanted to say I had a great time today."

I shake my head, trying to get back into reality.

"No, seriously," he says, taking my head shake for disbelief.

"That was the most fun I think I've ever had.

"You've got a strange sense of fun," I say.

"When you're dying, everything but death is pretty fun."

He kisses me again and climbs out of the car.

"Alex," I call after him.

He turns back. "Yeah?"

I swear, I intend to do it. I mean to flush his memory right there on the driveway. Instead, all I say is, "Good night, Alex."

"Good night," he says, slamming the car door and heading for his house.

I watch until he's inside, and then I bang my head on the steering wheel three times. "Stupid, stupid, stupid," I mutter in time with each head bang.

Backing out of his driveway, I turn for home, already dreading the rest of this night. I didn't tell Alex there would be repercussions for my actions today. He didn't need that guilt on top of everything else. But the list of what I've done wrong today is long. I didn't flush his memory, I jeopardized a human life, and I exposed the gods to a human. There's no way I can cover it up… and no way Zeus will ignore it. All I can do now is wait and see how long it will take Zeus to punish me.

118

CHAPTER 8

I DON'T HAVE TO WAIT LONG. IT'S TWO THIRTY IN THE MORNING, and I'm in my workroom catching up on the backlog of death left behind from my day of freedom. Chloe kept me company for the first few hours. She sat on the stool by the door and spun round and round while I told her everything that happened at Oz. In typical Chloe fashion, she saw only the bright side.

"But he kissed you. Three times," she said, sighing.

"Yeah, he did."

"Was it good?"

"It was better than good, Chloe. Better than Ares. It was awesome," I said.

"Well, if he can top Ares, whose womanizing skills are legendary, then he's a keeper. You did the right thing by not flushing his brain," she assured me. "Alex has the right to know who you are."

"Zeus isn't going to see it that way," I said.

She shrugged. "So what? You, out of all of us, deserve a little happiness. You've been miserable for a couple of thousand years. Grab it while you can."

I laughed at that, but I knew Zeus wouldn't care about

anything but the rules.

Chloe went to bed after getting all the details. Now I'm alone and boxing up lines for Thanatos. A sudden breeze blows through the room, and I look up to see the lifelines wildly blowing. I sigh. My punishment has arrived on winged feet.

I put the box I'm holding inside the delivery door and push the button. Then I wait, arms crossed. The breeze blows harder and Hermes, messenger of the gods, materializes in front of me. He looks exactly like the FTD logo, only not as shiny.

"Hello, Atropos," he says. The wings on his feet beat rapidly, and he hovers a few feet off the ground in front of me.

"Hello, Hermes," I say. I don't wait for him to speak again. "I know why you're here, so go ahead and say it."

He pulls a small scroll from his belt and unrolls it with a flourish. "Atropos, daughter of Zeus and third goddess of fate, you are ordered to report to Zeus' palace immediately. You are also to bring your mother," he reads.

"Tell Zeus we'll be there as soon as I reach a stopping point on all this." I wave my hand to indicate the lines all queued up and ready for cutting. "I'm behind."

"All right. But do it sooner rather than later. Zeus is angry and getting angrier the longer he waits," he says.

"And you're just loving that," I mutter under my breath.

Hermes hears me. "I take no joy in your suffering. I'm just the messenger," he says, but his smirk gives him away.

"Right," I say.

He poofs out of my room, and his chuckle echoes behind him for just a second after he's gone. I'm not surprised to be summoned to Mount Olympus. I've broken so many rules in the last twenty-four hours that even I've lost track. I am surprised that Zeus wants Themis to come, though. Mom isn't going to like that. She hardly ever returns to Olympus and being summoned there because her own daughter can't follow the rules is going to piss her off.

I take a quick look at the schedule for the day. I have a break later this afternoon that will be long enough to get to Mount

Olympus and back. Locking up my shears, I head upstairs to wake Mom. No sense in putting off the bad news. Might as well give her time to get used to the idea of seeing Zeus.

When I get to her room, there is light shining from underneath the door. I lightly knock.

"Come in."

I open the door and go inside, pushing it closed behind me. Mom is propped up in bed with law books and case files piled all around her.

"You're working late," I comment.

"I'm helping a friend with a civil case," she says. "Off the clock and off the record."

"Anything interesting?" I ask, pushing a pile of books out of the way so I can sit on the end of her bed.

"Medical malpractice," she says.

"Think how many lawyers would be out of work if they understood that things happen because we make them happen, instead of humans blaming humans for all their alleged screw ups," I say.

Mom laughs, and then asks, "Why are you still up?"

"Well, I'm in trouble. But it wasn't all my fault," I add, beginning my defense.

"Uh-oh."

"Yeah. I have to appear before Zeus as soon as possible. And he wants you there, too."

"Me? What did you do?"

I tell her about Alex and how I tried to push him away, about our day at the abandoned Land of Oz, about the Keres, and about how I didn't flush his memory. And why I didn't want to.

"So you left a human with full knowledge of your job, your sisters' jobs, your parentage, and various other aspects of our world?"

"That about sums it up. But I did and do think that Alex deserves to know who and what he's dealing with, especially since he's dying."

Mom is silent for a minute, but she stares at me while she

121

thinks. I know the look. It's the, "You are in so much trouble that I don't know where to start with you," look. Rarely is it directed at me. Usually, Chloe is the one receiving this stare. I try not to squirm or look away.

"You've never felt this way before. You've never had trouble concealing your identity from anyone that you've been friends with. Not that it has ever been a huge number of people," she adds. "I don't understand why you suddenly feel like Alex deserves to know."

"Because he kissed me," I say.

Mom's jaw drops at that revelation. "And you didn't run away? You didn't smack him? You let him?"

I nod. "And I kissed him back."

"Do you love him?"

"Mom, no, I—" I start and then stop. I realize now that it is kind of out there for all to see, except for me, who's been too busy denying it. "I think maybe I do," I whisper.

"Well, that changes things," she says.

"I just think that if he and I are going to be together until he dies, he has the right to know that I'll be the one killing him."

"A decision you've never had to face before, since you've never let a mortal get close enough for it to matter."

"It's kind of your fault," I say. "You're the one who thought it would be good for me to spend time with the humans. You pushed me toward him when I was doing everything I could to stay away from him. So did Zeus. Did it ever occur to either of you that this is exactly why I don't get involved? Not only is it painful, but it also gets me in trouble."

"You're half right. You'd think after three thousand years that Zeus and I could have seen this coming. Maybe we should have respected your decision to remain aloof. You were managing just fine. But you still should have known better and done what you were supposed to do. However, I can understand and even sympathize with why you chose to do what you did."

"Well," I begin, seeing the unfairness of blaming anyone but myself, "even if you hadn't pushed me, I still probably

122

would have wanted to spend time with him. He's just so damn interesting. Not like any human I've ever met."

"We'll explain it all to Zeus. I'm sure he'll understand."

I snort. "You and I both know that he won't understand anything beyond the fact that rules were broken. Do you think he'll punish me?"

"Probably, but I doubt it'll be too bad. Just prepare yourself for the likelihood that Alex's memory will be flushed, either by you or by Zeus. He won't abide a human knowing so much, and he'll fix it.

"Just come get me when you hit a stopping point later. I'll stay home from work so we can go. You're staying home from school to catch up on work, anyway, aren't you?"

I nod, reaching across the bed to hug her. It's nice to have her on my side in this. I go back downstairs, dreading the rest of this day only slightly less.

I finally get my break, and Mom and I get in the car and head for Mount Mitchell. We fill the drive with talk of her cases and my workload. Anything but what awaits me on Mount Olympus.

When we arrive at the park, we change into our hiking boots and then take off through the woods. There aren't many other hikers about on a Monday, and we have no trouble slipping off the main trail unnoticed. We hike in silence, both of us nervous for different reasons. I know it's not easy for Themis to come with me to Mount Olympus and face the man she loves but can never have. She's doing it because he commanded it and because she loves me, but it's costing her. I wish I could be a more comforting companion, but I'm wallowing too deeply in my own worries to ease her mind.

The best I can offer is a weak, "I'm sorry for dragging you into this," which she waves away. She keeps hiking beside me, face grim, and I feel terrible.

Once we are in the cave and standing before the pool, we slip off our boots. Ares' boots aren't here today, and I feel my chest loosen. At least that's one thing I won't have to face today. I roll up my pants, but Mom, who is never cold, has worn shorts and she simply steps into the pool. I hesitate on the edge, wishing for a miracle that will allow me to skip this trip.

"Just so I can prepare myself, do you think Zeus will strip me of my job and immortality?" I ask my mom.

I spent all night thinking about this possibility, and I finally decided it might be for the best. Being mortal is something I've considered and coveted for centuries. I'm nervous, nevertheless. It's never easy to give up the only life you know, even if it's for something that might be better.

She has clearly given this some thought, too, and she's smart enough to realize I might see mortality as a great idea.

"Don't you dare hope for that," she says. "You are my daughter, and I will not lose you to mortality. I know you struggle with the weight of your responsibilities, but don't you ever wish for that. Mortality is a death sentence, and I'm not having it."

I sigh. "Still. Do you think he will?"

"No. Not for one infraction in three thousand years. Especially not since this one is fixable. I think you'll just have to flush Alex's memory, probably all the way back to the minutes before you met. And you might have to stay away from him until he dies. But if Zeus is really angry, you never know what he'll do. If he tries to make you mortal, I'll fight him and every other god on Olympus. I won't let him kill you or let you kill yourself." She holds her hand out for mine.

I inhale deeply, take her hand, and step into the pool. We fly through the fractal universe and land softly in the pool in front of Zeus' temple. I slip on the provided sandals, but Mom opts to go barefoot. Probably just so she can track up Zeus' carpet with her mossy feet, her passive aggressive way of annoying him.

When we enter the temple, there is none of the foolishness that was going on the last time I was here. No dancing, no reading, no movies, and Zeus doesn't have his headphones on. The few gods and goddesses who are here stand silent, watching as Mom and I approach Zeus' throne. Clearly, the word is out that I am in trouble, and most have found something to do elsewhere. The danger of spillover rage from Zeus is real, and only the very brave and nosy remain.

I notice that Hera is one of the missing, apparently choosing to ignore the fact that Themis is in the building. Just as well. A cat fight between Zeus' current wife and his former lover would really mess up the day.

When we reach the foot of his throne, Zeus greets us politely, but I can hear the suppressed rage in his voice.

"Themis. Atropos," he says, nodding at each of us.

We nod back but say nothing.

"I am deeply disturbed by Atropos' actions regarding the human boy. She not only allowed him to witness an attack by the Keres, but she told him the truth about her identity and other facts about the gods. She did not flush his memory, as required, leaving this boy free to talk and placing all of us in danger of discovery," Zeus says like a bailiff reading the charges against me.

"I didn't have a choice about the Keres," I say. "It's not like I invited them along on our outing. I don't even know how they knew we'd be at Oz. I only wanted to take Alex somewhere fun. What was I supposed to do? Let Ker have him so she could torture him?"

"No, but after saving him, you should have immediately removed all memory of the events. Instead, you launched into a full explanation of your identity. You know the rules. Why did you not obey them this time, when you have always done so in the past?"

"Because it isn't fair to him."

"Fair? Bah. We have rules that must be obeyed!" Zeus roars.

Themis speaks up. "I think she was right. She and this Alex person are forming a relationship that stretches beyond simple friendship. Of course she had to protect him from the Keres. Having done that and revealed herself, she wanted him to judge her on her own merits, not on some false identity. She had to tell him the truth."

Leave it to the lawyer to distill the case down to its simplest facts. I silently cheer her speech.

"Had he run screaming from me, I would have flushed him," I add. "I wouldn't leave him burdened by the knowledge if it scared him. But he stayed and promised to keep silent. A human knows what I am and what I do, and he isn't repulsed. That's never happened before."

"Still, I would be within my rights to strip you of your powers right now, you know," he says.

"I know it." I look down at the floor, more to hide my smile at the thought of freedom than in shame.

Zeus thinks for a moment. "But I won't. This is your first serious transgression since I gave you life."

Themis lets out the breath she'd been holding while she waited for Zeus' judgment. Then she clears her throat. Loudly.

"Since *we* gave you life," he amends.

He leans back on his throne, considering. I meet his eyes and wait, knowing there will be more.

"Since the boy will die soon, I will not force you to remove his memories unless he becomes a liability. You can see the relationship through to the end if that is your wish," he says. "Just make sure that it has an end," he adds.

I let my breath out in a whoosh, and Themis squeezes my hand in support. I'm getting off easy, but mortality would have been nice. I try to look happy for Mom's sake, but any relief we feel, real or fake, is short-lived.

"It would be wrong to punish you for my shortsightedness," Zeus continues. "I should have more clearly foreseen the consequences of Lachesis' actions."

I look at Mom and whisper the words, "Lachesis' actions?" She shrugs, clearly having no idea what Zeus is talking about, either.

"What exactly are you talking about? What did Lachesis do?" I ask, although given a moment to think about it, a sick thought is beginning to poke at the edge of my brain. I look at Mom and see that she's beginning to think the same thing. Her mouth is hanging open, and she's breathing quickly.

Fear mingled with rage makes me nauseous, and I wrap an arm around my midsection. I pray that Zeus will say anything other than what I'm afraid to hear, but I know my luck for the day has run out.

"She came to me eighteen years ago and asked me if it would be all right if she fated a human boy for you, Atropos. She said she wanted you to experience the same feelings she felt for her beloved Charlie. I reluctantly agreed because I knew you'd been alone too long. You were becoming cold and unpleasant.

"I thought fating someone for you would give you a chance to experience a relationship in a less-threatening way. I never dreamed she would pick someone who would die so soon after you met him."

Anger makes my stomach heave, and I'm afraid of embarrassing myself by puking all over Zeus' marble floor. This is the secret Lacey is keeping in that password-protected document and why she looked so smug when I asked her about it.

She fated Alex for me, which means the only reason he likes me is because he has to. It also explains why he wouldn't go away when I was nasty to him and when the Keres attacked him. Lacey programmed him to overcome common sense. He was made for me, and she gave him an early death for one reason—*revenge*.

"She didn't do it so I could 'experience love' or any of that crap. She did it to get even with me. I killed Charlie, the human she loved. She knew all along I'd have to kill him, and she still hated me for it. The grief she felt was of her own making, and she blamed me. She fated Alex for me for revenge," I shout at Zeus. "She wanted me to experience pain, not love."

I'm beyond furious now. I hurt all over. I hurt for me, but mostly, I hurt for Alex. He's nothing but a pawn in Lacey's game. The only reason he's dying is because he's mine. She didn't give him an early death to balance the scales or fulfill Zeus' master plan. She did it to get back at me. Alex should be living his life, but instead, he's caught in this farce. Fresh rage washes through me, and I want to hit something. Somebody.

"I wondered as much, but she was sincere when she asked for permission," Zeus says. "She denied anything other than the purest motives."

"Well, she was full of shit, wasn't she?" I say. "How could you not see that? You're supposed to be omniscient. Your skill failed you on this one, Zeus."

"Careful," Themis warns, but I'm beyond caring. She puts a restraining hand on my arm.

"No, Mom," I begin, twisting out of her reach. "If we're on the subject of rules here, how about the one that Zeus broke? We, as Fates, are never to meddle in each other's lives. Clotho can't create someone because I ask her to. I can't kill someone just because one of my sisters wants me to. Lachesis can't fate someone for Clotho or me. We are not allowed to screw around like that. It was the first rule that Zeus set down for us when he gave us our jobs. We are to serve him, not our own interests.

"Lacey fating Alex for me was surely a violation of that first rule, and Zeus here giving her permission was even more wrong. She should be the one up here getting reamed out, not me."

"Atropos," Zeus warns. Lightning crackles at his fingertips. For one second, I'm afraid. And then I'm not.

"Do you think I care?" I roar. "Do you think you scare me with your little parlor tricks? I came here expecting to be punished for my one mistake. Instead, I discover that you and my sister have been breaking the rules all along. You even encouraged me to get closer to him because you knew it would work out. I can't believe you would mess with my feelings like that.

"You want Alex's memory flushed? Consider it flushed. I don't want him now. I don't want a relationship that's poisoned. You wanted to teach me about love? Well, this certainly wasn't the way to do it because I hate you, I hate Lachesis, and now I hate the very idea of love because I know that none of it is real. I was better off alone. I knew that, but I let you all push me into this and I shouldn't have."

"You don't mean that," Themis says. "You've been so happy

these last weeks."

I turn to her. "I do mean it. Did you know about this? Is that why you were pushing me to have fun with the humans? Because if you did—" I threaten.

"No. I swear. This is the first I'm hearing of it, and I'm as appalled as you are." She turns to Zeus. "I can't believe you."

"Well, you certainly didn't seem to be taking a hand in her life. You let her drift along, growing angrier and lonelier each year. I thought it was nice that Lachesis was concerned for her sister."

"Atropos was doing just fine without our interference," Mom says.

I roll my eyes. I know they'll bicker for hours, and I don't want to hear it. I'm done. I turn and run out of the temple and back to the pool. Mom can find her own way home. She can call a cab or hitchhike from Mount Mitchell. I don't care. The only thing I care about is getting home so that I can pummel Lacey until the rage passes. After that, I have to find Alex and flush his memory.

When I get home, Lacey and Chloe are working quietly in the basement, the strains of some old Big Band song—Chloe's genre of choice—the only noise. Lacey is poring over astrological charts, setting up the fate of some poor human. Probably planning to screw him or her over, too.

"Picking out another boyfriend for me since mine will soon be dead?" I hiss as I stride down the center aisle toward her. "I wouldn't recommend that."

I have the satisfaction of seeing her face go white and then bright red. She's busted, and she knows it. Good.

"How did you find out?" she asks.

"Good old Dad ratted you out."

She squares her shoulders and faces me. I feel a surge of adrenaline. At least she's not going to cower down. I'm going to get a good, soul-cleansing fight. "I'm not sorry."

"I didn't expect you to be. But you will be," I say, moving closer and standing toe to toe with her. I have two inches in height on her, and I love that she has to look up at me.

"Hey," Chloe cries, getting up from her spinning wheel and coming to stand between us. "What's this all about?"

"Our dear sister fated Alex for me so that I could experience the joy of love or some such crap. But I think we all know it was revenge, don't we?" I say to Lacey.

"Whoa," Chloe says. She turns to Lacey. "You really did that?"

"With Zeus' blessing," Lacey says with a smug smirk on her face.

"Only because you lied about your motives," I say.

She only shrugs. "So?"

"So, you condemned Alex to suffer and die young for no other reason than to get even with me. Does this not strike you as even a tiny bit wrong? This is not what we do. Human life isn't to be treated recklessly. We serve Zeus' plan, not our own petty agendas. Or we did, until you threw all that out the window."

Lacey waves a dismissive hand. "He'd have died someday anyway. They all do."

That's it. Something in my brain snaps, and I'm no longer rational. I push Chloe out of the way and tackle Lacey with everything I have. We hit the floor. She tries to scramble away from me, but I'm stronger. I sit on her chest and lean down with my elbow against her throat, pressing down with all my weight. She gasps for air and claws at me, but I don't let go. I can't kill her, but I can make her hurt.

Chloe tugs at my shirt, trying to get me off Lacey. I bear down even harder on Lacey's throat with one arm and brush Chloe off with the other. Lacey's turning purple, and I'm loving it.

Now Chloe is pounding on my back. "Let her go," she cries.

I keep the pressure on until the purple begins changing to blue. Then I let go. Lacey crawls backward, away from me, but not fast enough. I plow my fist into her nose. The bright red blood flows, and I finally let Chloe pull me up. My knuckles are split and bleeding, but I don't care.

"You are such an insensitive bitch," Lacey spits at me. She wipes her nose with the back of her hand, smearing blood all over her face. I can't help but smile at the sight.

"Charlie died, and you didn't care. You just snipped his line and walked away. You didn't care how much it hurt me," she says through tears.

"*It. Is. What. I. Do.*" I pronounce each word through clenched teeth. "Will no one ever get that through their stupid heads? Killing people is my life.

"The day you decided to love a human boy, you knew how it would end. And when. You knew you'd grieve, and yet, you did it anyway. That I had to kill him and cause you pain is your fault, not mine. You want to hate someone, hate yourself," I say to Lacey.

"You are my sister. You should have gone to Hades on my behalf and argued for Charlie's immortality. He's listened to you before."

I snort. "Once. And that was because of a very stupid mistake I made when I'd only been on the job a month. All Hades did was undo what never should have been done to begin with. He's never intervened in a case where fate has been assigned and correctly carried out. Nor will he. I'm not about to stick my neck out with Hades because you were too stupid to realize the consequences of your actions."

"I wasn't stupid. I only wanted to know what it felt like to really love someone and have them love you back. It was wonderful, but now he's gone and it hurts. It hurts so bad that some days, I can't stand it. Even after all these years, I miss him. Worse, it'll never stop hurting because I can't die and join him in the Underworld."

"Oh, please. Get your head out of the romance novels and look around. Love is not meant for us. It never was. We determine who loves and who doesn't, but it isn't meant for us.

I knew that and it's why I chose to stay away from the humans. At least until you mucked around in my life," I say.

"We can love," Chloe, ever the optimist, interjects.

"Sure, but it never works out," I say, turning on her. "Have you ever had happily ever after? No. And why? Because we exist outside of fate. Our relationships either end in breakups when the human finds the person they're really fated for, or they end in death and we go on living for millennia. Either way, we end up miserable," I say.

I turn to Lacey, who is now sitting in her chair and weeping, pressing tissues to her bloody nose. I roll my eyes. Any respect I have for her vanishes under contempt. "I can't stand it. Charlie was a hundred years ago. Get over it. The drama queen act is beyond old."

"Will you just 'get over' Alex?" she asks.

"You already know the answer to that question. You created this mess for the express purpose of making me hurt, so I think you know what will happen. I promise you this, however. I'll deal with it a hell of a lot better than you," I say.

I start to walk away and then turn back to her. I have the brief satisfaction of seeing her shrink away from me. Her earlier bravado has faded, and now she's afraid of me. *Good.*

"You know what? We're done, you and I. I will work with you on matters of fate because I have no choice. But that's it. Stay out of my life. If I ever catch you fating a human to have any relationship with me, even if it's to be my garbage man, I swear I will beat you black and blue and then cut you in half, just like I did Ker. Do your damn job and leave me alone."

I flee upstairs, Chloe hot on my heels. She catches me as I yank open the front door. Grabbing my arm, she tugs me back into the foyer.

"What are you going to do?" she asks.

"What I should have done to begin with. Go flush Alex's memory. Slash and burn. I'll go back so far he won't even know I exist. Hell, he'll be lucky to remember his damn name."

"Did Zeus say you had to?"

"No. He's willing to let it go since Alex is dying, as long as he remains silent. But I can't have a relationship with Alex, not now. Everything is tainted. He didn't choose me. Lacey *made* him choose me. There's no honesty in that," I say.

"We'd all be better off if he forgot me. I can't undo the early death she threw at him because of me, but I can at least let him die in peace."

"I understand if you want to flush him," Chloe says. "But he has feelings for you. Whether they're programmed into him or not, they're real to him. Maybe he will be happier spending his last days with you, the person he's fated for, than spending them without you."

"But how will I ever know what's real and what's not? Can I spend time with him, always wondering whether he would have chosen to spend that time with me if Lacey hadn't thrown him at me? What if he only loves me because he has no choice?"

"Sometimes, you just have to accept what is. You like him and your actions are your own because you have no fate. Lacey couldn't make you like him back, yet you do. Maybe that's all that matters right now. Maybe you can just love him until he dies and enjoy it for the pleasure it brings both of you without worrying about his fate. He doesn't have to know why he likes you. Only that he does."

I look down at Chloe. "Damn it. When did you get so wise?"

"I've always been that way. You just never notice. Don't go charging off to flush him right now. Cool down and think about it. Make the decision you want to make, not the decision that Lacey is pushing you toward."

She has a point. I'm usually guilty of rushing into decisions and regretting them later. Exhibit A—the whole Alex debacle. If I hadn't given in to my impulse to go after him that first day, none of us would be in this mess. Chloe is right. A cooling-off period is in order.

"I'll think about it," I promise, and I get a huge smile out of my sister.

"By the way, where's Mom?" Chloe asks. "I thought she went

to Olympus with you."

"Oh, damn," I say. "I was in such a hurry to get away from her and Zeus that I left them bickering at the temple. She's probably back at Mount Mitchell by now, fuming because I took the car. I guess I'd better go get her."

"No, you go cool off. I'll go. I'll talk her down so she won't be so angry at you for leaving her with Zeus longer than necessary."

"Thanks," I say.

"No problem. Everything will work out. It always does, and we have reason to know that better than anyone."

I smile at her. "I hope you're right."

"Of course I am," she says, pulling the door closed behind her.

CHLOE'S RIGHT. I'M NOT CAPABLE OF RATIONAL THOUGHT RIGHT now. I need to go where I can think without interruption. I decide to head for the mountain church that Alex showed me on our first outing. No one will bother me up there.

It's late afternoon, and the day is perfect for a drive and a hike. The only hiccup is that I have trouble finding the turnoff without Alex's guidance. I have to double back twice on the Blue Ridge Parkway before I find the small, open spot among the trees that marks the road to the church. The hike seems easier this time, probably because I know where I'm going and can pace myself better. I use the extra energy for swearing and ranting at Zeus and Lachesis for their scheming and for the impossible situation they've created.

When I get to the church, I spend the better part of an hour wandering through the cemetery, reading all the tombstones. Tommy Andrews remains the only name I clearly remember, but I feel a kinship with everyone buried here. They're all here by my hand, after all, so it's comforting to see that they ended up in such a picturesque final resting spot. Many aren't as fortunate.

After I've burned off the worst of my anger, I enter the

church and sit down in a pew toward the front. The sun has temporarily gone behind the clouds, and it is dark and cool inside. The darkness matches my mood and I let it and the stillness blanket me. My thoughts gradually slow down, my breathing evens out, and my thinking becomes more objective.

Lacey isn't my main problem. I've been working with her without liking her for centuries. I can keep going. Alex is my more immediate problem. I want to believe that Chloe is right and Alex will be happier with me than without me. But is it not fairer to let him live out his last days with his family and without the drama that comes with knowing me? Probably. But I can't ignore how happy he makes me, either. I've always made a show of preferring to be alone, but being with Alex reminds me that I don't want to be alone forever. Even if this feeling can only last a few weeks and even if there's going to be hurt at the end of it, I still want it. I want him.

Decision made, I close my eyes and let myself relax for the first time in days. I don't know how long I sit there, drifting and almost meditating, before the sounds of crunching leaves and snapping twigs from outside break my trance. Standing, I unfasten my sword pendant from around my neck. I nick the barely healed scab on my palm and rub the blade in the blood. My sword extends to its full length and I hold it up, ready to strike.

If it's a bear or a mountain cat, I'll only fight it if I can't get past it any other way. That's the funny thing about being the Death Fate—I don't like killing anything that doesn't absolutely have to die. Strangely, I don't worry about it being another person. After all, who else would come up here, much less at this late hour? I'm surprised, then, when the silhouette of a man darkens the doorway. The faint light shines behind him so I can't see his face, but a quick inventory of his lean build and the way he slumps against the doorframe in exhaustion reveals that it's Alex. I lay my sword on a pew and jog up the aisle to meet him.

"What are you doing here?" I ask.

When I get close enough to see his face, I can tell he shouldn't be up here. The hike up the hill physically cost him. His skin is pale and a light sheen of clammy sweat covers his face, despite the chill of early evening.

"I stopped by your house to see if you were okay. Chloe told me you were upset and that you'd gone to cool off. I took a guess that you'd come up here. When I saw your car in the lane, I knew I was right."

"Still, you shouldn't have hiked all the way up here. You should have waited for me down below."

"Yeah, it's not a good day," he says. That's an understatement. Not only is he pale and clammy, his labored breathing scares me. "I didn't think I was this bad off until I was halfway up. Then it was either keep going or turn back. I kept going."

"Idiot," I say, shaking my head at his stupidity.

"Come on, sit down," I say, propping him up against me and helping him to the nearest pew. I sit down next to him and rest a hand on his shoulder, ready to catch him should he pass out. Slowly, his color comes back and his breathing slows, so I withdraw my hand.

"Are you in big trouble?" he finally asks.

I sigh and slump back against the pew. "Not as much as I thought I'd be. I'm not being punished for telling you about myself, and I'm not in trouble for defending you against the Keres. Zeus didn't like any of it and he let me know it, but he's letting it go because of extenuating circumstances."

"Like the fact that I'm dying."

"That and the fact I like you and I haven't liked anyone in over two thousand years. Zeus seems to think it's a good experience for me."

I debate telling him of Lacey's trickery, but I decide against it. Chloe is right. There is honesty and then there is over-sharing. Alex doesn't need to know why he likes me, only that he does. To tell him that he was fated for me will only confuse things further and give him a burden he doesn't need to bear. I can bear it alone. I don't want him to feel obligated to me. He should remain free to make whatever choices he can with the time he has left. I might tell him the truth someday, but today isn't the day.

"So you don't have to memory flush me? When I got home last night, I was afraid you'd do it after all."

"No. Unless you want me to, and I think Zeus is hoping you will."

"I couldn't sleep last night because I kept expecting you to slip through the window and flush my head. I couldn't stand the idea of waking up and not knowing you. So, no, I don't want you to do it. Zeus'll just have to be disappointed."

"Then I won't. But if you change your mind, if knowing me gets to be too much, the option is always open," I say, half hoping he'll take me up on it.

"I understand, but I'll pass. I've got a tumor the size of a peach in my head. I don't need you rummaging around in there, too."

I nod, and we slip into silence. Alex leans back against the pew and closes his eyes for a few minutes. I let him be while he gathers what little strength he has left.

"So you like me, huh?" he asks after a while, showing me a wicked, sidelong grin.

"I thought that was obvious after yesterday. I didn't let the Keres take you, after all," I say, trying to match his joking tone.

"True," he says. He turns in the pew to face me. The grin disappears, replaced by a serious look. "But I want to hear you say it."

I inhale. This is it. The point of no return. If I admit my feelings, I can no longer avoid the tsunami of grief that will break over my head in a few short weeks. There'll be no going back, no returning to my cocoon of bitchiness and indifference. I will be opening myself up to pain like I've never known. Even the end of my relationship with Ares, bitter as it was, cannot compare with the finality of death. But if I do this, there might also be joy that makes the pain worthwhile. The humans find it to be so, at least. I let out my breath and step off the edge.

"I like you, Alex. I really do like you."

I bow my head in defeat. I've fought so hard to keep my feelings from overtaking common sense, and yet here I am. I'm happy and sad, frustrated and relieved. And terrified because I know how this story ends. There will be no happy ending, no fairy-tale romance. Just death, carried out by my own hand, and endless separation. A single tear tracks down my cheek, and I curse my weakness.

Alex places his hand under my chin and lifts my face so that I have no choice but to look at him. "I like you, too. And not just because you're a badass."

I choke out a laugh.

He picks up my hand, which is resting on my thigh, and brings it to his lips. Planting a kiss on the back of my hand, he turns it over and kisses the well of my palm, folding my fingers closed over it.

"You can keep that," he says.

I sigh and try not to embarrass myself by tearing up further, but the tenderness of the gesture leaves me no choice. Tears well up and spill over. Alex catches one and wipes it away with his thumb.

"You should be happy, not sad. I'm happy. Happier than I've been in a long time," he says.

Alex releases my hand and puts his arm around me, gently tugging me down until I'm resting my head on his shoulder. It's comforting to just rest here, to let someone else share my exhaustion and confusion. The irony of the dying boy supporting the immortal goddess isn't lost on me, and I'm humbled.

After a few minutes, he brushes a kiss across my hair and gently pushes me back so we face each other again.

"I have something for you," he says.

"Besides the kiss?" I ask, showing him my still-clenched fist.

"Besides that," he says.

He reaches into the front pocket of his jeans and pulls out a small jewelry box, but he doesn't hand it to me. He keeps it in his lap for the moment.

"I did a little Googling last night. I wanted to learn more about you."

"And did you?"

"Yep. I learned a lot."

"Probably nothing good," I mutter, knowing that he probably learned more than I'm comfortable with, much of it likely wrong.

"Oh, it was quite informative. And entertaining. Those paintings and sculptures of you as an old crone are a hoot. Of course, I'd rather hear it all from you, someday, but for now, I know enough."

He hands the box to me.

"Open it," he says when I take it but simply stare at it.

I crack the lid and gasp when I see the necklace resting on the velvet. It's a gold chain with a scissors charm dangling from it. The scissors aren't as ornate as my work shears, but the handles on the charm have delicate filigree work curling and swirling along them.

"It's beautiful."

"Here," he says, taking the box from me and pulling the necklace out. He leans in close to me and, sliding his hands behind my head, fastens the necklace around my neck. As he pulls back, he kisses me gently on the cheek.

"Thank you," I say, fingering the small charm that now hangs between my collarbones. It's the perfect complement to my sword pendant.

"Now, if you accept this, there is one condition," Alex says with that wicked grin again. "And since you're wearing it, I take that as acceptance."

"Uh-oh. That wasn't fair, you know," I say.

"Never claimed to play fair," he says. "You have to promise me something."

"If I can," I cautiously say.

The smile fades, and seriousness takes its place. "Will you see that I'm buried up here?" he asks.

That stops me. Of all the things he could ask, that's the least expected. "I can try, I guess, but where does your family want you buried?"

"Next to my mother in the Methodist churchyard. But I'd rather be up here. It's peaceful. And meaningful," he adds as he leans over and kisses my cheek.

"There aren't any recent graves up here, and the church is abandoned. I doubt there's any way to get permission."

He leans back in the pew and raises an eyebrow at me. "Who said anything about permission?" he asks. "Let my family conduct the service and bury me in the churchyard. Then you find a way to get me up here. Everyone will be happy."

"You do realize you're asking me to essentially rob your grave and bring you up here, don't you?"

"You mean you can't do it? I thought a goddess would have her ways."

"Oh, I didn't say I couldn't do it. Just be sure you want me to. Won't it bother you to have your father and sister visiting an empty grave?"

"It's what I want. What does it matter where my family mourns? Only my body will be in the hole in the ground. There's no difference between them visiting an empty grave and visiting a grave with an empty body in it. The part of me that is me, that will appreciate their thoughts of me, will be somewhere else, at least according to a very reliable source," he says, poking my thigh.

I think for a moment. He's sure he wants this; I can see it on his face. He knows what he's asking and what he is risking if his family ever learns the truth.

"Okay, then. After your regular funeral, I'll get you moved up here. I promise."

He leans his forehead down and rests it against mine. "Thank you," he says.

We sit like that for a few moments until I raise my head and kiss him. I'm surprised at my boldness, and I think he is, too. He eagerly kisses me back, and both of us abandon ourselves to the moment.

His arms come around me and pull me closer; I shift on the

141

pew so that I can do the same. This kiss is more intense than our first. It's as though, having asked and received permission with the first kiss, we are now free to fully explore. His hands roam over my back, and he brings one hand up to cup the base of my skull and hold me close to him. I feel his tongue against my lips, and I open my mouth against his. He lets out a little moan against my mouth, and I sigh with pleasure.

I lose myself completely in Alex. My job is forgotten, as is his impending death. There is only this moment, too soon to fade. We kiss each other fiercely, as though trying to force time to stop with our urgency. It's nonsense, of course, and when the moment finally ends, I rest my cheek against his and am content to just breathe in and out with him.

"I changed my mind," he says against my cheek.

"About what?"

"I don't like you."

I pull back, confused and stung by his words. A replay of Ares' cruelty flashes through my mind.

"I love you," he says.

I'm stunned. For a moment, I just gawp at him. "Oh, Alex," I finally say, shaking my head. If it's possible for a heart to swell with love and shatter in pain at the same time, mine does just that.

"I know it's not convenient and I know it sucks for you because we have no time, but there it is. You don't have to say it back if you don't want to. I'll understand," he says.

"It doesn't suck, Alex."

He hugs me close to him. In the warmth of his embrace, I'm forced to amend my statement. "Well, it does kind of suck," I say against his shirt, and I feel his chest rumble with a chuckle.

"Yeah, it does. I'm in love with death."

"And I'm in love with a mortal with a short shelf life," I answer, tears tracking down my cheeks.

Releasing me, he pushes me away from him, keeping his hands wrapped tight around my arms. He studies my face, taking in my tears and the shaky smile I give him.

"Say it again," he demands in a husky voice that doesn't sound like the Alex I know. His voice is serious, devoid of all the teasing that is usually there.

"I'm in love with you, Alex," I say.

This time, it's his turn to bow his head, hiding his emotions from me. "Thank you," he finally says. "I'd always hoped to hear a woman say that to me before I died, and now I have. I can die a happy man."

"You've never—"I start, but I falter. There's no polite way to ask this question.

"No. I've never been in love before, much less had anyone other than family say they loved me."

"That makes two of us," I say. "Well, I was in love once, but he certainly never said it back."

He chuckles. "This is really pretty sad when you think about it. To be as old as we are. Ancient, in your case." I playfully try to smack him, but he ducks out of my reach, laughing.

"And have never been loved outside of our families before," he continues. "Now we're in love and it can't last. I'm sure there's some karmic god somewhere just laughing his ass off over this one."

I wince. He doesn't know how close to the truth he is; only it's not a god who's laughing. It's a goddess, Lacey, who is having her fun watching us come together only to be torn apart. She's getting her revenge, and all she has to do is sit back and watch me unravel. I'm trying not to give her the satisfaction, but every hour I spend with Alex is bringing me closer to the despair she wants me to experience. *Shit.* I really am screwed.

My phone buzzes at my hip, and I sigh. "I have to go home, Alex," I say. His face falls. "I don't want to, but I have to."

"I know you do. Death won't wait forever, will it?"

"Sadly, no," I say, meaning more than just the people I have to kill tonight. It won't wait for us, either. Our time together is already limited, and my damn job just makes everything more difficult.

Something has to give, and I can only see one thing that

is optional. School. I've already been, and Alex doesn't really need to go anymore. A brainstorm hits me and I turn to him, excited by my new plan.

"Are you going to keep going to school?" I ask. Seeing what the trip up the mountain did to him, I can't imagine that sitting in school and doing homework every night is good for him.

"Dad wants to pull me out. There are only a few weeks left in the year, and I can do the work from home and still pass. He thinks school is too taxing for me, but I don't want to just spend all my days in bed, either. It feels like giving up. I'm not ready to give up yet."

"What if you could spend your days with me, instead? If you quit going to school, I'll quit, too. It'll free up more time for me to spend with you. I can quit trying to fit you in around school *and* my job, and just fit you in around my job. It's not ideal, but we'd have a lot more time together and you wouldn't have to spend all day in bed, either."

"Won't it raise suspicion about your family when you disappear from school?" he asks.

"Probably not. I miss so much school already that the teachers all wonder about me. Themis can come up with some believable excuse to get me out of the last few weeks."

"Will she do it?"

I think about how she owes me for her part in pushing me toward Alex. "Probably."

"Okay, then. I'll let my dad pull me out."

I nod and stand up. That's at least one problem solved. There are about a thousand more, but I feel better knowing that we'll be seeing a lot more of each other without school in the way. "I've got to get you home," I say.

"You go on. I can make it down."

"Are you nuts? It's almost dark, and you're ill. Don't argue with me," I say when I see him open his mouth to protest. "I'm not taking chances with you."

"It's not like I can kill myself, is it?"

"Well, no, but fate doesn't cover other things like the broken

144

legs, ribs, or arms you might get from falling down a mountain. You need your strength, not to be camped out in the hospital in traction. Besides, what would be the point of us dropping out of school if you end up in the hospital? Come on," I say, extending a hand to him.

He gets up and waits while I retrieve and shrink my sword. I hang the pendant around my neck so that it rests next to his shears. We walk hand in hand out of the church and to the edge of the clearing. When we get to the head of the trail that leads back to our cars, I look over at Alex. Just walking across the clearing has made him ill. He's already white and panting.

"Okay, here's what we're going to do," I say to him. "I'm going to carry you down the mountain. And you're going to like it."

He snorts. "I think I'm a bit heavy for you."

"Trust me. You're not."

Picking him up in my arms, I carry him the way a groom carries a bride over the threshold after the wedding. I would be able to carry him easily even if he was well, but his illness has made him thin and highly portable. I'm dismayed that I can feel almost every bone poking me through his clothes. The long pants and shirts of winter have camouflaged how much weight he's already lost.

"God, this is embarrassing," he says.

"Don't think of it that way," I say as I pick my way carefully down the trail. "Think of it as a privilege that few have ever had. Being carried by a woman is one thing, but being carried by a goddess is something special. We don't carry just anyone."

"You're not even breathing hard," he complains. "Could you at least act like you're struggling? Make me feel a little manlier?"

"I could, but I'd probably trip and injure us both. Just relax, Alex. Let me do the work and don't complain."

He gives up and rests his head against my shoulder.

"That's better," I say.

I carry him in silence the rest of the way down the mountain, putting him down when I reach our cars. "Can you drive?" I ask him.

"Yeah, that's no trouble. I'm not seeing double or anything."

"Okay. I'll follow you home," I say.

The drive is uneventful, but slow. He clearly shouldn't be driving. I can tell he's driving super slow to keep from making mistakes. It's like following an old man with a revoked license or a drunk who doesn't want the attention of cops.

He finally turns into his driveway. I pull in behind him and crank down my window. Getting out, he comes to my window. "Thanks, Atropos," he says.

I smile. "I think you're the first human to call me by my real name. I like it."

He leans in and kisses me again, gentler this time.

"Will I see you tomorrow?" he asks.

"Sure. In fact, I have a plan for tomorrow if you're feeling well enough. I'll call you in the morning."

"Uh-oh. Another plan. Will I get to see you beat up on some more bad guys?" he jokes.

"I sincerely hope not. Good night, Alex."

"Good night, Atropos."

I watch until he's inside the house, and then I drive home. When I get there, Chloe is sitting on the sofa, flipping TV channels and munching on popcorn. I hang my coat on the hall rack and flop next to her on the sofa.

"Well?" she asks. "Did you flush him?"

"Nope."

"Good. You deserve this, Atropos. Even if Lacey started out with bad intentions, I think this is wonderful for you. And for him."

"Yeah, but it's gonna hurt like hell when it's over," I say.

"And I'll be right here with a big Band-Aid," she says. "You know I'll be here for you. And for him, if the two of you need anything."

I lean over and hug her. "Thank you." I lean back and settle into the corner of the sofa. "He called me Atropos tonight."

"That's big."

I nod. "Yeah. I don't mind going by other names. I understand why we have to do it. But there's nothing like hearing your real name uttered by someone special. I haven't heard that since Ares. And Alex is the first human who's ever uttered my real name without it being a curse word."

"I know what you mean. I hate being called Chloe or Karen or any of the hundreds of other names I've used over the years. Sometimes, I forget who I'm supposed to be."

"I know. Tonight, I felt, I don't know. Whole, I guess."

"It's a great feeling, isn't it?"

"Sure is. But I'd better not get used to it."

"Don't do that," Chloe snaps.

"What?"

"Don't block yourself off from the experience because of how it's going to end. Just enjoy it and be present with him. You'll regret it if you don't."

"Thank you, Clotho," I say, intentionally using her real name. "You're a good sister."

"I try."

I push up from the sofa and blow out my breath. "Now I've got to go upstairs and apologize to Mom."

"Don't worry. She's pretty calm about the whole thing. I think she's way more pissed at Lacey and Zeus than at you."

"Good. Because I need her to get me out of school for the rest of the year."

Chloe raises her eyebrows. "Good luck with that," she calls after me as I trudge upstairs.

I don't have to battle too hard with my mom. She's surprisingly understanding about me not finishing the school year.

"We're all partly responsible for the mess you're in. The least we can do is to help you see it through to the end," she says, sighing when I explain what I want to do and why.

"It's not like you've ever skipped out on your lessons or failed to act like a normal student, no matter how many times you've had to endure an education. I think this one time I can come up with something to allow you to complete the year from home," she says.

"Of course, if you don't do the work and you flunk out, you'll have to go to summer school after Alex is gone. You still have to uphold the illusion that you're a normal kid," she adds.

I sigh. Of course I have to appear normal. I agree to her terms. I can do the coursework in my sleep and probably bang out all the assignments for the rest of the year in one night if I can get some uninterrupted time. I'm just grateful that Alex and I will have more time together.

Back at my desk in the basement, I glance at the calendar hanging on the wall. May fifteenth is circled in blue ink. Alex has about five weeks left. He doesn't know that, but I do. He's blessed not to know, not to have the countdown constantly ticking away in his head as it is in mine. May fifteenth haunts my dreams.

I trudge up to my bed, resolved to make the most of these remaining weeks. Before I fall asleep, I take off the necklace Alex gave me and place it carefully on my nightstand. I stare at it until sleep finally overtakes me.

I wake up early the next morning, quickly take care of some deaths, and set up my workroom for the rest of the day. Then I call Alex.

"Are you able to go out today?" I ask.

"Yeah, as long as whatever you've planned isn't too tiring."

"I told you you were an idiot for coming up that mountain yesterday," I say, sharper than I intend. I immediately hate myself. I shouldn't scold someone who is clearly trying to make the most of the life he has left. It's his time to do with as he pleases. That I wish he'd take it easy and preserve himself is my reality, not his.

"Don't worry," I continue in a softer tone. "What I've got planned isn't that tiring. I'll be there in five minutes," I tell him.

I get to his house a little after ten. I've managed to carve out about two hours before I have to be back in my workroom. I hope it's enough time.

Alex is waiting for me on his front porch when I pull up. Is it my imagination or does he seem slower to get up and walk to the car than he did the other day? I try to let it go. I'll make myself nuts if I spend the next weeks trying to discern every telltale sign of his decline. It's enough that I know the date.

Alex gets in the car. I turn and give him a quick kiss.

"So, what's the plan today?" he asks.

"We're going to the SPCA to get you a dog."

"Atropos, that's generous, but you don't have to. I know you said you'd take care of it when I'm gone, but I don't want to burden you with an animal."

"And I told you, it's no problem. You're getting a dog, so shut up and like it."

He tries to look disapproving, but I catch the hint of his little-boy smile.

"Can I ask for one more favor? One more thing to make this day great?" he asks.

"What?"

"Can I drive this car? I've lusted after it ever since you picked me up that day after school. Please," he adds when I don't agree right away. He turns on his pitiful look, and I'm helpless.

"Okay," I say. "But if you dent her—" I threaten.

"No way. I love her too much to damage her."

"All right, then."

We get out and switch places. Before backing out of the driveway, Alex caresses the steering wheel and the dashboard. He takes in every gauge and detail. He sighs, clearly a man in love.

"You know, even goddesses get jealous," I tease.

He leans over and lightly kisses me.

"There's no competition here, Atropos. Just a different flavor of lust."

I roll my eyes. "Guys and cars," I sigh.

He finally puts the car in gear and backs out of the driveway. His eyes gleam for the whole ride to the SPCA. He takes the long way to prolong the joy, but I don't nag him. We don't have to hurry. I'm just glad that I can make him happy. Or at least that my car can.

When we get to the SPCA, the attendant tells us that we're free to head on back to the kennels.

"There are leashes on the wall next to each pen, if you want to take a few dogs out to the meet-and-greet area and see how you get along," he says.

Alex and I wander up and down the length of the dog area. I try not to get depressed by the sheer number of hopeful faces that we pass. Most of them rush to the front of their pens, and I swear all of them are saying, "Please, take me. Choose me!" Today isn't supposed to be a sad day, and I resolutely push the sadness away. Hopefully, we'll rescue one dog today. That has to be enough.

"See anyone you like?" I ask Alex.

He walks back to a kennel that holds a small beagle-corgi mix. She looks like a corgi that's wearing a beagle suit.

"She looks interesting," he says. The dog comes to the front of the cage. She sits and stares hard at Alex, as if sizing him up. Her brown eyes look him up and down. I snicker. This looks like a case where the dog is going to do the choosing, not Alex. He doesn't realize that he's not in control of this situation.

I read from the card next to her cage. "She's about seven years old and fully house trained. Her owner had to move into a nursing home and couldn't take care of her. She's listed as good with kids and of mellow temperament. Her name's Maggie."

"That's what I want," he says. "Puppies are cute, but I don't have the energy to chase one around. I just want a dog that will hang out with me."

I take down the leash, and we take Maggie outside. Alex sits down at a picnic table in the yard and tosses a ball for the dog to chase. Maggie looks at him like he's lost his mind and instead of chasing the ball, walks over to Alex and lies down on his shoes.

Alex reaches down and scratches behind her ears. The dog rolls over onto her back for a full belly rub.

"I think mellow may be an understatement," I say, laughing at Maggie's shamelessness.

Alex picks her up and places her on his lap. They sit together for half an hour, getting to know each other. After a while, I leave them alone and go in search of the attendant.

"I think we've found a winner," I say, pointing out the window to where Alex and Maggie are sitting together on the bench.

"Great. I just need you to fill out these forms," he says, handing me a stack of papers, "and we'll evaluate your ability to be pet parents."

"There might be a complication," I begin, "and I want to be honest with you, but I hope it won't jeopardize his chance to adopt this dog."

I explain the full situation to the man, covering Alex's terminal illness and the fact that I will take Maggie upon Alex's death.

"So there's no danger of the dog coming back here when Alex dies," I explain. "My family and I are fully willing and able to take care of her. Alex could use the companionship and love of a good dog here at the end. I know this means a lot to him."

The man thinks about it for a few moments.

"Well, it's not standard," he says. "We usually like for our animals to go to one home and remain there until they die. But I can see the problem here."

He looks back out the window to where Alex and the dog are now sprawled out in a sunbeam on the grass together.

"And I'm sympathetic. I can see that the dog will be loved. If you love the boy enough to explain this to me and to be willing to take the dog upon his death, I don't think either home will be short of love. The only thing I ask is that you spend a lot of time with the dog, too, and introduce her to your home so that it's not so jarring for her when you take over. Will you do that?"

"Of course. I'll do whatever I can to make the transition easier for her."

"All right, then. Fill out those forms. Oh, here, let me give you a second set so you can fill out both addresses and home information."

I take the pile of paper back outside to the picnic table and hand Alex his half. I explain the arrangement, and his face lights up.

"I can't believe they agreed. I was afraid they wouldn't let me have her," he says.

We write in silence, the little dog passed out on Alex's shoes. When we're finished, I gather up the papers and Alex leashes the dog. We walk back to the main office, give the man the papers, and pay the adoption fee. He, in turn, gives us Maggie's veterinary records.

"Are you going to keep her name?" he asks. "Might be best since she's already used to it."

"I'll keep it," Alex promises. "It's beautiful."

Alex, Maggie, and I walk back to the Thunderbird. Alex and Maggie climb in the backseat and snuggle up together. I try not to think about paw prints, claw marks, and dog drool on my upholstery. I should have brought a blanket.

Our next stop is the pet warehouse store where we drop a ton of money on food, treats, and other necessities. After Maggie's needs are met for the foreseeable future, I drive Alex home and help him unload Maggie and all of her new stuff.

"Can't you come in and spend some time with us? I could make you lunch," he offers when I open the car door and sit down in the driver's seat.

"Sorry. I'm late as it is. But maybe I can get back tonight."

"This sucks," he says as he lightly pounds his fist on my door. I wince at the metallic thunk.

"I know it does. But there's nothing I can do about it."

"I could come watch you work. I swear I won't tell anyone anything."

"I wish you could, but it's not allowed. Zeus would fry all of us."

"I know. I was just hoping."

I sigh. "You go on in and get acquainted with your new friend. I'll be back when I can," I say.

Alex squats down in front of me and places his hands on my knees. "What if I don't let you go?" he teases.

He reaches up and brings my head down so he can kiss me. I rest my hands on his shoulders, squeezing lightly. I wish I could stay here like this, but my phone vibrates in my pocket and I pull away from Alex.

"That's my last warning. I really have to go."

He stands and backs away, but I can't miss the hurt and resentment on his face.

"I'm so sorry. It's not like I enjoy this. But it's what I have to do."

"I know. It's just sad that the only day I'll get your undivided attention will be the day that phone rings for me."

That stings. "That's not fair. You know what I am. I gave you the chance to leave, but you didn't take it. Now you're throwing something that I cannot change in my face."

"Sometimes I wonder if I made the right decision. I still love you, but I hate your damn job and I hate competing with everybody else who's literally dying for your attention. And I hate myself for being so pissed off about it. It seems like just when we're getting closer, we get pulled apart again. How much of this am I supposed to take?"

I shake my head. "You're angry. I get it. Probably less at me than at the shortened, unfair life you've been dealt. But please, don't spoil what has been a wonderful morning."

"Me spoil it? You're the one running off and leaving me behind!"

"Who's leaving who?" I yell. "You're leaving me, too, you know. Permanently." I clap my hand over my mouth, horrified that I've spoken the truth.

"I didn't mean that," I say.

"Sure you did. And it's your fault that I'm leaving. You're the one who's killing me with this damn tumor!"

I reel back, as if he's slapped me. "Well, now that we've both spoken truths that should never be aired," I begin, trying to calm the situation before it gets any further out of control.

"Truth is truth," he says. "Whether we speak it or not, it's there, isn't it?"

"Alex—" I start, but he cuts me off.

"You'd better go," is all he says, gesturing toward the road.

I turn to face the steering wheel and crank the engine. "Do you want me to come by later?"

"Sure," he says without enthusiasm.

I look in the rearview mirror as I pull away. Alex has already gone inside. Maybe what I am is too much for him to deal with, after all. That would have been great news a couple of weeks ago. Now it just sucks. Big time.

CHAPTER 10

I HEAD STRAIGHT FOR MY WORKSPACE WHEN I GET HOME. AS I
stalk past her desk, Lacey glances up at me. "Problems?" she
asks, a gleeful smile on her face.

"Hell, no," I say and keep walking. I'm not about to confide
in her. She's just one more thing on an ever-growing list of
things that piss me off.

I lock myself in my workroom and crank my iPod to its
maximum volume. The stirring strains of "Summa For Choir"
fill the cavernous space. The piece usually calms me, but today
it doesn't even begin to soothe my churning emotions.

I put in several hours' work before there's a knock at the
door. Stomping over, I yank it open, thinking that if it's Lacey
I'll get the thrill of slamming it in her face.

It's not Lacey; it's Chloe. She covers her ears against the
wall of sound that spills out the door, and I reach over to crank
the volume down.

"Ah, I can come back later," she says. Chloe knows that
music this loud signals a bad mood.

"No, it's okay. I've pretty much worked off most of the mad.
Now I'm working on the depression."

She pulls the door shut behind her and takes a seat on the stool by the door.

"So what's up?" I ask when she doesn't immediately say anything. I snip a few more lifelines and let them drift to the floor.

"Nothing much. It's getting late, and I wanted to see if you wanted me to bring your dinner down here."

"No, thanks. I have a break coming up in a little while. I'll raid the fridge later."

"Want to talk about it?" she asks, spinning around and around on the stool.

"About what?"

"Whatever's got you blasting down the walls with that music."

"Alex is mad at me," I say as I sweep lifelines into boxes for Thanatos.

"For what? I thought things were good with you two."

"For this," I say, waving my hand to encompass my desk, my shears, the lines hanging from the ceiling, and the ones on the floor.

"Ah. He hates your job."

"Not so much the job. He's surprisingly cool with the fact that I kill people. It's the time that the job requires that's the problem. He wants more time than I can give."

"Oh."

"Yeah. And there's nothing I can do about it. I've only got one more day this year that I can take off from work completely. I don't have a substitute or any kind of helper. And I can't even invite Alex to spend time with me while I work because it violates yet another one of Zeus' rules."

Chloe doesn't answer right away. She just keeps spinning. While she thinks, I take the boxes of lines to the delivery door and send them off.

"Here's my idea," she finally says. "Invite him down here."

"Which part of 'That's not allowed' did you miss? Zeus would go ballistic. I'd probably be struck down by a lightning bolt before Alex could clear the basement door."

"But what if Zeus doesn't know?"

"You're kidding, right? Zeus knows everything. Omniscient god, remember?"

"Not everything," Chloe says.

I stop and turn to her.

"Do you really not know that our workspace and, by extension, this house, are shielded from him, just as they are shielded from everyone but us? No other god can know what the Fates do. It keeps them from trying to influence us… and us from being influenced by them. Zeus only knows what we tell him, and Hermes is the only god allowed in our workspace, and he can come only when he has a message from Zeus. In other words, this space is private."

I'm floored. Sure, I vaguely remember Zeus saying something about the sanctity of our work and about being immune to outside corruption, but I missed the part about him not knowing anything that goes on in our workspace. I'm not sure he was ever that explicit, but I'm guessing that Chloe tested it somehow. Three thousand years of paranoia for nothing. *Damn.*

"Get over your rule-breaking phobia and bring Alex here," she continues. "Zeus won't know. He'll know when you bring Alex to the house, but not what happens after he clears the front door. If he asks, just tell him you had dinner together or played on the Wii. That's not illegal, and Zeus can't prove otherwise. Anyway, he trusts you. His natural assumption will be that you're telling the truth."

I stare at Chloe. She's the good girl, the one who never breaks the rules, and here she is concocting a devious plot. "I think my respect for you just shot up about ten notches. You've got a bad-girl streak in you."

"I've done it before, you know. Brought someone to our workspace? Just to test the limits. Remember when we lived near Kilimanjaro, and I was in heavy like with that Sherpa?"

I nod. I knew she'd tested this somehow.

"I invited him to hang out with me a few times when you and

157

Lacey were out. I knew he would be discreet. He thought my job was witchcraft, and he was too scared to tell anyone from his village, anyway. Of course, when we broke up, I had to flush his memory, but you won't have that problem since Alex is dying."

"And no one ever found out?"

"Nope. Not a soul knows, except you. Go get Alex. Bring him here. Mom's gone out and Lacey's in her room, probably planning how to doom someone else. No one will know but me, and I won't tell. You two can lock yourselves in here, and no one will know."

I rush over and hug her. "You are the best," I say.

"I know," she says, a mischievous smirk on her face.

After more hours of work than I care to count, I finally reach a stopping point. I slam my shears into their drawer, lock it, and dash upstairs and out to my car. Speeding the mile to Alex's house, I run to his front door and lean on the doorbell. I hope it's not so late that everyone's gone to bed.

Emily comes to the door after what I consider to be an eternity, but which is probably only a minute. She's in her pajamas, but she doesn't look like she's been asleep. Maggie stands behind her, tail wagging madly at me.

"He's not here," Emily says before I even have a chance to ask for Alex or say hello. She's blocking the door, restricting my view into the house.

"Are you sure?" I ask.

"Yeah," she says, but her eyes dart to the side, refusing to meet mine.

"Right. You can tell him you tried to keep me out," I say, pushing past her and jogging down the hall. I slam open Alex's door and put my foot out to keep it from rebounding off the wall and into my face. Alex is propped up in bed, reading on the Kindle I bought for him.

"Shouldn't you be at work?" The nasty tone in his voice

shocks me. This isn't the kind, gentle Alex that I know.

"I don't deserve that and you know it," I say. "But you're sick, so I'll let it slide. Get dressed and in my car. I'll wait for you outside."

"And why would I do that? I'm comfortable here. As I recall, you don't have time for me."

"I'm about done taking that tone from you. Now, if you want to come with me, I have something to talk to you about. If not, I can't force you, and we can just call it quits right here. I'll wait outside," I repeat.

I leave his room, slamming the door hard behind me. Emily is in the hall, staring openmouthed at me. "We're working on it," is all I say as I walk past her.

Alex finally comes outside, and I instantly regret my sharp words. He's moving slow, clearly having a little trouble balancing. I get out of the car and go to him, offering my arm for him to lean on. I'm a bit surprised when he takes it and leans on me.

"Okay?" I ask.

"Yeah. Sometimes, it just takes me a while to get moving," he says.

I get him settled in the passenger seat and close his door. Once I'm settled in the driver's seat, I turn to him.

"I'm sorry," we say in unison. Then we laugh at the absurdity of the situation.

"I owe you an apology," he says. "I'm sorry I blew up at you. It's not you running off and leaving me that makes me crazy. It's that no matter how much I want to, I can never stay with you. You were right. I'm going somewhere you can't follow, and I hate it. Plus, the medication makes me crazy, and sometimes the tumor presses on some behavioral part of my brain. I'll probably get a lot more unpleasant before it's all over."

"I figured it was something like that. That's why I didn't kill you," I say.

He chuckles. "Yet. What do you want to talk to me about?" he asks as I put the car in gear and back out of the driveway.

I shake my head. "Wait until we get to my house. It's a

surprise."

"More surprises," he mutters.

I know I cannot say anything out here. For Chloe's plan to work, I cannot discuss it anywhere other than in my house. Zeus could be listening to me here, but anything I say in the house will be private. I have to wait until we get home to confide my plan.

Alex crosses his arms over his chest and looks frustrated at the wait, but he doesn't say anything more. I hold up one finger, wordlessly begging him to be patient.

Once we're back at my house, I open the front door and look around before motioning Alex in behind me. There's no sign of Mom or Lacey.

"Come on," I say. "Move as fast as you can and follow me."

I take Alex's hand and pull him across the living room and through the kitchen to the basement door. We hurry downstairs, and I pause at the bottom to make certain that Lacey isn't down here.

"Hey," Chloe calls from her workspace. "You're all clear."

"Thanks."

"Whoa. This is your work area?" Alex asks when he finally gets a good look at the space.

"Yep."

"Am I allowed down here?" he asks.

"I'll explain in a minute. Come on," I say, urging him forward.

As we pass Chloe's spinning wheel, I take time for hurried introductions.

"Alex, this is my sister, Chloe. Also known as Clotho. She spins out the lifelines and then passes them on to my other sister, Lacey, who assigns a destiny to every life."

"Cool," Alex says, shaking her hand. "I've seen you around school some. You play on the softball team, right?"

"Yeah, I have a little more free time than Atropos does. You're right. He is cute," she says to me.

I roll my eyes, but Alex laughs. "Good to know," he says.

"Come on," I say to Alex, tugging his hand toward

my workroom. I don't need Lacey coming down the stairs unexpectedly, and I don't need Chloe making any more embarrassing comments.

"Good to meet you," Chloe calls to Alex as we walk away. He gives her a wave over his shoulder.

"That's Lacey's area," I tell him as we pass her tables crammed with scales and charts. He pauses to take a closer look, but I drag him on.

"Keep moving," I urge him.

"What's the damn hurry?" he asks, panting slightly as we cover the long distance to my workroom. I feel bad for exerting him, but I don't have a choice.

We reach the end of the basement. Immediately, his eyes fixate on the door to my workroom.

"This is incredible carving work," he says, running a hand over the wood. "Did you make this?"

"No. I'd cut my hand off if I tried. Zeus had it commissioned for me when he made me a Fate, but I don't know who the artist was."

"What does it say?" he asks, pointing to the Greek words carved across the top of the door.

"Death waits for all."

"Creepy, but apt," he says. Then he asks, "Is this you?" He runs a hand lightly over the carving of me. I shiver, imagining him caressing the real me that tenderly.

"Yeah."

"What happened?"

"Excuse me?"

"Well, in this carving, you've got such long hair and you're dressed in that beautiful gown. Not that you're not beautiful now," he adds hastily when I turn to him and simply arch one eyebrow in his direction.

"This just isn't the Atropos that I know," he says with a shrug. "You look softer, almost delicate, in that carving. You don't have the hard edge that's in you now."

"About three thousand years happened, that's all," I say,

shrugging.

"Time changes people, even immortals. That's how I looked when I lived on Mount Olympus, just after I became the Death Fate. I thought it was an honor, at first. Everything was new, and I was naïve. After you spend centuries killing people in every way imaginable and being hated by all of humanity and most of the gods, things aren't as rosy."

"Makes sense, I guess. The long hair was nice, though."

I shrug. "It's easy to maintain when the world's population is only a few thousand. Now that we're up to billions, I don't have time to deal with it anymore."

I enter my code into the security panel and place my finger on the scanner. When the door opens, I gesture Alex inside ahead of me and close the door behind us. Now I can relax.

"So what's the big surprise?" Alex asks.

"I've found a way for you to spend time with me while I work."

"Isn't that against your precious rules?"

"Zeus' rules, not mine," I clarify. "And, yes, it's against the rules. And no, the rules haven't changed. Chloe gave me an education in rule-breaking, though. Long story short, you can be down here as long as neither my mom nor Lacey catches us, and you cannot speak of anything that happens down here outside of my house. You can't talk about it with Emily, or even talk about it with me outside. Understand?"

He nods. "But what if you get caught? Aren't you sort of already down one strike for telling me the truth about yourself?"

"Yeah, but what's the worst thing that Zeus can do to me? Fire me? Make me mortal? I've thought a lot about it, and those aren't terrible fates. I'd be closer to normal than I've ever been. I could get a real job, have a normal life. It's not the end of the world. Right now, having you mad at me and not spending time with you feels like the end of the world."

"I don't know. Wasn't it Zeus who sentenced that guy to push the rock up the hill forever? What if he did something like that to you?"

"Sisyphus. Yes, that was Zeus' work. It's possible he could punish me that way or with something worse, but I don't think he will. At any rate, it's a risk I'm willing to take because I think he's wrong in our case. So I've made my choice. Are you in?"

He smiles, and he's back to the Alex I love. "Thank you," he says simply. "For trusting me enough to let me in."

I'm embarrassed by his words, so I keep my face down as I open my desk drawer and pull out the box that holds my shears. Laying the box on my desk, I pop the clasp.

"Wow," Alex says when I open the box and pull out my shears.

He reaches out a finger and tentatively touches the gemstones inlaid in the handles.

"Don't touch the blades," I warn. "The slightest touch will kill you."

"May I?" he asks, holding out his hand for the shears. I pass them to him, handles first, and watch as he admires the craftsmanship.

"This is a historic moment, you know," I say. "You're the first person, human or god, except me, to handle those shears since Zeus gave them to me."

"Seriously?"

I nod. "Yep. I've never even let Chloe or Lacey handle them."

He hands them back to me, and I reach over his shoulder and adjust the dimmer switch so the overhead lights come up to full power.

"Whoa," he says, looking at the billions of lifelines that are now clearly revealed and shimmering in the bright lights. The scope of my work is now obvious, and I watch Alex as he processes the reality of my life.

"There's a line for every living person in the world."

"Can I see mine?" he asks.

"Sure. But it looks pretty much like all the others."

I punch Alex's name into the computer and the racks whir and spin, bringing his line to the front of the room.

"Here it is," I say, unclipping it from the rack and handing it to him.

Taking his line, he dangles it in the air, examining it from all angles. He holds it next to another line that is on the rack for today's work. That line is much longer than his; it belongs to a ninety-year-old man who is about to die of natural causes in a nursing home. It's the life I wish Alex could have. I see the knowledge register on Alex's face.

"Well, crap," he says. "Kind of sucks to see that I literally got the short straw."

"I know. I hate it, too. It's part of the reason I wasn't sure you should come down here, rules or no rules."

"Well, it's not like I didn't know," he says, handing his line back to me. I hang it up and send it back into the recesses of the room. Alex is braver than I am. I don't want to see his line again until the end.

I point to the stool by the door. "You can have a seat there, if you want, or on the floor. Sorry there's not more comfortable seating. I don't have guests in here, other than Chloe sometimes."

"It's fine," he says, perching on the stool.

I turn the music on low and set to work. At first, I'm self-conscious about having Alex in my space. I know he's watching every move I make and wondering about every line I cut, every life I end, but I don't have the time to give him a play by play of today's deaths. To his credit, he doesn't pepper me with questions but stays silent, letting me work.

I gradually lose myself in the rhythm of the work, and I mostly forget he's even in the room. I'm dimly aware that he tires of sitting on the stool and he slides to the floor. Several hours go by, and I sense it's getting late. Or early, I'm not sure which, and I have to get Alex home soon. I'm boxing lines to send to Thanatos when he finally speaks.

"I'm sorry," he says.

"For what?" I ask as I place the boxes inside the door and push the send button.

"I apologized earlier, but I owe you another one for giving you a hard time about your work. You work harder than anyone

I've ever seen at what has to be an incredibly emotional job. And yet you do it with such grace and compassion that it's beautiful to watch. You move so fast, yet you're not careless with peoples' souls. I can't imagine that I'd have any compassion left after a week of this, let alone a few thousand years. I know I'll be in good hands when my time comes, just as all of these people are in good hands. I shouldn't have complained, and I'm sorry."

I stand there, dumbstruck by the kindness of his words. No one has ever complimented me on my work. Not even Zeus. No one has ever appreciated the fact that I do try to be respectful of the people I kill, whether they really deserve it or not. I've done a thankless job for thousands of years, and Alex is the first to appreciate the effort.

Tears track down my face as I walk to Alex and kneel down on the floor next to him. I take his hand in mine and press it to my cheek, letting him feel the tears that run freely there.

"Now it's my turn to say thank you. That's the first time anyone has ever spoken of my work with kindness instead of revulsion. Thank you, Alex."

I turn his hand over and kiss the well of his palm, folding his fingers closed over the kiss, deliberately mimicking his gesture from our day on the mountain. He pulls me over until I'm straddling his lap. Reaching up, he cradles my face with both hands.

"I see your softer side, Atropos. I see how much you care, even though you want everyone to believe you're so tough."

"It's what people expect from me," I say. "They expect me to be cold."

"I know, I know," he whispers, wiping the tears from my cheeks. "Just promise me you won't bury this side of yourself after I'm gone. Let someone else see it occasionally. It's not good for you to hold it in."

"Don't say, 'gone.' You won't be gone to me, Alex."

"Yes, I will. And I don't want you to be unhappy. So promise."

"I promise," I say as I lean down to kiss his cheek and then his forehead. I stare into his eyes, trying to memorize their strange color so I'll always remember.

He reaches to my shoulders, pulling me down to him. Kissing me thoroughly and well, his hands slide down my back. I jerk a bit when they come to rest on my butt, but I relax quickly, enjoying the heat of his hands through my jeans.

"I could kiss you all night," he says when we finally break apart.

"Technically, I think it's morning now," I say.

"Do you have more work to do tonight?"

"A bit. Do you want me to take you home first?"

"No. I'm good."

"Your dad won't mind you being out so late?"

"He'll never know. Ever since Mom died and I got sick, Dad hardly knows what Emily or I do at night. He locks himself in his room after dinner with pictures of her and their favorite music, and he looks at the pictures until he falls asleep. Trust me. He won't know whether I'm home or not."

"That's sad," I say, and Alex shrugs.

"It is what it is. I'm used to it. I think he deliberately spends time away from me so it will ease the grief when I'm gone. He stayed with Mom until the end, and it crushed him. He's separating from me now, rather than feeling it all at the end."

I should have a private conversation with Mr. Morgan about the value of appreciating what you have while it's still here, but I let it go for now.

"I won't be long," I say, kissing him lightly as I get up.

Alex settles himself on the floor, and I go back to work. Before I resume cutting lines, I pull up Mr. Morgan's file on the computer, angling the monitor so Alex can't see. If he's this depressed now, I'm concerned for him. Turns out that I have a right to be. He's scheduled to die in six months. Cause—suicide.

Even though I assigned this long before I knew the family, it still stings. I know that not everyone gets a happy life, but the relentless pounding that this family is taking is unfair. Especially since it's all designed to torture me. It makes me want to punch Lacey's nose in all over again.

I look up Emily's file next. At least her file gives me some good news. She won't die until she's eighty-four, and she'll die of plain old age. At least she won't be joining the rest of her family in an early grave. But she'll be alone. Probably end up in foster care or the care of some well-meaning relative. That sucks.

I close all the files and return to work, my heart heavy. There's nothing to be gained from telling Alex about his father. There's nothing I can do to stop it, and it would only make him worry more. He doesn't need that. I simply vow to help Emily however I can once all of her relatives are dead.

I'm cleaning up after finishing for the night when I glance over at Alex. He's slumped against the wall, eyes closed. At first, I fear that he's unconscious or in a coma, but then I realize he's just asleep. I check my watch. No wonder. It's three o'clock in the morning. I shake his shoulder. No response. I call his name. Still no response.

The heavy sleep is probably the result of some medication he's taking or just simple exhaustion from the cancer. He's either going to have to spend the night here, or I'm going to have to get him home. Since getting him out in the morning without Lacey or Mom noticing will be difficult if not impossible, home it is.

I lock up my shears, check the outer room for signs of Lacey, and then come back for Alex. Hoisting him into my arms, I carry him up the stairs and out to the car, where I lay him out across the backseat. He mumbles something and then falls back asleep. I drive to his house and realize that now I'm faced with the problem of getting him inside without waking everyone up.

Getting out of the car, I walk around the small house. I know which room is Alex's, and if I remember the floor plan correctly, Emily's room is the one next door. Standing on tiptoe, I look through that window. Emily is sitting on her bed, writing in a notebook by flashlight. I'm pretty sure that she's supposed to be asleep, but I'm glad she isn't. I tap on the window and she jumps, but she relaxes when she sees that it's me.

She opens the window and leans out. "Is everything okay?" she whispers.

"It's fine," I whisper back. "I have Alex, but he's out cold. Asleep," I clarify when she looks worried. "I need to get him inside. Quietly."

Emily immediately understands. "Get him and come to the back door."

Going back to the car, I retrieve Alex. I cradle him to my chest, and he stirs.

"Are you carrying me again?"

"Don't get used to it," I say. "Remember that it offends your manliness."

"I've decided I don't mind, after all. I like being close to your breasts. Nothing manlier than that."

I laugh, but I don't know what to say to that. Fortunately, I don't have to come up with anything. He sighs and falls back asleep.

I carry him to the back door, which Emily is holding open for us.

"Good grief, you're strong," she says, watching me guide Alex through the door.

"Not really. He's just light," I say, trying to deflect her interest in my strength. She closes the door behind us and returns to her own room, leaving me to handle Alex and get out of the house unnoticed. *Thanks, Em*, I think resentfully.

I carry him down the hall and to his room. Laying him down on his bed, I pull off his shoes and cover him with his blanket. Maggie comes in. She jumps up on the bed, spins three times, and curls up next to him. Alex's face relaxes even more. He knows he's home. Turning over, he whispers, "Stay," before falling deeper into sleep.

I want to stay, to lie down beside him and hold him close, but I know I can't be found here. I'm so tired that I know I'll fall asleep and not wake until morning, making it likely that his father will find me. Mr. Morgan might have checked out of his son's life emotionally, but I'm pretty sure that finding his underage son in bed with a girl would bring his parental instincts back in a hurry.

Instead, I sneak quietly out of Alex's house and drive back to mine. On the way to my room, I notice light coming from under Chloe's door. I knock lightly, figuring that she's still up.

When she calls for me to come in, I stick my head in the door and say, "Thanks for the lesson in rule-breaking."

She beams at me. "You're welcome. Did you have fun?"

"Yeah. It was nice to have some company."

"Even better that it was him and not me, right?"

"Well, you're great and all," I begin.

"Yeah, but I'm not going to kiss you," she says.

"Right. Thanks again."

"Any time."

I back out of her room and slip into mine. Unlacing my shoes, I fall asleep the minute I hit the bed.

ALEX AND I SPEND AS MUCH OF THE NEXT FEW WEEKS TOGETHER as we can. He hangs out in my workroom if I can sneak him in around Lacey and Mom. While I work, I keep him entertained with stories about life on Olympus. I can tell that while he believes me, much of my life seems like a fairy tale to him. Strange and fanciful, but not quite real. I can talk to Alex about anything, including my mixed-up relationship with Zeus and my hatred of my job. He never judges me or treats me like I'm a pariah for being the embodiment of death.

If I'm not working, I'm at his house, reading to him and helping him with the schoolwork he insists on keeping up with. It's a losing battle. I can tell his mind is slipping away. The solutions to math problems don't come as easily as they once did, and he often forgets things we went over not five minutes ago. But he insists we keep trying, so we do.

No matter how easy the conversation or how engrossing the work, the shadow of his illness always lurks in the background. There are many days where he doesn't feel well enough to come over, or where I simply sit by his bedside, hold his hand, and watch him sleep. In an effort to make him more comfortable,

I go to Target and buy a futon for my workroom so he can stretch out and nap instead of sitting on the floor. Even as I'm signing the credit card terminal in the store, I know it's only a temporary fix. The day is coming when he won't be able to come over at all.

No matter how much I try to pretend that we've got all the time in the world, it's obvious that Alex is dying. He gets thinner and paler every week, at least until the doctors put him on steroids that cause him to dramatically swell up. The number of prescription bottles on his nightstand grows, but nothing seems to slow down the disease, or even properly manage it. The number of days when he feels well enough to come to my house shrinks. Some days, his speech is slurred because the tumor is pressing on something and seizures leave him unconscious for hours. I'm losing him, and there is nothing I can do about it. Denial is no longer available to me, or to the rest of the Morgans.

I know that Mr. Morgan and Emily see and feel the same things I do. When I join the family for meals, I sometimes catch Mr. Morgan or Emily staring at Alex with sadness and regret in their eyes. There is so much pain there that it's hard to even look at them. Of course, I know that their eyes are a mirror of my own. When Alex looks our way, we laugh or look away to hide our pain. We try to act like everything is fine when it so obviously isn't. We're idiots, and it's shameful. Why can't we just acknowledge the awfulness of it all?

I carry my own private shame, too. With about three weeks to go until Alex dies, I'm ashamed to find that I actually want to be away from Alex more than I want to be with him. It takes so much out of me to be with him, to bear witness to his deterioration, that I have to get away sometimes. I desperately want to be with Alex for every moment that he has left, but I can't lie and say I'm not grateful sometimes when Emily calls to say he doesn't feel well enough to come over and I'm too busy to go to him. I'm supposed to be strong and capable, not sniveling, weak, and cowardly. It's practically human behavior, and it's shameful for a goddess.

171

One day, after I drop Alex off at his house so he can have a private dinner with his family, I realize I have some free time. I decide to take a walk in the nearby park and get some fresh air for a change. The walk will give me time to unload some of the misery that I'm carrying so I can make room for more. That's what my days amount to now. Unloading one pile of misery to make room for more.

It's not that late and with the longer days, I still have a couple of hours of daylight left. The park isn't crowded. It's dinner time for most, and the evening crowds haven't yet arrived for their nightly exercise. I take the trail that winds around the lake. I'm halfway around when someone appears next to me. I drop into a defensive stance until my brain registers who it is. Thanatos. I rise and force my heartbeat to slow down.

"Announce yourself or something next time, why don't you?" I say. Silence from Thanatos.

"Come to deliver another warning?" I ask as I resume walking. "You know, you really should consider wearing clothes," I add, taking in his appearance. "One day, someone's going to notice that you're wearing only a loincloth."

He shrugs. I figure he doesn't really care, but it's in both our interests for him to keep a lower profile. If someone ever sees him dressed like this, he's going to cause a riot.

Still, he says nothing. "Are you going to say anything? Or are you just here to annoy me?"

"No warnings," he finally says. "I wanted to speak with you. Since you're rarely away from that human these days, I took advantage of your solitude."

I don't like the way he emphasizes the fact that I'm alone out here, but I let it go. Thanatos is weird, but he's not dangerous.

"Well, what is it?" I ask, guiding him off the main trail and into a grove of trees so some poor jogger won't see him in his current state of undress.

"I want to ask you to marry me."

I think for a second that a bus must have run through the forest and nailed me. My breath whooshes out, and I can't say anything. But, no, the trees are still standing so it wasn't a bus. Whatever I was expecting him to say, it wasn't this. I brace my hand on a nearby tree for support.

"Excuse me?" I finally manage to wheeze out.

Even when we were dating, Thanatos never came close to proposing. Things were never that intense—or long lasting— between us. Well, at least not romantically intense. Anger is an intense emotion, but it's not the same as love.

"I know I was a real asshole when we dated, but it wasn't because I didn't care for you."

"What was it then? A genetic predisposition to being a jerk? You just couldn't help yourself?"

"I was young and new to the job of ferrying souls. Zeus told me once that you and I were made for each other, that his plan was for us to marry and rule the world of death together, maybe even overthrow Hades. It sounded like a good deal. He made it seem like all I had to do was approach you, and everything would fall into place. I never tried very hard with you, and I should have."

Ah-ha. Now it all makes sense. I've always wondered what possessed Thanatos to try to date anyone, let alone me, given how much contempt he has for both gods and mortals. Now I know that it was more of Zeus' meddling.

Zeus has always had a fractured relationship with his brother, Hades, and he saw his chance to depose him as the ruler of the Underworld and replace him with Thanatos and me. Zeus saw us as more malleable than Hades, and easier to control. Thanatos saw me as his chance to gain a little power of his own, something he'd always craved. It must have put a serious dent in both their plans when I dumped Thanatos.

The thought of all this scheming going on behind my back makes me furious. Bad enough to make me the Death Fate, but to try to force me into an arranged marriage? *Wow*. I don't mention my anger to Thanatos. I'll keep that to myself for now until I can take it out on the proper person—Zeus.

"Look, thanks for the apology and everything, but you and I

never got on well together. Remember how it ended?"

"Of course. You nearly ran me through with that barbaric sword of yours when you caught me trying to enter your workroom. I only wanted to see it, you know, to see what the woman I loved did all day."

I'd never believed that he only wanted to see my workroom. That distrust was a small part of the huge gulf between us. I'd always suspected that he was more loyal to his sisters, the Keres, than to me, and that he wanted to find a way to make me feed them. Breaking into my room only proved the point, in my eyes. Maybe he did only want to see what I did, but a curious person would ask, not engage in B&E.

Of course, now I knew the other side of the story. Not only was he working for his sisters, he was working with Zeus, too. Had he succeeded in marrying me, he could have controlled the Underworld and had significant influence over death and me. I'm sure he thought that family loyalty would have swayed me to feed his sisters more often. Frankly, the thought of having the Keres as in-laws makes me ill.

"You forget that you started it when you wrestled me to the floor and tried to choke me when I screamed at you because you'd damaged my beautiful door with your inept lock picking attempt," I say. "These are not the actions of two people who are meant, in any way, to be married, Thanatos."

"Be that as it may," he says, "I've never given up wanting you."

What he wants is my power and my ties to Zeus and Hades, but I don't say that.

"You and I are alike, Atropos," he continues. "Well, we were until you started hanging out with that human boy. Now it seems that you prefer humans over gods, which is a mistake on every level. We're superior to them. They need us, not the other way around." He shakes his head like a teacher who's disappointed in his star pupil.

I snort. "This isn't about your feelings for me. This is about power and jealousy. You want my power, but more than that, you can't stand that I don't want you. You don't love me; you just don't want anyone else to have me."

He opens his mouth to protest, but I hold up a finger and keep going.

"I don't give a crap whether Alex is human or not. I'm not on some pro-human crusade, and most of them still annoy me to no end. But whether I like humans or not doesn't matter. What matters is that you and I tried to be together, and we failed. I'm not going to try again."

"What if I've changed? What if I know that it was a mistake to go along with Zeus, and I only want you for you?"

"Then great for you. The more immune you are to Zeus' meddling, the better off you'll be. That's a lesson I'm learning the hard way. But I don't think you're telling me the truth. I think you want something from me, and it isn't love. So let's both just go back to work and forget this conversation."

His eyebrows lower and his mouth turns down. He's getting pissed off. He really thought that if he just asked me to marry him, that I'd say yes. He didn't plan for rejection. *Arrogant jerk.*

"Look," I say, trying to diffuse his anger. "I appreciate your coming here and talking to me. It's good to clear up some things from the past. But it doesn't change the fact that I just don't want you. You only wooed me then because Zeus told you to. You're only proposing now because you can't stand that Alex is in my life. You don't really want me."

"I did. I do," he says.

"Okay, whatever," I say. Since reason isn't working, I turn to leave. I know from experience that once he digs in on a position, leaving is the only course of action unless I want a fight.

He grabs my arm and jerks me back to him.

"Ow, damn it," I say. "Let go."

"Not until you listen."

"I did listen. You just didn't like what I had to say."

"You'll be sorry if you don't marry me."

"I'd be sorrier if I did," I say.

I know I've gone too far the second after the words leave my mouth. I've triggered the same instability that had him choking me on the floor all those years ago. He shoves me up against the nearest tree and holds me there, both of his hands digging into my biceps.

Strangely, I'm not afraid of him. Here is a fight I can win. Maybe I picked it with him just so I could fight something tangible for a change.

"I wish I could kill you," he says. "Damn immortality."

"Not helping your case," I chide. "Marriage proposals don't usually include death threats. And can you imagine what Zeus will say if you maim his daughter?" I shake my head. "So much for ruling the Underworld."

He slaps me so hard that I feel the skin of my cheek split over the bone. I taste my own blood as it drips into my mouth. Before I can react to that, he pulls back and slaps me again. This time, his hand hits the side of my eye and I know I'm going to have a black eye to go with the cut on my cheek.

"Well, that's enough of that," I say.

I bring my knee up into his groin, ridiculously unprotected in the loincloth, and jab my elbow into his windpipe. When he jumps back, I tug my sword pendant from around my neck. I rub it against my bleeding cheek, and it extends to its full length.

Thanatos backs away and I advance on him, claymore held high. I see a hint of fear in his eyes, and it makes me happy. I can't kill him, but I can hurt him. And I really want to hurt him. It's a little scary how much. I take a couple of experimental swings, taking pleasure in the whimper that escapes from his lips.

"You need to leave right now," I say.

"And if I don't?"

Before he can even defend himself, I lunge forward and cut two slices across his torso. Not deep enough to seriously wound him, but enough to cause him some pain.

"Well, there's that," I say, advancing on him again.

"You're making a mistake," he says, hands up in surrender.

"No. The mistake would have been to believe anything you

said here today. Now, go. Or I will run you through this time. I'm much more proficient with my sword than I was the last time. I won't miss."

He glares at me, trying to save some pride, and I glare right back. Finally, he vanishes as silently as he appeared. I wait in the woods for the better part of an hour to make sure he's really gone before I return my sword to its original size and head back to the main trail.

No one else is home when I get back to my house. There's a note from Mom on the counter letting me know that she's at some work function and that Chloe and Lacey have gone to dinner and a movie. Everyone will be home late.

Sighing, I crumple the note in my hand before lobbing it at the trash can. I miss. It must be nice to have the uncomplicated lives that my sisters have. They can go to dinner and the movies. They can play on sports teams and socialize. Even without Alex in the picture, I can hardly find a spare moment to sleep or eat.

I can't work ahead like Chloe and Lacey and buy myself some free time. Chloe can spin as many lines as she wants at any time and simply put them in storage. Lacey can create a destiny any time, and it won't become active until the day of that person's birth. But once that person is alive and in my workroom, they march inexorably toward death. I can't kill someone early, can't work ahead, and I can't get behind. I'm on alert all day, every day. And gods, I'm just tired.

Not for the first time, I wonder what life as a mortal might be like. Alex knows that he would be a veterinarian if he could live long enough, but what would I be if I could be anything I wanted to be? I have no idea. My life has been consumed with death for so long that the idea of doing anything for the joy of it is beyond me.

I know I'm whining, but the encounter with Thanatos exhausted what little energy reserves I have left. He wants my power; that's nothing new. What's new is how far he's willing to go to get it. Something or someone is pushing him harder, making him beg and attack me when I know he'd never lower himself to that on his own. The question is—who or what is driving him? I'll have to figure it out, but right now, I can't think straight.

My eye is throbbing, and the cut on my cheek pulls and tears every time I move a facial muscle. I drag myself up to the bathroom where I clean my wounds and bandage what I can. A quick look in the mirror doesn't improve my mood. I look exactly like what I am—someone who's been in a brawl.

I go back down to the kitchen to look for something to eat. First, I grab a bag of peas out of the freezer and hold it to my eye. The cold makes me sigh in relief. I open the fridge, intent on food, but end up just hanging on the open door, staring at nothing. Little looks good and anything that does look promising, well, I'm too damn tired to deal with preparing it. I shut the door and wander back into the living room, peas still clutched to my face.

I really want to collapse on the sofa and nap or watch some mind-numbing reality TV, but I have to work. My walk kept me out longer than I planned, and people have to die soon. I'm about to trudge downstairs to start cutting when the doorbell rings. I toss the peas onto the coffee table and go to the door.

I look through the sidelight and see that Alex is outside. I'm surprised; I thought he was in for the night.

"What are you doing here?" I sound snippier than I intend, and I rub a hand across my face. "Sorry," I say.

"I can go if it's a bad time," he says, turning to walk back to his car.

"No, wait," I say, reaching for his arm. "I'm just tired. Don't go. Are you all right? I wasn't expecting you tonight."

"I'm okay. I just needed to get out of the house. My family is in rare form tonight. They're watching every move I make like I'm going to keel over any second. If not that, they're studying me like they're trying to memorize every feature of my face. It makes it worse, you know? I know I'm dying. I don't need to have them being so obvious about it."

"Well, if this is a meeting of the down on life club, count me in," I stay, standing aside so that he can come inside.

"What happened to you?" he asks once he's inside and the bright lights reveal my messed-up face. He reaches up to trace the bandage on my cheek with his fingers.

"An asshole hit me."

"Who?"

"Thanatos. This is his misguided way of saying he loves me."

I see the fury bloom in Alex's eyes. Whether it's because Thanatos claimed to love me or because he hit me, I'm not sure. Probably a bit of both.

I put a hand on Alex's arm. "There's nothing you can do," I tell him. "Even if you were healthy enough to take him on, you can't find him unless he wants to be found."

He breathes deeply, struggling for calm. "Then is there anything I can do?" he asks.

"Unfortunately, no. But having you here makes me feel a bit better. If it's any consolation, I took some strips off him, too."

"It's not, but I'm glad. You said he claims to love you. Is there something you want to tell me?" he asks, uncertainty in his voice.

"No," I say, pressing Alex's hand to my cut cheek. "Thanatos and I dated once, so long ago. It ended badly. Today, I learned that the only reason he even dated me was because Zeus was pushing him toward me. Thanatos showed up today, professing love, but there's nothing there, on either side. Trust me. He's got a reason for coming after me today, but it isn't love."

Alex nods, content with my answer. He doesn't say anything else for a moment and I wait, knowing he's thinking about something.

"Can I tell you the truth? About why I came over tonight," he clarifies when I cock my head at him in question.

"Only if it's something good. Anything bad will have to wait till tomorrow. I can't deal with any more crap tonight."

179

He reaches out and pulls me to him, resting his chin on top of my head. "It's good. It's true that my family is annoying, but I came over here because I just couldn't stop thinking about you. I know I should spend time with Dad and Emily, but I just want to be with you."

I push back and look up into his face. "Okay. If we're being honest, then I get to be honest, too."

"Hit me," he says, mouth lifting into a cheeky grin.

"I'm selfishly glad that you want to spend the time with me. I get jealous when you're with your family. I know it's wrong and I hate myself for even thinking it, but I can't help it. I want you with me, not them."

Leaning down, he kisses me. He strokes my hair, and I sigh in pleasure. After today, I want nothing more than to be touched gently, to be loved. I slide my hands down his back and slip my hands into the back pocket of his jeans, pulling him against me. We kiss until my phone vibrates in my pocket, demanding I go downstairs to work.

"Damn it," I whisper against Alex's mouth.

"I'll come with you," he says.

I take his hand and lead him downstairs to my workroom. He stretches out on the futon, and I get busy cutting lines. I keep my back to him because I don't want him to see that I'm crying.

I'm so frustrated and angry about everything. The unfairness of Alex's impending death. Thanatos' abuse. My sisters who get to have lives. Zeus' meddling. It all comes out as tears. I should scream or throw something, but I'm too tired. All I can do is cry silent, painful, and embarrassing tears.

The rhythm of work helps me pull it together. *Snip, snip, snip.* It's calming. I finally feel that I can turn and look at Alex without embarrassing myself. He's sprawled out on the futon, his eyes focused only on me. I can't read exactly what he's thinking, but there is heat in his gaze and, what is it? An invitation. I stand, rooted in place by his gaze for a beat, and then two.

"Screw this nonsense," I mutter.

I toss my shears on the desk, for once heedless of damaging

their beauty, turn off my phone, and flip the lock on the door. Approaching the futon, I stand before Alex.

"You were crying," he says.

"You weren't supposed to notice."

"I notice everything about you." He extends a hand to me and when I take it, he draws me down to the futon. I stretch out next to him, and he holds me in place on the narrow cushion.

"Are you crying over what Thanatos did you to you?" he asks, stroking my cheek.

"No. Well, not exactly. Mostly, I'm just feeling sorry for myself and hating my life, and then feeling bad because it's not like I should be complaining."

"You mean at least you aren't dying," he says with a smile.

"Well, yeah. I really don't have room to bitch about much."

He pulls me closer and kisses me. "You don't have to be so strong all the time. It's okay to feel like you got a raw deal out of life and throw a pity party for yourself. I do it all the time."

"You do not," I say. "I've never met any human who has accepted death with as much grace as you."

"Ha. You see what I want you to see. I pity myself all the time. But then I remind myself of all the good things I've had. You. My family. Sure I got a raw deal, but plenty of people have it a lot worse. Surely, you've got something good in your life that you can focus on when things get really crappy."

"He's lying right in front of me," I say, reaching up to caress his face.

We watch each other for a moment. Alex takes a deep breath and lets it out, creating a gentle breeze through my hair.

"Atropos, there's something I want to ask you. You can say no if you want, and I won't hate you for it or anything."

I know what he's going to ask, just like I also know this is the real reason he came over tonight. And I know what my answer will be.

"You don't have to ask," I whisper, snuggling closer to him and gently kissing him. He pushes away.

"Are you sure?" he asks, searching my face. "I don't want you to do it out of pity. I don't want it to be like, 'Hey, I feel sorry for the poor virgin, so let's get him laid before he croaks.'"

"It's nothing I haven't thought of a million times already," I say. "I'm sure. If you were going to live a thousand years, I'd still want you tonight."

He pulls me to him and I relax into his touch, letting him pull me gently on top of him. I look down, seeing that his face is red and his eyes won't quite meet mine.

"What is it?" I ask.

"God, this is embarrassing," he begins.

"It's okay. Just tell me. Am I hideous or something?"

"Oh, no. I'm sorry, Atropos, but you'll have to take the lead. I don't have enough strength these days to hold myself up for long, and I get tired easily. I don't want to collapse on you."

I place a finger over his lips. "Don't be sorry. I'm honored," I say.

I lean down and kiss him. His fingers are undoing the buttons on my shirt. Mine are doing the same to him. For the first time, we are skin to skin and I revel in it. I try not to focus on just how thin he is beneath his clothes. He's concentration-camp-victim thin, and it scares me.

I kiss his eyes, his neck, his mouth, unable to get enough of him. Trying not to think that this might be the only time we will ever do this, I fight to take in as much as I can, to enjoy every aspect of him. Of us.

I pull away from him so that I can help him with his pants, and he gives me a shy smile.

"I'm so stupid," he says. "I didn't think you'd say yes. I don't have protection."

I chuckle and sit back on my heels. "No worries. Since we're both virgins and I can't get pregnant, I don't think it's a problem."

"Whoa," he says.

I expected that reaction. "Which part? The 'I'm a virgin part,' or the, 'I can't get pregnant part?'"

"Both."

"First, yes, I'm a virgin. Nobody worthwhile ever asked. Ares was the only man I ever considered having sex with, but I waited too long and he got frustrated, I guess. He dumped me for another woman who *would* have sex with him. And you can see how well things with Thanatos went," I say, waving toward the cut on my cheek. "After those debacles, I just kind of gave up."

"Bastards," Alex interjects.

"Yeah, well," I say, deflecting the subject, unwilling to dampen this moment with awful memories. "Second, no, I can't get pregnant. It's part of the whole 'goddess of death' thing. I can only end life, not create it. It's not what I would have chosen, but there it is. At least it comes in handy now."

He laughs and pulls me back down until I'm lying on top of him. I can feel his readiness between us, so I raise myself up and over him. After that, it's only the two of us, lost in each other and the moment. For once, there is no death, no buzzing phone, no annoying relatives, and no rules. There is nothing pulling us apart. We are coming together, enjoying the experience of each other, and reveling in joy instead of sorrow and pain. It's terrifying and glorious.

Because Alex is sick, we move slower than I assume most couples do when it's their first time. Instead of wild thrashing, there is only slow motion, exploration instead of conquest. Time is slowed, as if the world is simply waiting for us. I know that no matter how many more centuries I might live, I will forever cherish the tenderness of these moments and I abandon myself completely to the experience, vowing never to forget one detail of Alex's touch upon my skin.

When it's over and we're lying exhausted in a heap on the futon, I pull the blanket off the back and drape it over us. We lie there, lightly dozing in each other's arms. I'm not sure how much time has passed but I have to get up. Never before have

I turned my back on my job, and the guilt tugs me off the bed.

As I move to get up, Alex's arm tightens around me. "Thank you," he says simply.

"Don't thank me. It makes it sound like I did something I didn't want to do, which is completely not the case."

"I've always wondered what it would be like, to make love. I was afraid I wouldn't live long enough to find out. Now I know. It was awesome."

I smile. "You think you've waited a long time? Try three thousand years. Give or take a few."

He laughs. "You win."

I lean over and kiss his collarbone, then his cheek, unwilling to break the intimacy between us. But I have to. I sit up, and a frown crosses Alex's face.

"Do you have to?" he asks, reaching for my hand as I stand up and put on my jeans.

"Yes. I've left it too long as it is."

"Will you get into trouble?"

I shrug. "Probably not. Zeus doesn't know you're down here, so he can't really know what we've been doing."

"You look worried."

I sit back on the futon and button my shirt. "Not worry. Guilt," I clarify. "It's the same dilemma as always. Job versus love and life. Tonight, love won, but there's a price and it's guilt. I let some people down."

"How so?"

"Most people can stand to live a little longer. Hell, most of them pray for it. But there are some who want to die. Some are suffering, and they count on me to end it. By making them wait, I disrespected them and made them suffer needlessly while I was having fun. It's selfish and cruel."

"You're entitled to a life, too," he says gently, stroking my arm.

"That's just it," I say as I pick up my shears and resume cutting, working extra fast to catch up. "I'm not entitled to a life. I'm a goddess, a servant of Zeus. I have a lot of blessings in my life, but everything I am exists for the sole purpose of making sure that the dying die on time and in accordance with Zeus' plan. That's all I am and all I'll ever be."

"You're more than that to me. Much more."

Tears are running down my face again. "But I'm not supposed to be."

"Maybe you need to think bigger," Alex says.

I let out a snort. "Why bother, when I can't have any of it?"

"I think you just did," he says.

We're laughing and crying when the lifelines begin to flutter, then blow wildly around.

"What the—" he begins, but I'm already looking around the room as if there is some action I can take to stave off the coming disaster.

"Shit," I say, because it's all I can do. It's too late to try to hide Alex or send him away.

Hermes appears in front of us.

"Whoa," Alex says, beholding Hermes in all of his FTD gold glory.

"I thought as much," Hermes says, looking at Alex as though he is something he found in a litter box, something that must be dealt with but which is unpleasant in the extreme.

"I bet Zeus that you were with the human, but Zeus assured me you wouldn't neglect your job for him. He sent me to see what emergency kept you from your job. Looks like I win," he says gleefully.

I sigh. I am so busted.

"Alex, this is Hermes, messenger of the gods," I say in an effort to bring some civility to the discussion. "Hermes, this is Alex Morgan."

Alex extends his hand to Hermes, but Hermes turns away with a sniff. "I don't care who he is. Atropos, you are to come with me immediately."

"What's the message?" I ask. "Just tell me and go."

"There is no message. I'm here to collect you. Zeus sent me to investigate when the sands stopped flowing through the hourglass. If the neglect of your work was due to silly reasons, like this," he says, taking in Alex's state of undress, "I was to bring you directly to him."

So that's how Zeus knew what I'd been doing and why he sent Hermes. In my haste to believe that Zeus wouldn't know what Alex and I were doing in the basement, I forgot about the damn hourglass. And Chloe hadn't known about it to warn me when she'd given me her course in rule-breaking. That was my responsibility, and I blew it. Zeus might not know what goes on down here, but when that hourglass went still, he knew I wasn't working.

I turn to Alex, who is sitting, draped only in a blanket, on the futon. He's just staring at Hermes. Other than my sisters and me, he's never seen any other gods. My sisters and I take steps to tone down our appearances to better blend in with regular humans. Hermes doesn't bother and he is inhumanly beautiful, almost painfully so, to mortals. He hovers just slightly above the floor, the gold wings on his feet fluttering rapidly.

I kneel in front of Alex, breaking his trance. His eyes drift to my face. "Alex, you have to go home. Get dressed and let yourself out the front door."

He stands, still clutching the blanket around himself. When he sways a bit, I bite my lip to keep from expressing the concern I know he does not want.

"No way. I'm going with you. This is partly my fault."

Hermes laughs. "As if any human boy would ever be allowed into Zeus' chamber. Much less one who looks like that," he adds, pointing at Alex's state of undress.

"Shut it," I say to Hermes. "Or I will take my shears and clip off those wings you're so fond of."

I turn to Alex again. "Please. I'll be fine. I'll call you when I get back."

Alex hesitates. I don't want him to go, but there is no other choice. I don't know how severe Zeus will be, but whatever awaits me on Mount Olympus is my burden, not Alex's. His presence would only infuriate Zeus more. I only hope I'm not lying to Alex when I tell him that I will be back.

"Now," Hermes says impatiently, holding out his hand for mine. "I have things to do and a bet to collect."

I look pleadingly at Alex and he gets the message, although I can see by the defensive set of his shoulders that he doesn't like it. He dresses quickly, opening the door to my workroom. When he leaves, he mouths, *I love you*, over his shoulder at me as he goes.

I lock the door behind him and take Hermes' hand. He dematerializes, and we fly through the fractal universe to Mount Olympus where my punishment awaits.

*

HERMES TRANSPORTS ME DIRECTLY TO ZEUS' CHAMBER, AND WE touch down in front of his throne. I don't even get the reprieve of the walk from the pool to the temple to compose myself before Zeus tears into me.

"What were you thinking?" he bellows as soon as my feet hit the ground.

His anger sends most of the curious onlookers scurrying away, including Hermes, who apparently decides he can collect on his bet later. As much as the other gods might want to see the drama, they have the good sense to get out before Zeus finds a reason to turn his rage on them.

"Never mind," Zeus says when I open my mouth to defend myself. "You obviously weren't thinking. What is your sole purpose? Why did I create you?"

"To kill the humans," I mumble.

"Did I create you to have relationships? To love? Did I create you to get involved with the humans in any way?"

"No."

"Then how do you explain this?" He gestures to the unmoving black sand in the hourglass.

"I don't—" I begin, but Zeus cuts me off again.

"I'm not an unreasonable man. I let it go when you told this boy the truth about yourself. I thought it might be good for you to have a little fun. I trusted you to control it. Never did I dream that you would let him into your work area, and I certainly didn't think you'd let him interrupt your work."

"He didn't," I say. "I did it. I made the conscious decision to put down my shears and spend time with Alex."

"And I don't understand why," he shouts, leaning down from his throne to bellow in my face. "What is so damn special about this boy that you have defied every rule that I set for you?"

"I love him," I say simply.

"You don't know anything about love."

"And you do? You tried to pair me off with Thanatos, who's an abuser and about as unstable as they come. Did you do that for love?"

"No, I did that because it would have been good for you."

"Good for you, you mean." Zeus raises his eyebrows at that, and I see a flicker of uncertainty cross his face. "Yeah, I know all about your little plan to overthrow Hades. Thanatos talks too much. Maybe someone should tell Hades about your duplicity, by the way."

"Careful," he warns. "That would not be wise. There would be unpleasant repercussions."

I say nothing, but I mentally file the information away for later use. I'm sure there will come a time when telling Hades the truth will outweigh any punishment from Zeus. I can wait.

"You may think you love this boy, but I highly doubt he loves you in return. Would he love you if Lacey hadn't fated him for you? If she hadn't intervened, do you think he would care for you? It's impossible for a human to really love a killer."

Zeus' words sting. It's the one thing I wonder above all else. Would Alex love me if not for Lacey's interference? In my heart, I think not. But I won't admit that to Zeus.

"I don't know," I shout, climbing the steps to Zeus' throne so I can argue with him face to face. "But maybe you should have thought about the consequences before you allowed Lacey to carry out her ridiculous plan of revenge. Then none of us would be in this mess."

"Get down," he says, pointing toward the lower level. The one where the supplicants grovel. I stand my ground. I'm not about to give him the satisfaction.

"No. If I'm going to be bellowed at, you're going to do it on level terms. I refuse to cower down there like a criminal or an underling. This is as much your fault as it is mine, and I refuse to take all the blame. Or the punishment."

Zeus' face turns purple, and lightning begins to ripple from his fingers. *Good. Get good and mad*, I think. Maybe his rage will meet mine, and we'll knock Olympus and all its stupid rules right off its foundations.

"I don't know if Alex could love me without Lacey's interference," I say in a calmer tone. "And it's not like there's a way to find out, now. But I love him. Lacey didn't mess with my fate because I don't have one. I have no life at all, remember? The idea that I can love him gives me hope that he might love me, too. Anyway, as you've repeatedly pointed out, he'll be dead soon, so what does it matter to you whether he loves me or not?"

Zeus sits back on his throne, breathing heavily through his nose, like a bull snorting before charging. He's thinking hard. I put my hands on my hips and wait for whatever he says next.

"I let your foolishness slide once before, but now you have invited the boy into your sacred space, dishonored your work, and disrespected those who were supposed to die today. Those actions must be punished."

"Get on with it, then," I say. "If it will make you feel better and absolve you of your role in this, then go right ahead."

He raises his hand and, for a moment, I think he might actually hit me. I don't flinch, though, and that makes me proud. Either because I don't show fear or because he loses the urge, he lowers his hand and points at me instead.

"You and your workspace will be moved back to Olympus and away from this boy until he dies. You will not spend any more time with him. Instead, you will dedicate yourself to your work. If you need to consult with your sisters or mother, they will be brought here. You will not return to your home until the boy is dead."

I lean back as if he'd slapped me after all. Of all the things Zeus could do to me, and history shows he has an impressive imagination, strangely, this one hadn't occurred to me. Buzzards eating my liver? Expected. Separation from Alex? Not expected. In shock, I make a reckless decision.

"Fine. Then you can go ahead and create another Fate to do your killing for you. I quit. Furthermore, I demand mortality," I say, throwing out the last demand on impulse. Yet, I know it is what I want, and not just because of Alex. Living and killing for as long as I have is unnatural. I'm so tired, and I just want it all to end.

"Absolutely not," Zeus roars, turning purple again. "You will do your job and you will remain here. As an immortal. I will not even entertain the idea of mortality, which is tantamount to suicide, for any daughter of mine."

"We'll see. I think Hades owes me a favor. Might as well cash it in and have him rip out my immortal soul," I say.

Hades is the only god who can revoke immortality, although it's never been done. No one's ever wanted to give up their immortality and besides, from what I understand, the process is beyond painful. Hades once told me that it involves ripping out the immortal soul and replacing it with a mortal version. Sort of like being attacked by the Keres, except you aren't dying when it happens, so you get to experience all the pain and confusion, unrelieved by the comfort of death.

Zeus waves his hand dismissively. "You forget that my brother works at my command. He won't do it."

"He might. He's never respected you all that much, as I recall. And he doesn't know about your attempted betrayal, either. There's bound to be a reward for telling him that. I'm not making an idle threat. I no longer want to be immortal. I'm sick of my job, sick of you, sick of Lacey, and sick of living if the

191

only life I'm ever going to have is nothing but killing. I've had a taste of a normal life, and I want it. I don't want to be your Death Fate any longer."

"You are my daughter," Zeus says slowly, as if speaking to an idiot. "And my servant. You have no choice in the matter. It hurts me that you don't value the gifts you've been given, but I will not relieve you of your job. And I will not lose you to mortality."

"Fine. I'll go find my uncle."

I turn to leave Zeus' chamber, bound to seek out Hades, but two guards who look like they've been taking too many steroids appear beside me. Each grabs an arm and holds firm. I twist but can't get free.

"If you won't accept your punishment, I'll simply imprison you until you do," Zeus says.

"You bastard," I scream at him. "I'm your daughter, and this is how you treat me?"

Zeus cocks an eyebrow at me. "I grow tired of repeating myself. You are my servant, Atropos, and disobedient servants are punished."

He waves a hand, and I see a spark of lightning shoot from his fingers. It's the last thing I see before I black out.

When I regain consciousness, I'm lying on the floor of the cottage that I once shared with my mom and sisters. I sit up and rub the sore spot on my chest where the lightning bolt hit me. Zeus' answer to the Taser. I look down and see a purple bruise with a little singeing around the edge, but the damage isn't too bad.

Glancing around, I see that the cottage is in good repair. Someone's been taking care of it in our absence. I'm in the common area. Three bedrooms branch off from the main room and there's a small kitchen, as well. A set of stairs at the back of the room leads to the underground workspace. The stone walls are still the same bright yellow that Mom painted them years ago. She said she wanted to make the place glow from within, but I find no joy in the warmth.

Despite its cheerful appearance, the cottage is a true prison. There's a curtain of lightning over each window and door, courtesy of Zeus. I know that any escape attempt will end with me fried on the floor but, of course, I have to test it because I am an idiot. As a result, I spend the next day and half recuperating from electrical burns.

Mom visits once. She tries arguing with Zeus for my freedom but without success. "I'm so sorry, Atropos," is all she says as she caresses my hair and lets me cry on her shoulder. "So sorry."

True to his word, Zeus has all of my work dragged up to Mount Olympus. I take one trip downstairs to see the setup. The room is dusty and musty from disuse. The space has none of the technological conveniences of my workroom on Earth. No computers and no moving racks for the lifelines, meaning everything will have to be done manually. The last time I worked under such conditions, the population of Earth was much smaller and the workload more manageable. My body aches just thinking about the physical labor involved in locating and cutting thousands of lines each day without the conveniences I'm used to. That's almost more of a punishment than being separated from Alex, and I'm pretty sure Zeus knows that. *Sick bastard.*

Zeus' moving crew just dumped the lifelines into piles that need sorting, except for one. Alex's lifeline is taped to the wall, a cruel reminder of my punishment. Someone printed out my cutting schedule and piled the pages on the desk. My shears are still in their box, but it lies on the floor as if it were trash. I take one look at the mess and walk out without cutting a single line.

It's petty and juvenile, not to mention unfair to the dying, but I'm going on strike. I don't care anymore. Alex only has a couple of weeks left, and I'm a prisoner. I'm missing out on what little time we could have had together, and I'm beyond bitter. The only leverage I have is my refusal to do my job, and I use it well. It only takes two days for the circle of life and death to lie in ruins. You wouldn't think it would take so little time, but there is a balance to the universe and it doesn't take long to throw it off.

When hundreds of thousands of people worldwide don't die when they're supposed to, the population tilts dangerously into the overcrowded category. Things like water and food get scarce in a hurry. Not to mention that resources such as healthcare become stretched too thin. The humans get nervous when things like this start happening. Unpleasant reactions include wars, looting, and global panic. Zeus' master plan descends into chaos.

Then there's the flak that Zeus gets from Hades and Thanatos. From my perch by the window, I can see them trekking back and forth to Zeus' palace every day to harangue Zeus about his failure to deal with me. If there's no death, Hades and Thanatos don't have jobs. Well, technically, Hades does since he gets to oversee the dead in the Underworld, but it gets boring when there aren't any new recruits coming in.

With his ordered world in shambles, Zeus shows up at the cottage on the third day of my strike. The lightning on the window sizzles, and the sound penetrates my nap. I sit up on the sofa and look toward the window

"Are you planning to work, Atropos?" he asks from beyond the lightning curtain.

"Nope," I say, flopping back on the sofa.

"I can make your punishment more severe," he says.

"Go ahead," I say, calling his bluff. "You've done the worst you can do. What's left? Make me push a rock up and down a hill all day, like Sisyphus? Fasten me to a burning wheel for eternity, like Ixion? I'd prefer physical torture to the mental torture I deal with every single day."

"Oh, please, you foolish girl. The hero act is getting old. I could hurt you. I could make you beg for mercy, and you know it."

I sit up again and meet his eyes. "You've already hurt me.

194

You gave me the job of killing everyone, every day. And worse, I don't know what I did to make you hate me so much that you had to give me that job. Then, when in the midst of the never-ending misery I find a tiny sliver of happiness, you take it from me and punish me for it. When I finally discover that I can be decent and kind, you do everything you can to make me regret the change.

"So go ahead. Do your worst. I'm already living a nothing life. A little more pain or suffering won't matter much. As for begging for mercy, you can forget it. I wouldn't waste my breath."

Zeus pulls his arm back, and a lightning bolt appears in his hand. This one is larger than the one he conjured in the temple. I think, *This is it. He's finally going to strike me down into nothingness.* It will be as if I never existed at all. Strangely, I don't care. I even feel a little hope. Nothingness might be better than being a monster.

I look straight into his eyes, lift my chin, and wait for the blow. Zeus breaks eye contact first, and I'm filled with pride. And knowledge. This is the second time since I arrived on Olympus that he's backed down from my challenge. I'm not foolish enough to believe that it's out of love for me. I know that it's because he needs me to do my job. That knowledge gives me power.

"It's too much trouble to destroy you," he says, clenching his fist and extinguishing the lightning bolt. "Make no mistake," he continues. "You are still the Death Fate. And you will do your job."

"Not until you allow me to return to Earth and be with Alex."

Zeus thinks for a moment before saying, "That's not going to happen. So until Alex is dead, who should I get to do your job? I'm sure you'll come to your senses after he's dead and there's nothing left for you to fight for. Until then, someone will have to fill in for you."

"Don't bet on his death turning me into a happy worker bee," I say. "Choose carefully because this substitute of yours will have to take on the job permanently."

"Oh, I'm sure his death won't make you happy. But when Alex is dead, I'll have the leverage. His soul will reside with Hades, and Hades will do what I tell him. Placing your Alex in the darkest corner of the Underworld with no one for company but murderers and thieves ought to inspire you to work. And if it doesn't, then remember that punishment and torture are not limited to the living."

The thought of Alex suffering in the Underworld strikes me with fear. I don't know if Hades will really go along with Zeus' plan but if he does, Alex will suffer because of me. I can't let that happen. Still, it's not enough, yet, to make me pick up my shears. Until I know for sure what Hades will do, there is still a chance that I can win this battle.

Zeus stands outside the cottage, waiting for me to recommend someone. I'm about to tell him to deal with it himself, but before I can tell him to get bent, inspiration strikes.

"Persephone. Get Persephone," I tell him. "As Hades' wife, she'll be perfect. She knows the ways of death and the Underworld." This is a lie. Persephone spends six months out of every year in the mortal world, so her knowledge of death is limited. I have a plan, however.

Zeus nods and stalks off. Ten minutes later, Persephone is in my basement, attempting to work. I go downstairs and perch on the bottom step to watch. As expected, she screws up everything she touches. She can't figure out my system, and she's overwhelmed by the sheer enormity of the task. She asks for my help, but I refuse. I have nothing against her and, in fact, we were once good friends until Mom moved us to Earth. But I'm not going to help her succeed. I need her to fail.

Let her leave some humans suffering in agony because she didn't cut their lines on time. Let her cut a few thousand lines too soon and wreck the fabric of destiny and fate. She'll just make more work for Lacey and Chloe and, hopefully, they'll add their voices to the cacophony of complaints that Zeus is enduring. I'm hopeful that other gods might join in as well. Without death, gods like Ares can't wage a decent war, and Charon has no one

196

to ferry across the River Styx. So each time that Persephone asks for help, I send her away with, "Figure it out yourself. It's not my problem anymore."

While Persephone finds inventive new ways to screw up the process of death, I spend my time worrying about Alex and reliving our last night together in my mind. At least up to the point where Hermes showed up, anyway. Every moment of that memory is precious to me, even more so now that it seems I won't even get to say goodbye. That night was our farewell, but it wasn't enough. Nothing would ever be enough. I only hope he knows how much I love him since I didn't get a chance to tell him before being dragged up here.

Finally, after a week and a half of Persephone's screw ups, the event that I've been praying for finally happens. I'm camped out on the stairs watching Persephone work when Hades appears in my workroom, angrier than I've ever seen him. I hoped that being without Persephone for a while would bring Hades up here to yell at Zeus, but I was afraid he'd be too stubborn to come this quickly. To my relief, Hades' obsessive need to have Persephone near him at all times trumps his dislike of his brother. He's currently bellowing at Persephone. I'm thrilled. Well, I'm sorry she's getting yelled at, but Hades knows this isn't her fault. He'll let her off easy.

"You never have time for me anymore," he yells. "You're up here, doing this damn job of killing humans. I only get you for six months out of the year as it is, and now I have to share you with Zeus and this bullshit job?"

"I couldn't say no, Hades," Persephone says. "You know I couldn't. Zeus didn't ask me to do this; he told me to do it. I had no choice. And it's turned into a mess, and she won't help me," she says, pointing at me.

"Well, it's over. As of right now," Hades roars. "Come on."

He drags Persephone past me and up the stairs. Near the top, he pauses long enough to say to me, "I'll be back to take care of you." I simply smile, knowing that things are turning in my favor.

I follow them upstairs and watch out the window until Hades reaches the palace doors and disappears inside. A flurry of figures comes rushing down the front steps. *Rats fleeing the disaster*, I think. No one wants to be in the room when this bomb explodes.

I figure that once they get inside the palace, I won't be able to hear the argument between the brothers, but I'm wrong. When two Olympian gods get good and pissed at each other, the shouting can be heard for miles.

"She's done being your death machine," Hades yells at Zeus. "I won't let you curse my wife like you cursed your daughter. I'm taking her home."

Watching the street from my window, I see heads poking out of cottages all up and down the street. Gods and goddesses stop whatever they're doing to listen.

"She cannot leave," Zeus roars back. "Atropos will no longer work because of that boy, and death must continue in the human world. You know that. You depend on that. Persephone must continue."

Now that they know the argument is about me, every god in the street turns toward my cottage. I give a little wave and shrug, but I make no move to hide. I'm neither scared nor ashamed.

"Fine. Death must continue," Hades says. "But you can find someone other than my wife to do that job. It's not like she's doing it right, anyway."

"Hey," Persephone interjects.

"How many gods are sitting up here doing nothing?" Hades asks, as though Persephone hasn't spoken. "Get one of them to do it. Better yet, why not just send Atropos back home? Stop being such a stubborn, sanctimonious ass and let her be with the boy. They only have days left. Even if she only works half time, it's better than the mess we've got now."

"She has defied me and must be punished," Zeus says.

Hades laughs. "Everyone here has defied you at one time or another, including me. If you punished every one of us, you'd have no one left to do your work for you. Then you'd really be in a mess. You'd have to get your butt off that throne and work, and that might kill you. My advice is to get over it. If Atropos will agree to work if you let her go home, let her go."

They quiet down after that so I'm unable to hear any more of their argument, but on his way back to the Underworld, Hades stops back by the cottage. He simply walks through the curtain of lightning as though it's nothing. That's one perk of being the god of death—immunity to many of Zeus' minor tortures. Persephone remains outside, although she shoots an angry glare toward the cottage now and then.

"I think Zeus will let you go home," he says.

"Thanks," I say, holding out my hand for him to shake. "I know you didn't have to get involved."

He takes my hand. "Don't thank me. I'm not too happy with the way you treated my wife. I know it was you who suggested her for the job. Couldn't you have helped her a little bit?"

I draw back and raise one eyebrow at him. "And if I had? Would you be here right now, arguing for my freedom?"

He studies me for a moment before he laughs. "You devious little death goddess. I see your plan, now. Damn, I can't believe I didn't see it sooner. You're right. I probably wouldn't have come. If she'd been good at your job and efficient enough to make it home to see me occasionally, I probably would have let her stay."

"Then I did the right thing. Apologize to her for me, please. Tell her it was nothing personal, but I needed you to get pissed off and come up here and make Zeus see sense."

He shakes his head. "It's hard to believe sometimes that Zeus is your father. You think more like me with every passing year. I shouldn't be proud of you, but I am."

I smile at him. To everyone else, Hades is scary and forbidding, but to me, he's always been a slightly eccentric uncle and surrogate father figure.

"I'll take that as a compliment," I say.

"Fine. But please just do your damn job so I don't have to have this conversation again. If I don't see my brother for another five hundred years, I'll be perfectly happy."

"If he lets me go home, you have my word."

Hades nods and then turns to leave. At the door, he stops and turns back to me. He clears his throat.

"I'm going to give you some advice, and I want you to listen."

I nod. Hades offering up anything other than bare facts is rare, so you pay attention when he does.

"You're going to have to kill the boy in the end. There isn't any way around it, and you know that. It's the hardest thing you'll ever have to do. Stop fighting everyone and everything and let him go gracefully. You can't win, and you'll only make yourself crazy if you try. You have to find a way to accept what is."

He's not telling me anything I don't know, but I appreciate the sentiment behind his words.

"I understand. Thanks," I say.

He pulls me in for a quick hug, which is even rarer than the advice. Letting me go, he steps outside and I watch as he takes Persephone's hand. The two of them poof back to the Underworld. Is it my imagination, or does Persephone give me a quick wink just before they disappear? I owe her. I'll have to make this up to her somehow. Later. After.

Thirty minutes later, Zeus' guards appear and remove the lightning enchantment from the doors and windows. At that moment, there is a bang and the floor shakes hard enough to rattle Mom's decorative pottery off the end tables. I recognize the noise as my workroom being moved back to Earth. When the shaking quiets, Zeus appears in the doorway.

"I'm sending you back to Earth on one condition," he says.

I wait, silent. Zeus' condition may not be one I can agree to.

"You will do your job to the best of your ability. You will not shirk your duties to spend more time with the boy. If you do, I will yank you back up here and you will remain here. Permanently."

"Am I allowed to see Alex, as long as my work is done?"

"As long as your work does not suffer, you may spend time with the human. I don't like it, but Hades was more than clear that death cannot continue to be treated so callously. Your refusal to work is impacting the work of too many other gods and causing chaos in the human world.

"Fortunately, the boy will die soon and the problem of what you've told or shown him will die with him. However, you are forbidden from having any relationships with humans that go beyond casual interaction after this. You have proven that you cannot be trusted. Do you understand?"

"Fine. I won't want anyone else, anyway," I say.

"You might. Eternity is a long time, after all."

"As long as you and Lacey stay out of my business for that eternity, I'll be fine," I say.

"Then you are free to go."

I don't have to be told twice. Shoving past Zeus, I run for the pool. I step into the water and let it take me back to Mount Mitchell. Navigating the cave as fast as I can, I start to run when I burst into the open forest.

As I jog through the woods toward the parking lot, I worry that I'll have to call a cab to get home from the park. There's no telling how long it'll take Mom or one of my sisters to get up to Mount Mitchell and get me home. Yet when I emerge from the woods, I see my mom leaning against her car in the parking lot. I smile and wave, so happy to see her.

I go from happy to thrilled when the car door opens and Alex steps slowly out into the sunshine. Taking off running across the lot, I throw myself into his arms. He staggers, but I steady us. I kiss him, but he is too weak to respond with anything more than minimal effort. Mom coughs politely, reminding me that she's still here.

"How did you know I'd be here?" I ask Mom when Alex and I break apart.

"Hades stopped by on his way back to the Underworld. He told us what happened and that he was willing to bet you'd be home within the hour. I stopped to pick Alex up on the way. I knew you'd want to see each other."

"Thank you," I say, giving her a big hug.

Now that the rush of reunion is over, I study Alex. It's distressing to see how far he's deteriorated in just under two weeks. He only has four days left to live, and it shows. He is alarmingly thin and pale. As soon as we get into the backseat of the car, he wraps himself in a thick blanket, despite the fact that it's close to ninety degrees outside.

I pull Alex close to me and put my arms around him. He's already asleep. I kiss the top of his head and hold him all the way home.

When we get to his house, I carry Alex inside, beyond caring that his father's jaw drops to see me carrying his son as easily as I'd carry a load of laundry. I carry him to his room and lay him on the hospital bed that has replaced his regular bed.

"I'll be back soon," I promise as I remove his shoes and tuck him in. I kiss him lightly before I leave, hating this new reality and cursing Zeus for the time we lost.

I go home with Mom and head down to my workroom to start repairing the damage done over the past weeks. And, hardest of all, to prepare myself to say goodbye to Alex.

THE NEXT FOUR DAYS PASS IN A BLUR. I SPEND MUCH OF THE
time running back and forth from Alex's house to mine. The car
might be faster, but running keeps me functional. Feet pounding
on pavement, wind in my hair, lungs gasping for oxygen. All of
it keeps the fear and grief at bay, at least for those minutes that
I'm running. Every day I get faster, until I can cover the mile
between our houses in under four minutes. I realize that I'm
trying to outrun my emotions and that I'll never be able to do
so, but still, I keep running. Chloe has even taken to calling me
"Forrest," after Forrest Gump. I don't find it funny, but since she
helped me rehang all the lifelines and get my workroom in order,
I don't complain.

Hospice workers now help manage Alex's care, but they
are kind enough to leave us alone when they can. Alana, the
day nurse, is especially kind, allowing me to help with some of
Alex's care. I spoon-feed him baby food, help him to and from
the bathroom when he's able to get up, and empty bedpans
when he's not.

"Most people retreat from this kind of care," Alana says one
day as I'm helping her clean up Alex's vomit after he was unable

to keep some food down.

I shrug. "This is the price of love," I say.

Loving Alex means being there until the end, not running from the wreckage that his body is becoming. The Alex I love is still here, even if his mind and body are betraying him. That's why I help the nurses when I can. He deserves that and more from me.

On the increasingly rare occasions when Alex is awake, passion is replaced by caution. Anything more than light kissing and cuddling is out of the question for us. Most of the time, I climb onto his bed and lean against the pillow, cradling him to my side while I read to him or simply stroke his hair. We talk a little, but for the most part, we are beyond words.

All I can do it wait for the end. Nothing I can do will slow the passage of time, but that doesn't stop me from obsessively checking the clock and mentally calculating how many hours, minutes, and seconds are left. I hate being so helpless, and I hate feeling like I'm losing a fight. Even worse, I'm not only going to lose, but I'm going to deal myself the loss. It's a twisted and frustrating feeling that no amount of running can erase.

Tempting—and logical—as it is to surrender, I'm not ready to give up. Problem is, I don't have many tools available to me. The human doctors have given up. I can't alter Alex's fate, and I can't stop time. Refusing to kill him isn't an option. If I don't, Zeus will just have someone else do it. And Hades won't interfere. He's already told me to give up.

There is only one god that might be able to help Alex. Asclepius. He was born human, the son of Apollo and some mortal woman we never knew. He became a gifted healer who perfected the healing arts to the point where he could bring people back to life. Unfortunately, Zeus, jealous and paranoid as always, killed him thousands of years ago as punishment for subverting authority and acting outside of fate. But, as with any good soap opera, the dead man wasn't really dead.

After Asclepius' death, Apollo approached Zeus and negotiated a deal. Apollo argued that Asclepius' service to humans merited some sort of reward. After all, the man wasn't all bad. He'd simply overstepped his bounds in his enthusiasm to use his gifts. Zeus agreed and allowed Apollo to journey to the Underworld to try to retrieve Asclepius. If Apollo succeeded, Asclepius would be raised into the pantheon of the gods on the condition that he never again use his abilities to raise the dead. Apollo succeeded, and Asclepius became a god.

While he's no longer allowed to raise the dead, he is allowed, on rare occasions, to perform a medical miracle for the humans. Ever see someone suddenly recover from a one-hundred-percent fatal disease or injury? That's Asclepius' work. He doesn't act alone, though. Lacey has to include that medical miracle in a person's destiny, and she's very stingy about it. Miracles are supposed to provide inspiration to the humans and show them that the gods can be kind, but personally, I've always thought they are simply a way to quell rebellion. How long would humans tolerate gods that never showed any benevolence? Not long. Miracles are a panacea for the masses.

Over the centuries, Asclepius and I have become friends. Well, maybe *friends* isn't the right word. Asclepius isn't the sort of friend that you go to the movies with or visit just for the hell of it. He's a recluse, and he doesn't seek out the company of either gods or humans. Who can blame him really, given his experiences? I think that's what forged the bond between us. We're both feared and reviled, even among our own kind.

Given his animosity toward Zeus, Asclepius chooses not to live on Olympus. I can't blame the man. After all, who wants to live close to the man who killed you once and who still harbors a fear that you're going to usurp him? That's asking for trouble. He lives instead on Stone Mountain, Georgia, only three hours from my house. Out of desperation, and against Hades' advice to let it go, I decide to visit Asclepius and plead for Alex's life. To plead for a miracle.

I'm torn about making the trip. It's a long shot that Asclepius can or will help me. He'd be sticking his neck out on the chopping block if he did, and I don't know that he even can.

And I hate to leave Alex. Every minute is precious and I'll be blowing the better part of a day on this fool's errand.

On the other hand, I feel like I have to try anything and everything to save Alex. Hades said that I had to find a way to accept what is. The only way I can do that is if I know that I've exhausted every option. If I don't ask Asclepius, I'll always wonder what might have been. If he says no, it won't make accepting Alex's death any easier, but at least I'll be able to say I tried everything. Maybe that'll bring some comfort on some far off day.

So, on the day before Alex is to die, I drive to Stone Mountain. I leave Alex before sunup, after a couple of hours spent reading to him and holding him while he sleeps. I don't tell him what I'm about to do. I don't want to get his hopes up, and I'm not sure that he's conscious enough to understand my plan, anyway.

I stop by my house on the way out of town and quickly cut a few thousand lines. I'm fortunate that today is a slow death day, and that tomorrow is similar. I'll do the best I can to keep up, but for once, I'm not worried about it if a few people die a little early or late. I'm more worried about Alex.

The drive to Asclepius' place is scenic and usually a source of joy to me. Today, I only want it to go by faster. I don't care that the trees are in full bloom or that the mountains are shining pink in the morning sun. I just want it all to go by much faster than the Thunderbird can legally cover the distance. Every five minutes, I curse Zeus again for not giving me the ability to poof in and out of places.

Stone Mountain is, among other things, a Confederate memorial. A huge carving depicting Robert E. Lee, Stonewall Jackson, and Jefferson Davis astride their horses dominates the north face of the mountain. When that carving finally comes into view, I relax my grip on the steering wheel and breathe deeply. I'm here. Now all I can do is hope.

Asclepius doesn't live in plain view of the humans as my sisters and I do. He actually lives inside the mountain, which means I have to hike through undeveloped land to get to his place. I dressed this morning in jeans and hiking boots so I wouldn't have to waste time changing.

I pull into the parking lot next to the hiking trail that leads up the mountain. There aren't too many tourists around yet since it's only nine o'clock in the morning, but there are enough park rangers that I need to be careful not to get caught in the restricted areas.

I hike about a third of the way up the mountain before the main trail intersects with the Cherokee Trail, which winds around the mountain rather than up it. This is where the tourists who don't want to climb any more get off. I turn left and follow the Cherokee Trail for about a quarter of a mile. The woods are thicker here but not thick enough that I can disappear quickly once I leave the main trail, as I can on Mount Mitchell. Here, I have to move fast to get under cover before I'm seen. Thank the gods I've been running for days.

When I reach the place where I need to leave the trail, I pause for a long moment and wait, listening for any sounds of nearby people. Hearing nothing, I step off the trail and sprint into the woods. I stop to catch my breath once I'm a safe distance away from the main trail. When I start walking again, I'm hiking along the lower face of the mountain.

I need to get to the carving, but there are no public access points. There are plenty of people who'd take great joy in destroying a Confederate memorial, so park management doesn't give anyone the chance. I snicker at that thought because Asclepius is living right behind that carving and no one knows about it. So much for security.

I walk about a half a mile before I'm far enough around the mountain to see the carving above me. There's a smooth chute running down the mountain face here that I cannot cross, probably the remains of some long dried-up waterfall. I don't need to cross it; it merely marks the end of my hike.

Looking up, I see the slight protrusions in the chute's face that act as hand and footholds. If any normal person looked, they wouldn't see anything more than rocks. Even if they do see it as a climbing wall, few would be stupid enough to try scaling a rock face without a harness.

I grab the first rock and haul myself up, climbing hand over hand up the chute. It's tiring, but nothing I haven't done before. I move quickly, careful to keep my footing. A fall won't kill me, but I can't afford the recovery time.

The chute extends all the way to the top of the mountain, but the tree cover only goes halfway up. Just before I climb past the tree line and become visible to anyone looking at the memorial, the handholds end and I climb onto a small ledge. There is a body-width sized crack in the rock face here. I slither through it and into a cave. Pulling a penlight from my pocket, I flick it on. It's pitiful illumination, but better than the pitch dark I'd be in otherwise.

I move forward, trailing a hand along the wall to keep myself oriented. Even though I've been here before, the darkness remains disconcerting. All I need is to miss a turn. I'd end up wandering through here for hours.

There are three tunnels at the back of the cave. I take the one on the left. The one on the right leads to the portal that Asclepius uses if he has to go to Olympus. I don't know what's down the middle tunnel and I've never been inclined to find out. Knowing Asclepius, it could be anything from experiments that I don't want to know about to a collection of old *LIFE* magazines.

The tunnel leads up toward the carving. Another quarter mile or so of hiking in the darkness brings me to the end of it. It looks like a dead-end rock wall, but if you know where to look, you can see the thin outline of a door.

I knock and wait. Finally, I hear the locks disengaging and the door opens a crack. The kind, weathered face of Asclepius peeks out at me.

"Atropos," he says, gesturing me inside. "What brings you to visit an old man? Although I bet I can guess."

I follow him inside and sit on the chair he indicates, gazing at the centerpiece of his living quarters. Asclepius lives directly behind the carving of the Confederate heroes. He thinned the rock on the back of the carving just enough so that he can see the details from inside the mountain, though reversed from what the public sees.

After he thinned the rock, he coated the inside of the carving with something similar to two-way glass, but with a textured finish that makes it look like rock if viewed from the outside. As a result of this little invention of his, light filters into his rooms but looking outside is like looking through thick, wavy glass. The view is distorted, and individual objects are indistinct. Anyone outside looking in only sees rock, as though the carving is unaltered.

During the day, enough light comes in through the carving so Asclepius can read and work. At night, he retreats behind his heavy bedroom door and turns on his oil lamps, keeping it so that no light shining through the carving betrays his location. He has a ringside seat any time he wants to watch the nightly laser show light up the mountain.

Asclepius sits down on the chair opposite mine. He doesn't offer food or drink. Not because he's not a nice man, but because such social niceties just don't occur to him. Why would they? He lives in virtual isolation.

He is an old man, alarmingly thin, and with a gray beard that reaches his collarbones. His skin is leathery, wrinkled, and ghostly white from living inside this cave for so long. He was already old when Zeus killed him, and his time in the Underworld didn't improve his overall appearance. His eyes still sparkle with intelligence and a bit of mischief, though. The lids are papery with age, but the gray-blue color is still clear and sharp. He may be old, but he isn't stupid or unaware.

He folds his hands on his lap and waits for me to speak. I try to think of how best to phrase my request.

"It must be serious if you've come all the way up here," he says by way of encouragement.

"The boy I love is dying," I say.

"I know."

209

"You know?" I ask, surprised.

"Girl, everyone knows about you and the boy. Word of your defiance of Zeus has spread to all the gods. I may live alone up here, but I'm not unaware of what goes on up on Olympus. Some are calling you a hero. Others think you're a traitor. I'm in the first camp," he adds in a whisper.

"Great," I say, but without enthusiasm.

"The question I believe you want to ask me is, 'What can I do about it?'" he says.

I nod. "Can you heal him? Or at least give him more time?" I ask.

Asclepius leans back in his chair and steeples his fingers, watching me over the tips.

"How did you get so involved with a human, let alone one that you have to kill so soon? It isn't like you to be so careless. I thought you had more sense than that."

I sigh. "No, it's not at all like me. It wasn't entirely my fault, either. It's Lachesis' fault. She fated Alex for me. She wanted to get back at me for killing some boy she loved hundreds of years ago. She wanted me to experience pain, and she got her wish."

He snorts. "That sounds like something she would do. Never liked that girl. She's always been uppity," he says. "What's the boy dying of, then?"

"Brain tumor. I don't know all the specifics because Alex rarely talks about it. All I know is that conventional treatments have failed, and I have to kill him tomorrow. Or find another way," I add hopefully.

"Hmm. Brain tumors are most tricky, especially in their advanced stages. Even I had a very low rate of success with them."

"Can you try?" I plead.

"I don't want to be unkind, Atropos, but you knew the answer to that question before you came here. I am not included in the boy's fate. There is no provision for a last-minute miracle, is there?"

"No." I know this, of course. I've read Alex's file a hundred times and know that there is no miracle for him. Lacey doesn't intend to simply take me to the brink and then let me off the hook. She intends to destroy me. I bow my head in defeat. "I hoped there was some way around that."

"I know. And I also know that you came up here for more than that foolish request, so let me hear the rest of it."

I take a deep breath and then rush through my next request. "Once he's dead, can you bring him back to life?"

Asclepius doesn't laugh, but he does snort a bit. Getting up, he walks over to stare out at the wavy world beyond the ass of General Lee's horse. He keeps his back to me when he speaks.

"There is nothing more that I would like to do," he says, and my heart jumps. "But I cannot."

I nod, even though he can't see me. I'd expected as much.

"You are my friend," he continues, turning to face me. "One of very few. I hate not being able to use my skill for your benefit. But you know that I have only a tenuous peace with Zeus. If I were to do this thing that you ask, he would surely destroy me with no hope of another resurrection.

"I may not have much of a life anymore, but having been to the Underworld, I know that this is preferable, limited though it is," he says, waving a hand to encompass his rooms.

"I know. I had to ask, though. If there was some way, secretly—" I begin, seeking some sort of loophole.

"There isn't. Zeus would know the instant I tried it." He lifts his pant leg to reveal a wicked scar running from his ankle to his knee. I've never seen it before.

"Underneath this scar is an enchantment that will alert Zeus if I try to resurrect a human. There is no way to remove or disable it. It was a condition of my own resurrection. I'm sorry."

I lean back in my chair, deflated and defeated. "Then it's over."

"Likely so," he says, but not unkindly. "I only have one thing that might be able to help you, but I would counsel you to think seriously about the consequences before deciding to use it."

"What is it?" I ask, sitting forward, hopeful again. "Anything would be welcome."

"Don't say that until you know what it is," he says as he walks over to one of the cabinets against the wall and begins rummaging along the shelves and muttering to himself.

"Ah," he says, as he pulls a small jar from one of the shelves. He returns to his chair opposite me and passes it to me.

"What is it?" I ask.

It is about the size of a jar of model paint you can buy in a craft store. It's small enough to easily fit in a pocket or purse, and it's filled with a silvery powder. My first thought is some sort of powdered mercury, but I don't know what use mercury would be in my situation.

"It's a concoction of my own invention, designed to restore a human's fate to their immortal soul."

"Wait? What?" I ask, confused. "Why would anyone want to restore fate to a dead person?"

"Granted, it wouldn't happen often," he says. "But there are cases, and yours might be one of them."

"I'm still not getting it," I say, holding the jar up to the light.

"You know about fate and free will, don't you, and why Zeus decided that humans needed fate?"

"Sort of. Zeus just told us that humans have to follow his master plan and the only way to ensure that is to give them a fate that fits into that plan."

"That's a half-truth," Asclepius says. "Zeus created you and your sisters because he didn't believe that humans deserved unrestricted free will. He didn't feel that the humans could be trusted with such a gift. And, being the paranoid despot that he is, he was afraid that free will would result in the humans rising up against him and the other gods. Therefore, you and your sisters control human lives until death. It's like keeping the humans on a leash of sorts. They can do a few things on their own, but fate will always yank them back into line."

"Leave it to Zeus to leave out the important bits," I mutter, yet again surprised at the depths of Zeus' machinations.

"Anyway," Asclepius continues, "upon death, a human's fate

is severed and their soul is gifted with true free will. Granted, there's limited use for it in the afterlife, but Zeus felt that it was a fair reward for a human life well-lived. And since the dead aren't a threat to Zeus, one that costs him little."

I turn the jar over in my hands. Suddenly, I see the possibility. "So, when Alex dies, the fate Lacey created for him will end. And he won't have to love me anymore." The thought is depressing.

"Correct. Once freed from Lacey's destiny, Alex may no longer love you. Or he might. It's difficult to say. But you could ensure that his feelings for you remain as they are by using that." He points to the jar.

"But what good would it do me? He'll still be dead and in the Underworld, out of my reach."

"Not necessarily. You might be able to convince Hades to allow you to visit him once in a while, or grant you mortality so you can join Alex in the Underworld, if that's what you want. That's between you and him. If you could, though, that," he points at the jar, "would ensure that Alex would love you forever."

"How does it work?"

"It's a powder. You must sprinkle half on the dead person's body and the other half on their soul. Even though the soul is mere spirit, it will work as long as the powder passes through the apparition."

I think about what Asclepius is offering. He can't save Alex. All this potion can do is ensure that Alex's feelings for me remain the same, in the unlikely event that we're ever allowed to spend any time together after he's dead. However, using it means that I'll take away his chance to experience free will. I'll freeze him in the same state he's in now. It's selfish and unfair. But yet, I don't hand the jar back to Asclepius.

Asclepius nods, understanding my unspoken thoughts. "As I said, it requires careful consideration before use. But if you think it will help you, it's yours."

"Thank you," I say, standing and pocketing the jar. I extend my hand for him to shake, but he pulls me into a hug instead.

"Go home and spend the last day with your human. When

the time comes, do your job honorably and well. That's the best gift you can give him. When it's over, then you can make the big decisions."

"It's so hard," I say against his shoulder. "It shouldn't hurt this much."

"Of course it's hard, dear, but I know you. You're stronger than this. You're not weak like Lachesis, who can't handle her own grief without dragging other people down with her. You'll deal with this and be better for it."

I pull back from him and wipe the tears from my eyes. While I appreciate his kind words, I don't believe them. He can't see the gaping hole that is slowly taking over my soul. He can't see the way my protective shell is cracking and falling away, leaving nothing but a woman shivering in the cold wind of death.

"You have to go back," he says, taking my hand and leading me toward the door. "Much as I enjoy your company, staying here with an old man who is powerless to help you just cheats you out of the time you have left with your human."

"Thanks for your time. And the gift," I say, patting my pocket. "I promise to think carefully before using it."

"I only wish I could give you more, my dear," he says. I nod, hug him quickly, and jog up the dark corridor toward the exit.

It's a wonder I make it back down the mountain and to the parking lot in one piece, given that I'm blinded by tears the whole way. When I get in the car, I allow myself a moment to get myself together before driving. Leaning my head back against the headrest, I breathe deeply. I knew this was a fool's errand, but I allowed myself to hope.

Hope, I've learned over the past few weeks, is a dangerous emotion, more dangerous than grief or fear. Those emotions can be dealt with, acted upon. Hope is something that is raised and dashed in minutes or even seconds, over and over. If you once allow yourself to hope and dream of what might be, you open yourself up again and again to disappointment. In many ways, it's better to never hope at all. Just accept what is and live with it. I was good at that, once.

I race back to Asheville, heedless of speed limits. Having failed at my mission, I have to get back to Alex as soon as possible. To be there for the end. Asclepius is right. The only thing I can do for Alex now is to make his passing as easy as possible.

When I get back to town, I stop by my house and snip yet more lines, so it's late afternoon when I squeal into Alex's driveway. He only has hours left. When I get inside, I see that Emily and Mr. Morgan are huddled around Alex's bed. He's pale and unresponsive, despite his family's constant questions and prayers. Alana is fiddling with the IV and checking Alex's vitals. She meets my eyes and shakes her head. No change and getting worse. Since there is no room next to Alex, I slide into a chair across the room and wait for his family to go to dinner. While they whisper to him, I watch his chest rise and fall with each breath. The rhythm is uneven, with long pauses and short puffs of air. He's struggling, despite the oxygen cannula that's pumping air into him at regular intervals.

Emily and Mr. Morgan finally head for the kitchen. I decline their offer of dinner, choosing to spend the time with Alex instead. Alana finishes her work, tucks the blanket firmly around him, and pats his hand.

"Do you want me to send the night nurse over?" she asks me as she gathers her things. I notice that she packs up some of the things she usually leaves each night, such as her books and personal medical equipment. She's not planning on coming back.

I look at Alex. No amount of nursing can help him now. Alana knows it, and I know it. "No," I say. "I'll be here. I can handle it."

"I think he's close," she says.

I simply nod. You don't have to be a Fate to know when death is near. She squeezes my shoulder as she leaves.

When everyone is gone, I slip carefully onto the bed next to Alex and gather him close to me. He stirs and opens his eyes. I brush the hair away from his forehead, kissing him gently.

"Atropos," he whispers.

"I'm here."

"Where'd you go? I wanted you. You weren't here."

That hurts. He was aware enough to want me, and I was off on some stupid, pointless trip. The truth can't help him so I smile and say, "Work. You know how it is."

He sighs and falls asleep on my shoulder. I pick up the book we're working on and begin reading, silently this time. I don't think there is much point in reading out loud to him anymore.

He's almost gone, bound on a journey I can't prevent and on which I cannot follow. I check to be certain that he's asleep and resting comfortably. Satisfied, I finally bow my head and let the tears fall onto the page in front of me.

EMILY AND MR. MORGAN RETURN AFTER DINNER. I SLIDE OFF
the bed and settle back in the chair with my book, giving them
time near Alex. He hasn't been responsive for most of the
evening, coming around only long enough to tell me he loves
me and to briefly smile at his dad and sister. Even though I'm
desperate to talk to him, to imprint his voice on my memory,
part of me wishes for him to remain out of it until the end. That
seems to be the most merciful thing I can hope for.

When I have to reach up to turn on the table lamp to keep
reading, I know that Alex has seen his last daylight. Death will
come tomorrow before the sun is fully up.

Emily and Mr. Morgan leave us alone around nine o'clock.
Maggie is curled up on the rug next to Alex's bed. She lifts her
head and wags her tail as I approach. I climb up on the bed and
settle in to wait. I'll have to leave about twenty minutes before
death time so I can get home and prepare to cut his line, but I
will stay until then, even if he can't talk or doesn't even know
I'm in the room.

Alex surprises me, though. I've been reading for a couple of
hours and I think Alex is asleep, but when I glance away from

the book to look at the clock on his nightstand, I see that his eyes are open.

"Hey," I whisper. "Do you want me to get your family?"

He shakes his head. His mouth is moving like he's trying to speak, but nothing is coming out. I lean down closer to him to try to hear better.

"It's okay," I say. "Don't waste the energy trying to talk."

He closes his eyes, and I can see him mustering his strength to try again.

"How long?" he whispers.

I feign ignorance because I don't want to talk about it. "Until what?"

"Don't," he says. "Don't lie to me now. I know it's soon. I can feel it. See it on your face."

"A few hours," I admit. "Six thirty-two in the morning."

He slowly turns his head to look at the clock. "Almost one," he says. "Five and a half hours left."

He turns his head again and stares up at the ceiling. I clutch his hand as the minutes pass, but I say nothing. What is there to say? Telling him that it's going to be okay is pointless. He closes his eyes, and I think he's drifted off again.

"I want you with me," he finally says, though his eyes remain closed.

"I'm here," I say, pressing his hand harder and kissing the back of it.

"No. I want you with me when you cut my line."

I lean down to whisper in his ear. "You know I can't do that."

"Can too," he argues.

"Even if I could, what about your family? They'll be here for the end, and you know they can't watch me kill you."

"Don't want them here."

"Well, it's not like I can throw them out of their own house," I say.

"I know. Take me to our place. Do it there," he pleads.

"The church on the mountain?" I ask. It would be difficult but not impossible to get him up there in the dark, but how can

218

he want that?

"No, Oz," he corrects me. "Take me to Oz. Let me die where we first kissed, under the witch's nose. Our perfect day."

"Except that you were nearly killed by the Keres," I remind him with a smile.

"But you saved me."

"You know I can't save you this time," I say. If he is hoping for some Oz-related miracle, I don't want him harboring false hopes. Asclepius was more than clear that there will be no miracles.

"I know. But I want the memory of that day to be what accompanies me on my final journey."

"Don't you think you should be here, where your family can say goodbye?"

"Better to be somewhere else, I think. Better that they not watch the end."

I think for a minute. He has a point. It might be better if his father and sister are spared the final act, although I'll catch holy hell for taking him away from them. Well, I can deal with that later.

Beyond that, should I grant his final wish? He isn't supposed to see me kill him. No human has ever seen their own line being cut. It's unnatural to see death coming that way, not to mention just plain weird. Most people wouldn't ask, would cower from the knowledge of their own death. But Alex isn't most people.

I don't see how it really matters if he sees me cut his line, though. He's already watched me cut thousands of lines. It isn't like the process is a secret to him anymore. And he sure won't be telling anyone about me after this night is over. If it's his wish to meet death with open eyes and full awareness, who am I to deny him that right?

"If you're sure," I finally say.

"I'm sure."

"All right, then."

I unhook his IV morphine drip and oxygen, and disconnect his catheter, silently thanking Alana for showing me how all the medical equipment works. Wrapping Alex into his blanket, I gather him in my arms. When I get to the door of his bedroom, he puts a hand on the doorframe and I stop. He looks back over my shoulder for a long moment, taking in his room one last time. When he lays his head back on my shoulder, I feel the dampness of his tears soaking through my shirt.

Through all of his misery, he's never cried, at least not in front of me. That he's crying now as he realizes that he is leaving his home and family for the last time moves me to my own tears. I try to check them but I cannot.

Maggie pads down the hallway after us. I stop and lower Alex to the floor so he can pet her one last time. He is too weak to do much more than rest his hand on her head. She whimpers softly and licks his arm. I have no doubt that she knows Alex won't be coming back. Dogs sense things that humans cannot. She looks to me as if for validation of her suspicion. I nod, and she nuzzles close to Alex. Tears are running freely down my face as I watch this final farewell, and I swipe them away with the back of my hand. Alex removes his hand from Maggie and nods once at me. I scoop him up again.

"You'll take care of her, won't you?"

"I promised, didn't I? I'll pick her up as soon as I can, unless your dad changes his mind and wants to keep her."

I carry Alex quietly through his house and out to my car. After I lay him gently on the backseat, I climb into the driver's seat. I don't want to wake anyone so I put the car in neutral and let it glide silently down the driveway, turning the ignition over only once I am on the street. I glance back at the house and see Maggie watching us from the living room window, saying goodbye to her master forever.

"I have to stop by my house first," I say, wiping away tears. There's no answer from the backseat.

Pulling into my driveway, I sprint into the house and down to my workroom. I retrieve Alex's lifeline, a big flashlight, and the velvet box that holds my shears, dropping them all into my backpack. On my way out, I quickly snip eight lifelines that are waiting for me. I'll box them later. *After*.

I'm up the stairs and almost to the front door when Lacey calls from behind me, "Where are you going at this hour? And why are you making such a racket?"

Turning, I see her standing on the steps that lead to our bedrooms. She's in her nightgown, and she has bed hair.

"Go back to bed," I say.

"Are you okay? You look like you're in trouble," she says, pointing to my overstuffed backpack.

"I'm fine. Just in a hurry. I'm going to kill Alex."

"At his place? You know you can't do that," she says.

"I know, but I'm doing it anyway. And I'm not going to his place. I'm taking him back to Oz."

"Your funeral," she says and turns to go back upstairs.

"Keep your mouth shut about it," I threaten.

"Of course," she says as she disappears at the top of the stairs. I'm not sure I trust her to keep quiet, but I don't have time to go upstairs and beat her into silence.

I get back in my car and drive like an idiot. Half-blinded by tears, I cut the drive to Oz down to an hour and a half by going way too fast and taking too many risks. Fortunately, the cops aren't out at this hour.

I use the drive to get myself together. I need to be strong to get Alex through this. I can cry all I want later. Right now, I have to be strong for him. My tears won't do him any good and will only make him feel worse. It's my job to make this easy on him.

By the time we get to the park, I have myself under control, though I'm not sure it will last. I pull up behind the same rocks I hid the car behind before, shoulder my backpack, and carefully help Alex out of the backseat. He can't walk, so I wrap the blanket tighter around him and carry him up the road toward the park entrance. As we enter the emerald-green gates, Alex lifts his head.

I can tell that he is trying to see the landmarks in the dark, to mark our progress toward the witch's rock. I haven't turned on the flashlight since I can't manage that and Alex, too, so there is only the light of the moon to show the way. Dorothy's house and all the other cottages and homes stand out against the night sky, but the details of each are lost in the darkness.

I have to slow down as we move further into the park. The remains of the yellow brick road aren't even, and I trip and stagger over loose bricks every few feet. I have to be careful not to drop Alex. He's in enough pain as it is.

Everything was quiet the first day we came up here, but that quiet was nothing compared to the absolute silence that reigns tonight. There is no breeze to ruffle the leaves and no bird song. I can't even hear a hoot owl or the chirping and buzzing of night insects. The only sound is that of my feet sliding along the path, seeking safe passage. It is as if everything has gone silent out of respect for what is about to happen in this place.

I finally reach the witch's rock and lay Alex down on the bench where we shared our first kiss. He mumbles something, but I can't make it out.

"We're here," I whisper to him.

I kiss his forehead and I think he gives me a small nod of acknowledgement, but it could be simply a reflex. There is no way to make him comfortable but I do the best I can, tucking the blanket around him and trying to roll enough of it up under his head to create a small pillow. That done, I sit down on the ground next to him and check my watch. It's just after three in the morning. He has just a little over three hours left.

I sit there watching his chest rise and fall, mentally preparing myself for the job I have to do. Strangely, up to this point, I haven't given this part much thought. I've been so busy helping him live that I haven't prepared myself to help him die.

Of course I've known all along that I'll kill him, but I assumed that I'd have the protection of distance. The plan was always that I would cut his line in the safety of my workroom where I would intellectually know that the deed was done, but I wouldn't have to bear witness to the finality.

Instead, it is just the two of us, and there is no hiding from what I am about to do. I unzip my backpack and pull out his lifeline. Running it through my fingers, I feel the softness and watch it shimmer in the moonlight. I've held millions of lines over the years, but I swear that Alex's feels different somehow. I know it's just my imagination, but it feels warmer. Softer. Almost like him. I return it to my pack, not wanting to look at it any longer.

I sigh, realizing for the first time that despite eons of meting out death, I have only an abstract understanding of what death means to humans. To me, death means that a human is simply there one minute and gone the next. Each line I cut is simply another in a very long procession of lifelines. While I try to be compassionate toward those I kill, death has never been anything to me other than work. *Cut the line, box it up, and send it to Thanatos. Repeat.* Here, in the silent darkness of Oz, I am face to face with the finality of death and the very human fact that death brings pain to those left behind. And I'm not sure I can handle it.

I check to make sure that Alex is okay. Satisfied that he's comfortable, I walk to the stone bridge overlooking a now-dormant waterfall and stream. Leaning on the remains of the bridge railing, I let the tears come, hot and fast. I try to be quiet. I don't want to wake Alex, but my sobs get progressively louder until I'm almost choking on my grief.

Sitting down, I lean back against the stone, wrapping my arms around my legs. I push my fist into my mouth to quiet my crying.

"I can't do this," I say into the darkness. "I can't. I'm not strong enough."

No one answers me, but I don't expect them to. There is no fairy godmother who can make any of this go away. No one else can cut Alex's line. Too late I think that I should have brought Chloe with me. She would be supportive, if not helpful. But then I think that Alex wouldn't have wanted that. He wanted to come here with me and me alone. He didn't even want his family here to witness his last moments. Only me. He chose to place his last moments solely in my hands. He trusts me to help him on to the next world. I owe him my best effort, not this mindless sniveling.

Struggling to my feet, I walk back to where Alex lies on the bench. I sit back down on the ground next to him and hold his hand. Dropping my head to my knees, I feel suddenly more tired than I have ever been.

"Don't cry," he whispers from above me.

"I'm not," I lie.

"Heard you," he says.

"Damn. Sorry. It won't happen again."

I think I hear him chuckle, but it's more of a wheeze.

"Is there anything you need?" I ask.

"Only you."

"I'm here," I assure him. "And I will be until the end."

"Thank you," he says. He closes his eyes and drifts off again.

Standing up, I lift Alex's head and shoulders off the bench. When I sit down, I lower him onto my lap. I readjust the blanket around him, kiss him softly on the lips, and settle in to wait, already alone in the darkness.

The birds that live in the remains of the aviary start to twitter and chirp as the sun turns the sky beyond from black to indigo to pale pink. I look at my watch. It's six o'clock and the sun is just about to rise. It's almost time.

I take a deep breath and lift Alex, slide out from under him, and place his head carefully back onto the bench. Standing there for a moment, I look down at him, memorizing his features one last time. Wrapped in the blanket that hides his thinness and with sleep removing the pain from his features, he looks like the boy I met in English class weeks ago, instead of the patient he's become.

I debate whether to wake him. It might be better to just let him die in his sleep, but he specifically asked to watch his line being cut and I'll honor that. I shake him gently. It takes a few more hard shakes to rouse him, and I know that he is almost gone. His body is just waiting for me to end the struggle.

When he finally opens his eyes, he looks around in confusion and I see the moment he registers that the sun is coming up. His eyes widen and meet mine.

"It's time," he whispers. Not a question. A statement.

"Almost," I say, reaching down and taking his hand in mine. I squat down next to him. "Is there anything you want?" I ask.

"Just you," he says. "Can you help me sit up so I can see the sunrise?"

Thinking for a second, I figure out how best to accommodate him. I drag the bench until it is perpendicular to the rock face. Then I sit down behind Alex and lean my back against the rock. Pulling him to me, I let him lean against my chest with his head on my shoulder. I wrap my arms around him.

"Better?" I ask.

"Yes," he whispers.

Together we sit there, watching the sun rise over the mountain. It would have to be perfect and beautiful. A day like today should be cloudy and depressing, not gorgeous.

Alex doesn't say anything more, but I feel his head turn against my shoulder. I look down to find him staring up at me. Leaning down, I kiss him, lingering over it and savoring the moment. I don't want to pull away, but my phone vibrates at my hip. I have to get ready.

I end the kiss and lean over to reach into my backpack one-handed, cradling Alex in my other arm. Pulling out the box that holds my shears and Alex's lifeline, I place them on the bench beside me.

I open the box and gather Alex's lifeline in my hand, then stretch it across his chest so he can see. He looks down at it and gives an involuntary jerk as he realizes that he is about to die. Thinking about the end of your life in the abstract is one thing. Seeing it lying across your chest is another.

"I can go over there, if you'd rather," I offer, pointing to the Cowardly Lion's den, which is almost out of view around the bend in the pathway. How fitting. Where else to go to be a coward?

He shakes his head and moves as though to reach for my hand. He's too weak to manage and his hand flops by his side, so I take his hand in mine. He looks up at me. In his eyes, I see sadness, but also a fierce desire to meet death head on. I also see his absolute trust in me. I squeeze his hand tightly.

"Love you," he says.

"I love you, too," I say, the tears beginning to fall.

I don't say that I'll see him later or anything like that. I will never join him in death as his human family will. This separation is forever and no trite words can change that fact, so I don't offer them.

My phone vibrates again at my hip, and I know that it is the final buzzer. Releasing his hand, I take his line in one hand and my shears in the other. Lifting his line so he can watch if he wants to, I move the open shears into position over the line.

I don't check to see if he is, indeed, watching. I don't want to know. I feel him stiffen in denial against me so I know he's at least seen me get ready. Rather than prolong the inevitable, I flex my hand quickly, once, and snip his line.

Immediately, his body goes slack against mine and I know it is almost over. He isn't dead yet, but he is dying. His brain and heart simply have to catch up to the fact that the lifeline is severed. It won't take long.

I drop my shears to the ground, horrified by what they've done. By what I've done. Not that I ever had a choice, but I've never felt more like a senseless killer than I do in this moment. All the lines I've cut, and never once has it been personal. It's always been mechanical and cold. Distant. Someone else's problem. There is nothing cold or impersonal here, right now. All I feel is the heat of my anger and grief, and the coldness of Alex's life slipping away.

Cradling the two pieces of his lifeline in my hands, I scream into the empty air, scattering the birds away from us. I scream until my vocal cords threaten to rip and then I sob, covering Alex's face with my tears as I lean over his dying body. So absorbed am I in my grief, I don't feel the air change or see it ripple.

"So you did the deed," Thanatos says when he appears beside me. "I was sure you'd chicken out."

I'm startled, but of course, I knew he would come. This is just the first time I've ever been present when he's come to collect a soul. I turn my head and look at him.

"You have to wait," I say. "He isn't dead. You can't have his soul yet." This is true. I can still feel a very faint pulse in Alex's wrist and a soft puff of breath on my cheek at odd intervals.

"I don't wait anymore," Thanatos says, reaching toward Alex.

"You can't. You can't take the soul of the dying, only the dead. He isn't yours yet. He's still mine."

"No. He's ours," Thanatos says.

I don't know what he's talking about, but then I hear it. The awful rushing of wings and the cackling laughter of Ker and her army of winged nightmares. I was too distracted to notice until now, when they are all but upon me.

"You can't," I say again, hoping it will help, but knowing it will not. This is what Thanatos has been alluding to all along. This is his new alliance. He's taken the side of his sisters against me, my sisters, and Hades. He's perverting the natural order of death in a sorry grasp for power.

Thanatos laughs as the realization dawns on me.

"I told you that you should have allied with me. You and I could have ruled the world of death together. We might have even dethroned Hades himself. Instead, I've chosen my sisters. They're always hungry, you know and I'm going to help feed them. We will control death from now on. Not you and not Hades."

Ker and her army lands in front of us. I stand, laying Alex down carefully on the bench and stepping in front of him so that my body shields his. I have no room to maneuver. Ker and

Thanatos are in front of me, and Alex and the rock are at my back. I know before it begins that I will lose the battle. I have no escape route to take Alex away, but I will fight anyway. For Alex.

I pray that he is dead. That is the only way that the Keres will leave him alone. If he is still alive, they'll feed on him. They have no taste for the blood of the dead. Only the soon-to-be dead. I have to buy him enough time to die peacefully before they get to him. That's all I can fight for now. Minutes ago, I was wishing for him to live. Now I'm wishing for him to hurry up and die.

I pull my sword from around my neck. Before I can cut myself and lengthen it to its full size, Thanatos is upon me. I curse myself for not thinking of my own protection before now. Basic battle tactics—always protect yourself first. I should have taken the time to ready my sword just in case. Now, it's too late.

Thanatos leaps on me and throws me face-first to the ground. The breath whooshes from my lungs and the pendant skitters away. He picks it up and hurls it down the mountain. Thanatos also pulls off the bracelet that can summon Hades' hell horses and throws it down after the sword. I kick and twist, but I can't get him off me. He doesn't seem inclined to hurt me, only to disarm me and hold me down.

That puzzles me, but only for a moment. Several of the Keres claw at me, ripping through my clothes and tearing strips of skin from my body. I scream in agony. Thanatos' job is merely to hold me while the Keres hurt me. Vengeance for my earlier victory over them, I imagine. Ignoring my own pain, I turn my head to see what is happening to Alex.

"No," I scream as I see Ker flex her talons over his chest.

"This time, he's mine," she says.

I redouble my efforts to get free, but it is no use. Thanatos merely latches on tighter, using his weight to hold me down, and the Keres rip at my back, legs, and arms.

As I watch, Ker drives her talons into Alex's chest and rips his soul free of his body. There is a tearing sound, and I scream as his body jerks with the pain of it. Ker turns and smiles a hideous, gloating smile at me as she holds Alex's soul aloft.

A soul looks like the human it belongs to, but it's like looking at a film negative version of that person. You can see their features and expressions, but everything is indistinct and all the wrong colors. I see the fear and pain on Alex's face, shadowy though it is. His mouth is moving, but no sound comes out. I don't know if he's praying or screaming in pain. Either way, there's nothing I can do.

Ker flings Alex's soul away, leaving it to find its own way to Hades. Without a guide, Alex's soul might wander for days or even months, trying to find its way to the Underworld. Even if I manage to find him, I cannot help him. Only Thanatos can guide a soul to the Underworld, and it looks like he isn't performing that service anymore. Without his guidance, Alex will have to find his own way. Until then, he'll be a ghost in this world, alone and shunned. My heart breaks for him.

As if desecrating his soul isn't enough, Ker turns and rakes her talons down Alex's chest, opening gaping cuts. Blood wells to the surface and I retch as she begins to feed on him, slowly licking each cut. She takes her time, knowing I am watching. She isn't just feeding; she's rubbing my face in her intimacy with Alex. Her feeding is almost sexual, and I fight the urge to vomit.

"Don't hang on, Alex," I whisper. "Please. Let go." I pray he will hurry up and die so they will leave him alone.

One by one, the other Keres approach Alex. Ker allows each to feed for a moment before shooing them away. Once each of the Keres has had a taste, Ker licks up what is left, turns to me, and smiles, her lips dripping Alex's blood. I gag.

She wipes her mouth with the back of her hand and then steps back, allowing me an unobstructed view of Alex's mutilated and mangled body. He's still breathing, shallow and intermittent, and I watch, tears running down my face and into the dirt. Finally, after what seems like an hour but is really only minutes, I see his last breath leave his body and I drop my head to the ground. It's over.

But not for me. Thanatos lifts my head by my hair.

"Watch," he commands.

Ker picks up Alex's body and surges into the air with him. She flies out past the edge of the mountain and drops his body into the vastness below.

"No," I scream, which only brings out laughter from Thanatos and the other Keres.

Ker returns and hovers in front of me, wings beating softly.

"Just go," I say. "You got what you wanted."

"Oh, no, honey," Ker says, landing and squatting down next to me so she can stare into my eyes. I see nothing but blackness. No love, no hate, just nothingness.

"Alex was just the first course, so to speak. I came for something more. Something very valuable that your stupidity and loyalty to the human boy has cost you." She glances toward the bench.

My shears. The gold blades glint in the sun, shining from their place next to the bench. I struggle against Thanatos, but all that happens is that one of the Keres slices deep into my leg, exposing the muscle, and Thanatos bounces my head hard, once, on the ground like a basketball.

It is then I realize the enormity of my errors. I not only left Alex and myself unprotected, I left my shears unprotected, as well. I brought them here, into the open where they are vulnerable. The one thing I was never, ever to do, I've done, and there will be no forgiveness for this.

Ker saunters over, picks up the shears, snips them mockingly in my face, and then flies into the air, headed for who knows where. Her sisters fly after her, laughing all the way.

"You should have chosen me," Thanatos whispers into my ear. "I would have spared your human this desecration, at least." I feel Thanatos' weight lift from my back as he, too, flees the scene.

I am alone. Well and truly alone. I roll slowly on to my back, hoping that somehow, I might die, too, even though it's impossible. I've lost the boy I love, and I've lost my shears. My grief is unbearable, but even worse is the guilt I feel. Everything that happened here today is my fault. I was too caught up in Alex to appreciate the dangers around us, dangers that now threaten the entire human race.

Now that the Keres have my shears and Thanatos on their side, they'll be able to kill whenever and whomever they want. They don't have access to the lifelines, but it doesn't matter. A human life can be ended with just one cut from those shears. The lifelines are nothing more than a means to keep me from having to travel around the world like some kind of Santa Claus of death. The shears are the killers. With them, the Keres will have no trouble killing to suit their whims.

With the Keres in charge of death, every death will be bloody, violent, slow, and painful so they can feed their hunger. Humans have never experienced anything like the disaster that is about to befall them. I only hope that the Keres have enough sense to at least go slowly so as to not exhaust their food supply too quickly. Otherwise, the humans will quickly become extinct.

I know I have to get up, both to retrieve Alex's body and get to Zeus to ask him to intervene in this mess, but I am so tired and hurt that all I can do is lie on the ground and weep for my losses while I wait for my wounds to heal.

15

THE SUN IS HIGH IN THE SKY BY THE TIME I FEEL WELL ENOUGH to move. My tears are baked onto my cheeks, and I am a bloody, sticky mess. I roll over slowly and get to my knees. That sends the world tilting on its axis, so I stay still for a minute until the dizziness passes.

I finally make it to my feet and head toward the edge of the mountain where Thanatos tossed my pendant and bracelet. I comb through the vegetation while trying to keep myself from sliding down the mountain. A solid half hour of searching finally turns up both items stuck in some weeds. Not wanting to make the same mistake twice, I use some of the blood still seeping from my leg to lengthen the claymore. It's cumbersome to carry through the wilderness, but if I find anyone on the growing list of people I want to kill, I'm going to be prepared.

Properly armed now, I slip and slide down the mountainside in the general direction that Ker threw Alex's body. There's no way I'm leaving him down there for the buzzards and other carnivores to eat. I promised him that I would bury him in the graveyard at our church, and I'm keeping that promise.

At one point, I slip and tumble down a particularly steep

part of the mountain. I land in a patch of Cherokee roses, and the thorns poke fresh holes in my already-raw skin. I wince, expecting pain, but it's strangely painless. I figure that everything else already hurts so badly that a few more pricks make no difference. I've become that old joke about how you get a broken leg to stop hurting—by breaking an arm. Ha-ha.

My sword comes in handy as a brush cutter. I hack viciously at the overgrowth of vines and scrub as I make my way down the mountain, searching for any sign of Alex. Every few feet, I stop and look back up the mountain to make sure I'm still on the same line as the witch's rock. Then I continue down, constantly checking to make certain that I don't stray too far from that line.

Finally, I find a patch of grass and weeds that's been recently flattened. A few feet farther on, I find another one. These are the points where Alex's body bounced. I wince at the image but keep moving, still tracking flattened patches of flora. The patches eventually become closer together until finally I'm following an unbroken path of mashed weeds and grass. Alex's body stopped bouncing and simply rolled down the mountain from here on out.

I find him lying at the bottom of the mountain, his body half in and half out of a stream flowing through the ravine. His legs are bent at odd angles, and it looks like his neck is broken. After I drag him from the water, I kneel down beside him and gently straighten his limbs so he at least doesn't look so grotesque.

The rest of him is unfixable. I can't erase the damage done by the Keres and his trip down the mountain. He has a large hole in his chest where Ker ripped out his soul. There are cuts and slashes made by the Keres' talons, and there are bite marks all over him.

If I take his body back to his family, they are going to ask questions that I can't answer. I don't know what to do. His father needs to know what happened to his son, but this damage is too much for him to take in, even if I were free to explain things.

I sit by the stream for a while, thinking and listening to the burble of the water as it flows down the mountain. No answers are forthcoming, so I finally give in to the waters' call, strip off my disgusting clothes, and wade into the stream. It is cool but not frigid, and it feels wonderful on my cuts and aching muscles. In the center of the stream, the water is up to my neck. Dunking my head underneath a few times, I let the water refresh my body and mind. I drag my clothes into the water, too, and rinse them of the blood and dirt that cakes them.

I finally climb out of the water and spread my clothes out on the bank to dry. Stretching out on the warm rocks beside Alex, I take his hand in mine and lie there, letting the sun warm my aching body. I close my eyes and try to relax, to think clearly.

"So beautiful," says a voice beside me.

I smile without opening my eyes. "Alex," I say.

"You always were so beautiful," he says.

"I know I'm dreaming because you're dead," I say. "But please, stay with me."

"You're not dreaming. I'm here."

I sit up and open my eyes, hope flaring for just a moment that the impossible has happened and Asclepius has stepped in after all. I'm brought back to reality in a hurry. It is Alex talking, and it isn't. It's his soul and only his soul. He stands beside his body, looking down at it with wonder and revulsion.

"Alex." I sigh. "I'm so sorry."

"I'm dead," he says, still looking at his broken body. "It's not what I thought it would be. I thought I'd be in heaven or the Underworld by now. Somewhere. Instead, I'm here talking to you. I don't feel dead. What happens now?"

I stand and walk toward him. "You have to find the Underworld," I say.

"Isn't Thanatos supposed to take me there? You said that's what would happen."

"Thanatos is part of the reason you aren't in the Underworld right now. He's joined with the Keres and stopped helping humans. He won't be coming for you."

"Then you'll take me," he says, sure that I'll help him.

I shake my head. "I can't. I don't know how. Only Thanatos

knows how to take someone to the Underworld."

Alex thinks for a moment. He seems to be trying to fit the pieces of the puzzle together and failing.

"What happened after you cut my lifeline? I can't remember. When I came to, I was up there," he points to Oz, "wandering around the witch's castle. I don't know how I got there. Then I saw you down here, so I followed you." He shrugs.

Well, that's a blessing, at least. I'm guessing that oxygen deprivation limited his memories of the attack. I'm not going to tell Alex the whole truth if I can help it. I opt for a sanitized version of the last few hours.

"Thanatos showed up with the Keres as you were dying. They stole my shears and now the Keres are in control of death." He watches my face for a moment. I try to look innocent and truthful, but I fail.

"And?" he asks. "You're not telling me everything."

I sigh. Leave it to Alex to see right through any attempt at evasion. "Nothing else," I lie again.

"Liar," he says without heat. "I can always tell when you're lying. You suck at it. Besides, my body is too damaged for 'nothing'," he says, putting air quotes around nothing with his fingers.

He's right, and I can tell by the stubborn set of his face that he's not going to let it go.

"The Keres ripped your soul from your body, fed on you, and then threw your body down here. Since Thanatos is with them now, you'll have to find your own way to the Underworld," I say.

"How?"

"I wish I could tell you, but I just don't know."

"You are immortal. Hades is your uncle. You have to know. You can help me. Please," he says, reaching toward me. "I don't want to be stuck here."

He sounds so lost and pitiful that my heart breaks all over again.

"Maybe I'll just stay here with you," he says. "I can follow you anywhere now."

"You can't stay, Alex. You have to go to the Underworld. There's nothing for you in this world. You're a ghost."

"Nothing for me here? What about you?"

This is a problem. He knows he's dead, but he thinks that because he's still here in some form that things can go on as usual. I've never seen this, but Thanatos told me about it once. He always said he had a hell of a time getting the ghosts to the Underworld. If a soul lingers in this world too long, and too long can be just a matter of hours, it becomes comfortable and doesn't want to leave. It thinks that it can keep a piece of its former life by staying in its house or visiting its loved ones. Of course, all the soul is really doing is scaring the crap out of everyone by "haunting" them. Yet trying to explain that to someone who still feels alive and part of this world is a problem.

"I can't help you. I want nothing more than for you to stay with me, but it isn't right for you to be here. You have to go. You have to find your place."

"So I'm doomed to wander aimlessly until I find some mystical portal or path to the Underworld? And you can't help me? Is that about it?"

I'm crying again, this time out of anger and frustration, but through my tears, I hear something snap. Actually, it sounds more like a twang and it comes from Alex's soul. That would be his earthly Fate severing itself and free will taking over. Now I'll find out the truth about his feelings for me.

"Alex," I begin, planning to offer some more words of comfort or explanation, but he cuts me off.

"No. You can't or won't help me. Fine. I get it. I guess your love for me ended when you cut my line. I should have expected as much from an immortal. Death means nothing to you. You'll just move on while I'm stuck here like some monster."

He turns to go.

"Alex—" I call after him. He turns slightly toward me.

"What?" he snaps.

There is so much I want to say, but nothing comes out. The

right words aren't there. I just shake my head.

He nods once, and then asks, "Is it too late for you to flush my memories of you?"

"Yes. I can only do that to living humans. Not the dead."

"My mistake," he says. "I should have let you do it when you offered instead of foolishly clinging to the memory of every kiss and touch that we shared. If I'd known that you'd abandon me now, I would have chosen to forget you."

The cruelty and the truth of his words slice my heart open. I knew all along that the kinder, smarter path would be to let him go, but I was too selfish to do it. He'd clung to me as the only refuge in a world rapidly going to hell and I'd let him do it, only to betray him in the worst ways possible at the end.

"Alex, I—" I try to speak through my tears, but the coldness of his eyes quiets me. There is nothing I can say that he wants to hear.

"I love you," I say softly. "And I'm sorry."

He stares at me for a long minute, and I think he might soften. Instead, he says, "I've got an Underworld to find. I'd best get to it. I don't know what I ever saw in you."

He turns and stalks off, his feet passing soundlessly through the weeds and leaving no imprints in the underbrush.

"Go safely," I whisper to the empty air.

I can't really fault him for his anger. He trusted me and in my stupidity and selfishness, I betrayed him. I told him how death works and promised him the better experience. Then, because of my actions, he got the worst possible outcome.

I turn back to the rocks and get dressed in my damp clothes, hating myself. I can't turn back time, but I can at least do the right thing going forward. Bending over, I heave Alex's body onto my back so that he rests across my shoulders and begin the laborious hike back up the mountain to Oz.

It takes an hour to get back up the mountain. When I get to the top, I have to lay Alex down on the bench under the witch's nose and rest for a few minutes. It's got to be late afternoon by now. I'd love to linger in the sunshine and let it soothe my aching muscles, but it's been a long, crappy day, and I still have things to do and distance to cover. If I stay here too long, I'll cramp, so I force myself to stand and pick up my backpack, the blanket, and, finally, Alex.

When I finally get to the car, I slide Alex into the backseat and cover him with the blanket. After one last look, I pull it over his face and drive away from Oz.

Somewhere during this hellish afternoon, I decided that there is no way I can take Alex home to his father. I'm going to bury him in our churchyard, first, and then face his father. I don't know exactly what I'm going to say when asked where Alex is, but any lie is better than leaving his father with the image of Alex's broken and mutilated body with no explanation as to what happened.

Before I can bury Alex, I need some supplies, so I stop at the hardware store in Banner Elk. I need a shovel to dig a grave and some wood from which to construct a makeshift coffin. I'm not going to be able to build anything fancy, but I don't want to just dump his body in a hole. Predators will just dig it up, and I'm not having that.

I park in the far corner of the lot. I hope that if anyone passes by the car and looks inside that they'll just assume Alex is asleep. I don't want to think about the questions I'll have to answer if anyone realizes that I have a dead body in my backseat.

I blow through the store quickly, gathering wood, rope, a hammer and nails, a battery-operated lantern, and a shovel. After I have an employee cut the wood into the pieces I'll need to make a box, I'm back on the road in under twenty minutes, panels of wood hanging out of my trunk.

It takes an hour to reach the turnoff to the church, and I use the time to bury my sadness. I have a job to do, and I don't have time to wallow in my grief. While it's tempting to curl up into a ball and cry, I can't do that. Grief is fast turning to fury, anyway. I'm angry at Thanatos and the Keres, but mostly, I'm angry at myself. I caused these problems, and I'm going to have to fix them. I'm short on ideas about how that's supposed to happen,

238

but I'll figure it out as I go along. After I clean up my mess and get my shears back, I can grieve for Alex. Not before.

I turn off the Parkway and bump down the hidden road until I can take the car no farther. When I hop out, I take a deep breath. I have a lot of work ahead of me.

First, I carry the wood up to the church. That requires two trips. Both are hard, sweaty grinds up the mountain, the wood on my back bending me nearly double as I climb. Getting the nails and tools up only takes one trip, and then it's time for me to take Alex up.

I'm accustomed to his weight now and quickly shift him into the best carrying position across my shoulders. Even though I am gifted with the strength and stamina of an immortal, I'm still tired, sweaty, and sore by the time I get him to the churchyard. I want nothing more than to lie down in the cool grass and sleep for several hours, but that isn't an option.

Having learned from my earlier mistake, I remove my sword pendant from around my neck and nick my palm with it. When the blood flows freely, I rub the blade in it, extending my sword to its full length. I'm not leaving myself unprotected again. Not that I have much left worth fighting for, but still. I jam it blade-first into the ground and get to work.

I quickly assemble a rudimentary coffin and gently lay Alex inside, still wrapped in his blanket. Standing back, I study his face one last time, remembering him as he was before sickness and the Keres ravaged his beauty. I kneel beside the box, lean in, and kiss him once, softly.

"Goodbye," I say. "And thank you for loving me."

I remember Asclepius' jar in my pocket. He didn't say that the powder had to be used on the body and the soul at the same time. He made it seem like it could be used on two separate occasions. I'm still not sure whether I should use it, but this is my last chance to sprinkle some of the powder on Alex's body. Well, unless I want to come back up here and dig him up later. Which I do not.

I tug the blanket down, revealing Alex's chest. I uncap the

bottle and sprinkle half of the powder over the hole where Ker removed his soul, then replace the blanket. Nothing happens since I haven't completed both parts of the transaction, but I've preserved my chance to use it later on his soul if I want to. If I can even find him, of course. I carefully recap the bottle and put it back in my pocket. I look at him for a few minutes more before fitting the lid and hammering it into place.

That done, I begin digging the grave. I've chosen a place under a large oak near the back of the cemetery. The oak is gorgeous now, its canopy lush and green in the summer air. I think he'll be happy here, where the gentle breeze stirs the leaves in the summer and the bare branches will allow the winter sunlight to filter down and warm the earth.

The last of the daylight quickly fades as I dig, but I continue on, using the beam from the lantern to light my progress. The wind rises, but I don't pay much attention until Hermes materializes above me and perches on the rim of the grave.

"Oh, for crap's sake," I mutter as I heave the shovel out of the grave, purposely just missing Hermes with the toss. I climb out of the hole to face him.

"What?" I ask.

He takes in the grime and bruises that cover me, the open hole, and the waiting coffin with one disdainful glance. "I don't know why you're bothering with this," he says, waving a hand over the scene. "The buzzards and mountain lions will take care of the human for you if you just dump him somewhere."

Leaning toward him, I stretch myself to my full height so that I tower over him. I rest my hand on the hilt of my fully extended claymore so that he gets the message. I am in no mood for his prejudices tonight.

"State your business and get out of here," I snarl.

I'm pleased when he flutters backward just a bit, putting some distance between us.

"Zeus wants to see you," he says with the gleeful smile of someone who knows trouble is brewing and that he's not involved.

"I imagine he does. And he's next on my list after I take care of this."

"He said now," Hermes insists.

"You tell him that unless he'd like to get his fat ass down here and help me dig, it's going to be a while."

"He'll be angry," Hermes warns.

I pick up my shovel and sword and hop back into the grave. "When is he not? At any rate, I doubt he can be much angrier than he already is. Tell him I know I screwed up, and I'll be up to see him as soon as I keep my promise here. If he wants to kill me before then, well, he knows where I am if he wants to throw a lightning bolt down here. Grave's already dug. Makes no difference to me."

I go back to work, but Hermes still doesn't leave.

"Is there something else?" I puff out as I throw another load of dirt over the edge at him.

"No. I'm just trying to figure out how a human ruined you so completely. You used to be a goddess. Now you're practically one of them, wallowing in the dirt and muck to dig a grave. It's so beneath you, Atropos."

"Get out of here," I roar at him, tossing the shovel down and lifting my sword. "Get out, you little bastard, and don't come back even if Zeus orders you to. If you do, so help me, I will cut you in two and it'll take you weeks to put yourself back together," I threaten, waving the sword at him.

He poofs away, and I go back to digging. Minutes later, a thunderstorm rolls over the mountain. What had been a perfectly nice evening turns violent. Lightning sparks all around me, and the rain pours down in torrents. I'm quickly soaked, and the bottom of the grave becomes a mud bath. The wind whips the oak tree above me, and I worry that it might snap in half and finish me off, too.

Through it all, I keep digging.

"Go ahead, you monster," I scream at the heavens. "You think you're pissed? Well, that makes two of us. The longer you keep this up, the longer it's going to take me to get this done and get to you. So keep it up, asshole!"

The only answer is a lightning bolt that strikes a tree farther up the mountain, sending sparks and flames everywhere. The orange light casts ghostly shadows all around me. I'm truly in hell now, I think.

"You want to kill me? You've got lousy aim," I taunt. This temper tantrum of Zeus' is really ridiculous. He's reacting to my refusal to rush to him as if he is a child, not a god. Well, I'm not going to give him the satisfaction. I'll finish here or die in the effort.

Eventually, the storm tapers off to a drizzle and then it ends entirely. The wind dies down to a gentle breeze, and the moon peeks out from behind the clouds.

"Blowhard," I mutter. "All flash and no substance."

Finally, I finish the grave and heave myself out of the hole. I lie there, muddy, wet, and panting for a few minutes, then set about trying to figure out how to get the coffin into the grave. It is too heavy, awkward, and inflexible for me to lift it and gently place it in the hole, and I don't want to just shove it in and let it fall however it might. That seems disrespectful. I need something capable of moving a large load.

After some thought, I decide to try to call Hades' hell horses. Depending on how much I'm hated in the realm of the gods right now, they might not come. Hades may have restricted my use of them. But it's worth a try.

I open my bracelet and toss a pinch of the black powder into the sky. Nothing happens and I fear that I am truly on my own. Just as I am about to give up and push the coffin into the hole after all, the familiar black cloud rises out of the ground and Aeton appears before me.

"He only let one of you come, huh?" I say to the horse.

Aeton nods.

"Well, that was generous, considering," I say.

Aeton nods again.

"You're right. I'm a big screw up, but thanks for coming."

I cut the rope into lengths with my sword and fashion a

hammock of sorts around Alex's coffin. When I have it as supportive as I can make it, I tie one end of the hammock to the pommel of Aeton's saddle and pick up the other end. Aeton and I stand on opposite ends of the grave, the coffin between us and parallel to the open hole.

"Okay, boy, we're going to walk this sideways until it's over the hole. Then I'll lower my end into the grave and come cut your end free after that. You're going to have a lot of weight dragging you backward once I let go of my end until I can get over there and cut you loose. You okay with that?" I ask.

Aeton just tosses his head and rolls his red eyes as if I'm insulting him by even asking if he can handle it.

"I know, but I have to ask, don't I?" I say. I heave on my end of the sling and yell, "Go," to Aeton.

Together, we walk the sling sideways until it's suspended over the grave. When we have it centered, I lean over as far as I can and let go of my end. The bottom of the casket lands with a thud.

Aeton digs his hooves into the muddy ground as the load pulls him backward toward the open grave. Picking up my sword, I race to the other side of the grave. I swing hard and my sword cuts the rope on the first try. Aeton springs forward, and the coffin crashes to the ground. It holds together, much to my relief.

"Sorry, Alex," I say. "I'd have liked to give you a softer landing, but this was the best I could do."

Aeton stands puffing off to the side.

"You can go, now, unless you want to keep me company," I tell him. "You did well."

I turn and start shoveling dirt back into the hole. The first few clods thud on the coffin's lid. The sound brings home the finality of this moment, and my throat constricts. I battle back the tears and find it easier than before. Exhaustion and rage are quickly replacing grief. At least for now.

Aeton wanders over and butts his nose into my back. I turn and scratch him affectionately.

"Thanks, boy."

To my surprise, Aeton climbs over the mound of dirt and begins using his back feet to push dirt into the hole, helping me in the only way he can.

I smile for the first time all day. "Leave it to an animal to show more compassion than any god," I say.

We work together in silence until the job is done. When we are finished, Aeton returns to my side for one more affectionate scratch and then he disappears in a cloud of black smoke.

I stand alone by the grave. I need to go, but it doesn't seem right to just leave Alex here. He'll be all alone, and I don't like that idea. I know that this is the way things work. The living leave the dead. But I can't bring myself to just leave him.

A dozen times or more I turn and walk to the edge of the clearing, resolving to leave, but each time, I turn back. I tell myself I am being stupid, that there is nothing more I can do, but I just can't leave. The thought of Alex alone, in that dark box, is too much.

On what is probably my twentieth trip to the edge of the clearing and back, Persephone appears in front of me, blocking my path back to the grave.

"You have to go," she says.

"Did Hades send you?" I ask.

"No. But he's worried about you. When you called for Aeton, we started watching you to see what kind of trouble required Aeton. Hades didn't send me, but you know as well as I do what he'll do if he feels like you're shirking your duty to stay here with a body."

I know, all right. Hades might like me more than my own father does, but even he has a limit on how much he's willing to overlook. With death in the hands of the Keres and the Underworld soon to be overflowing with incoming dead, he'll have no patience for someone who chooses to sit beside a grave and keep a pointless vigil.

"I can't go, Persephone. He's out here all alone, and no one but me will ever know what happened to him because I can't tell his family the truth. I can't just leave him here."

"You have to. That's the way of the mortal world. The dead are left behind and the living go on."

She walks over to the grave. "This is only his body," she says, waving her hand over the fresh earth, making blue and yellow flowers appear over the grave.

"The real Alex lives inside you, and inside those who loved him. His soul is still intact and will soon be resting in the Underworld. You know we'll take care of him, don't you?"

"Of course I know that. But he's not there yet, and there's no telling how long he'll wander the Earth looking for the Underworld. Thanks to Thanatos' betrayal, Alex could wander for centuries before finding peace."

I sit down next to the fresh mound of earth. Persephone crouches before me.

"Even more reason why you must leave here. You can't do anything for him here. But if you get up and move, you can begin to avenge him and all the other humans who are about to die too soon.

"You haven't seen because you've been busy, but in the hours since Ker stole your shears, thousands of humans have died. Ker has released the Nosoi from Pandora's jar again to spread disease and pestilence. There are ghosts terrorizing the living because they cannot find their way to the Underworld. It's chaos out there, and you have to fix it."

I sigh. "I know. I know. But," I begin.

"He isn't here," Persephone says again. "Look inside yourself and you'll know that as well as I do. Do you feel him here? Do you feel anything more than the breeze and the grass beneath you? Do you feel the pleasure he brought you or the love you shared?"

I think for a moment. Closing my eyes, I reach out for Alex in my mind. She's right. There is nothing of Alex here, except some memories of better days. His body might rest beneath the ground, but Alex is not here. Those memories are inside me, and they will go with me. Alex is with me, not with his body.

"You're right. He's with me. Not here."

"Good. Then you'll go," she says, rising to stand and extending a hand down to me.

I take her hand and let her help me up. "You know, for someone who wasn't very good at handling death when you took over for me, you're a pretty good grief counselor."

"Who said I was trying when I helped you? Maybe I just wanted everyone to think I was terrible at it so Zeus would give you your job back."

I laugh, then, and it feels good. She outsmarted both Zeus and me. She was responsible for getting me back to Alex.

"But you acted like you truly had no idea what to do," I say.

"I'm a good actress. I knew you wouldn't have summoned me to do your job without a plan in mind, and it wasn't hard to figure out what that plan might be. So I played along and it worked."

"You and Hades are perfect for each other," I tell her. "I'm sorry, though, if he gave you any trouble over it."

"Don't worry about it. We're always fighting about one thing and another. It's how we get along."

I shake my head. "If my plan was so transparent to you, it's a wonder Zeus didn't figure it out."

She shrugs. "He's a man, and a bullheaded one at that. He sees what he wants to see. We women know the ways of love and the lengths we'll go to keep it. Men are clueless about such things. Now, come. Let's get you out of here."

With our arms around each other, we walk to the edge of the clearing. When we reach the edge, we turn and face Alex's grave. The sun is just rising over the mountain, and it gives the oak tree over the grave a pink halo. Persephone's flowers blow gently in the breeze. It seems a fitting beauty for Alex. I raise my sword in silent tribute, and Persephone bows her head for a few moments. Then I turn and head down the mountain alone while Persephone disappears back to the Underworld.

I STAGGER INTO THE HOUSE AS MY FAMILY IS FINISHING BREAKFAST.
I'm still covered in blood, mud, and sweat, and my wounds,
although partially healed, are still visible. My clothes are a
tattered mess and my hair is shedding leaves and dirt every time
I shake my head.

"Thank the gods you're safe," Themis says when I fall into
her arms.

"We got worried when we didn't hear from you. We didn't
know whether you were a prisoner or if you'd run off somewhere.
Or if Zeus had killed you."

Mom leads me to the couch and pushes me down, heedless
of the ick I'm leaving on her upholstery. Clotho sits next to me,
firing questions at me that my brain can't quite process. Finally,
Mom quiets her.

Themis turns to me and asks, "What happened?"

I tell them as much as I can, as clearly as I can. Their
expressions turn from relief that I am safe, to sadness over
Alex's death, to fury at what Thanatos and the Keres have done.
Finally, I see pride in their eyes when I tell them how I buried
Alex despite Zeus' temper tantrum.

When I confess how badly I've messed up in allowing the Keres to steal my shears, I'm relieved they don't scream at me. After I've explained it all, Themis says, "We knew it was bad. We knew you were no longer cutting lines, and we've seen the news reports on CNN about increasing wars, murders, and plagues among the humans. We knew it was the Keres when we saw a report about some ugly female-like creatures that sealed off an elementary school and slaughtered everyone inside, and then killed every cop that tried to stop them."

I shrug, not because the thought of innocent children being slaughtered doesn't upset me, but because I've become somewhat immune to pain. The last twenty-four hours haven't made anything that's happened any less horrible; they've only made me too tired to get worked up about it.

"I've only come home to change and clean up. I have to go give Alex's family some explanation about what's happened to their son. Afterwards, I have to go see Zeus, apologize for this mess, and beg for his help in cleaning it up. I can't fix it alone. I'll need his help and the help of the other gods."

Themis shakes her head. "He'll enjoy that a little too much. He'll enjoy seeing you grovel and beg for his help, but you'll just have to be strong and not let him goad you. Check your temper at the door."

"I'll try. Fortunately, I think I'm too tired to fight very hard."

"Good. I'd go with you but since I wasn't summoned, my presence would likely only anger him more," Themis says.

Clotho says, "While you're gone, we'll work on a plan. We'll contact some of the other gods and work out how we can get your shears back."

"Thanks," I say, putting a hand on her arm. "But I don't want you involved in this. It's not only dangerous, but it's also likely to have consequences for the future. A screw up this big is something Zeus will punish me for, and it may be eternal punishment. I don't want you all dragged down with me. You're better off just doing your jobs and keeping out of it."

Lacey, who has been standing off to the side since I entered

248

the house, shakes her head and says, "She's right. This isn't our fight."

"Of course it is," says Chloe.

"No, it's not. Atropos was stupid enough to get herself into this mess, so she can get herself out of it. I'm not willing to be punished for her mistakes. Let her deal with it."

"That's not fair, especially since you set these events in motion by screwing with Alex's fate. You bear some responsibility and the right thing to do is help fix it," Chloe says, coming to her feet and getting in Lacey's face.

"Stop it," Mom says, interrupting and stepping between them. "We'll figure out the right thing to do eventually. For now, we help your sister."

I can see that none of them are going to back down yet, but I hope they'll reconsider. I know that Zeus is going to take me down, and I don't want them to fall with me. They don't need to lose their jobs and status because their sister and daughter fell in love with a human, screwed up her job, and violated every rule of the gods.

I turn to Mom. "What do I tell Alex's family?"

"I don't know. You can't tell them the truth; at least, not all of it. I don't know whether it would be better for them to know he is dead, or for them to assume he's dead. I think you'll know what to say, though, when the time comes."

"I hope so," I say.

I let Chloe lead me upstairs to the bathroom. She helps me undress and get underneath the hot shower spray. Once I'm safely in, she leaves, promising to bring back food.

I stand in the shower for a few minutes, letting the water relax my sore muscles and rinse away the filth of the last twenty-four hours. Scrubbing the caked blood off my wounds, I wash my hair until the water finally runs clear. After I'm clean, I lean against the shower wall, close my eyes, and rest until the water cools. At one point, I think I may finally cry, but no tears come. I'm too spent.

When I get out, I'm happy to see that Chloe's laid out my

favorite black jeans, a black, long-sleeved T-shirt, and my newest pair of hiking boots. The outfit is appropriate for visiting Alex's family, but it's also suitable for trekking through the woods to the portal to Olympus. Not having to change will save me a trip back here. As I dress, I wolf down two sandwiches that she left on a plate by the sink and wash them down with a can of soda.

Feeling somewhat healthier, I head downstairs.

"Good luck," Mom calls as I open the front door. She and Chloe are huddled at the kitchen table, no doubt discussing how to best deliver a swift and decisive butt-kicking to the Keres. Lacey is nowhere to be seen.

"Thanks," I call back. "I'll need it," I mutter to myself. I pause to look at them one last time, not knowing when or if I might see them again.

I hop in the Thunderbird and drive the short distance to Alex's house. Mom said that I'll know what to say, but I don't share her confidence. I hope I won't blow it; that I'll be able to strike the right mix of truth and lies that will provide them comfort and closure but not scar them too badly.

My heart sinks when I see the police cars in Alex's driveway. *Well, what did you think would happen?* I ask myself. He's been gone over twenty-four hours. Of course they called the cops.

The presence of the cops makes my decision much easier, though. Since I don't want to answer anything the cops might ask, I just have to pretend that I have no idea what happened to Alex. I review last night in my head, making sure anything I say won't contradict what the cops already know. Emily and Mr. Morgan left us at nine o'clock. They hadn't checked back in before I took Alex to Oz around one in the morning. That means there are four hours that they can't be certain where I was or what I was doing. Perfect.

I get out of the car and walk toward the front door. Before I can ring the bell, the door flies open so fast that I'm almost sucked into the foyer by the sudden whoosh of air.

"Where is he?" Mr. Morgan demands, grabbing my arm and hauling me inside the house.

"Alex?" I ask, giving my best impression of ignorance. Fortunately, I'm so tired that my stupid look is likely believable.

"Yes, Alex. You were with him two nights ago, and he's been gone ever since."

I look around the room. Three cops are watching me, waiting. Emily is sitting in a corner, crying softly and clutching Alex's faded Appalachian State baseball cap. I remember how much he wanted to go there.

"He's gone?" I ask.

"Yes, gone," yells Mr. Morgan. "And you had something to do with it."

"Sir, I don't know where he is. I left here around midnight. I read to him for a while. When he fell asleep, I went home," I say.

"Well, where have you been for the last day? You're always here with him and since you haven't come to visit before now, it looks a bit suspicious. You were together, weren't you?"

"No, sir," I say. "I went home, and I've been home ever since. Mom said I had to stay home and catch up on homework and chores. I was only planning to come by yesterday if he got worse."

I know Mom will back up the lie and since she is the D.A., the cops will likely take her at her word. There are perks to living with the law.

"Well, in his condition, he didn't unhook himself from his IV and walk out of here on his own," Mr. Morgan says.

"Did he tell you anything before you left? Give you any indication that he might be planning something?" the youngest of the cops asks me.

I act like I'm thinking hard. Pacing over to the living room window, I stare out at the tiny, weed-filled flower bed. Maggie comes to me and rubs herself against my legs, hoping for a scratch behind her ears. *I have to take her home*, I remind myself, adding Maggie to my lengthening to-do list.

Without turning around, lest the evasion be visible on my face, I say, "He did make it clear to me over and over again that he didn't want to die here. He didn't want his father and sister

251

to find him dead. As close as he was to death the other night when I left, I can't imagine that he walked out on his own, but he was determined not to die here."

There. That's honest to a point, with no mention that I was the one who took him away.

The young cop turns to his buddies. "Then it sounds like he somehow left this house to die," he says to them.

"Did he ask you to take him somewhere?" another cop asks me.

"He did. But I refused." I did refuse. Several times. Until I gave in, that is. Half-truths are working well for me.

"Do you know if he asked anyone else?"

I shrug. "I don't know. I don't think he knew many people. Maybe he asked one of the nurses?"

I'm not proud of throwing someone else under the bus, but I have to give the cops and Mr. Morgan somewhere else to look. Mr. Morgan hasn't taken his eyes off me since I entered the house. I have a feeling that he knows exactly what I've done, but with no way to prove it, he can't accuse me outright.

While everyone is pondering who else could have helped Alex, a fourth cop comes in from the back of the house carrying a tool kit and wearing gloves.

"I can't find any definitive evidence that he walked away. Neither can I find any evidence that anyone else besides family and caregivers were in this house. It looks likely he either walked out on his own or he had help from within his inner circle. But unless anyone wants to admit it, we can't prove anything."

I look at Emily and Mr. Morgan and they look right back at me, accusation in their eyes. I say nothing.

"We'll keep looking for him," the young cop assures Mr. Morgan. "If he went out on his own, it's unlikely that he made it far. For now, we're going to assume that he's alive. We'll put out an Amber Alert for him and bring in teams to scour the neighborhood."

Mr. Morgan nods.

"I can help you look," I offer, hoping to sound innocent and concerned. "I know the area well."

"Fine. Just stay out of our way and don't get yourself into any trouble. Mr. Morgan, you and your daughter should wait here in case he comes back."

The cops leave and I follow behind them, not wanting to endure the accusing glare of Mr. Morgan any longer. Besides, I have to get to Mount Mitchell to complete the rest of my torturous day. As I'm climbing into the Thunderbird, Emily comes flying out of the house. I slam the door, but I roll down the window so she can talk to me.

"Where is he?" she whispers.

"I told you, I don't know," I say.

"You know. Of course you know. Look, I'm not going to say anything to dad or the cops. A few days ago, Alex told me that you'd be able to tell me the truth if anything strange happened. He said that you were special and not like us, that you specialized in death. I asked what he meant, but he wouldn't explain any further. He said you'd be able to take care of him at the end, and that I should trust you to do what was best."

Tears run down my cheeks. I'd known, of course, that he trusted me, but I hadn't realized how completely. I sigh and reach for her hand.

"I have to know. Please," she begs.

What the hell, I think. I can't get in much more trouble, and I trust her to keep her mouth shut. "He's dead."

She nods, and fresh tears start. "I figured. Can you tell me what happened?"

"Someday, I promise I'll tell you. Right now, there's a lot going on that I have to sort out before I can tell you everything. But I will tell you when I can. For now, all you need to know is that I honored all of his last wishes."

I don't need to tell her that I have no idea if he is okay or not, or that his last moments were brutal. Half-truths.

"Thank you," she says, squeezing my hand. "It's good to know for sure, you know?"

"I know," I say. "Remember your promise. You won't say

anything, right? Those cops wouldn't hesitate to throw me in jail and I still have work to do."

"I swear it. I won't say a word."

I turn to face front and crank the ignition. Emily backs away from the car.

"Will you come visit me, now that he's gone?" she asks.

"If you want me to, and if I can," I say, thinking that I'm likely to end up imprisoned on Mount Olympus again, this time forever. "And probably only when your dad isn't home."

She looks back over her shoulder, wincing when she sees her dad watching us from the front door. "Good. I'd like to see you," she says, waving as I pull away.

As I drive toward Mount Mitchell, I keep a watchful eye on my rearview mirror, checking for any cops who might have decided to follow me. The last thing I need is to lead a cop to the portal to Mount Olympus. But I see no one.

I reach Mount Mitchell in the early afternoon and begin my hike toward the portal. It's a gorgeous early summer day, and there are plenty of other hikers sharing the path. I have to wait nearly twenty minutes, pretending to tie my boot laces, check a map, or study the flora before I can make it off the trail and into the woods without anyone noticing me.

When I finally reach the portal, I'm surprised and dismayed to find Ares waiting for me by the pool.

"The day just gets better," I say.

"I heard you'd be coming here today," he says.

"I'm sure everyone knows of my failure by now."

"Not everyone, but most." He says it with a smile, and I have to smile back. That's the thing about Ares. He might be a jackass and perfectly capable of gleefully reducing an entire civilization to rubble, but he is also boyishly good-looking and charming.

"What are you doing here?" I ask him. "If you've come to rub it in, or make fun of me, I haven't got the time."

"I'm here for neither," he says, and I'm shocked to hear sympathy in his voice. "There was a meeting this morning of the Olympians. That's why I'm here. I've just come back from Zeus' little conclave, and I have a message for you."

"Fabulous," I say, rolling my eyes. "Let's hear it."

"First, Zeus is so angry that he no longer wants to see you. You are not to go to Mount Olympus unless and until you complete the task that Zeus has set for you."

"Oh boy," I say, thinking of the thousands of twisted things Zeus might ask me to do.

"Yeah. I was surprised he didn't want to ream you out in person. He usually never misses a chance to yell at someone, but he's so angry at you that he doesn't even want to see you. It's a first."

"That's kind of good," I say. "I really didn't want to see him either."

"Not so good, Little Atropos. No one has fucked up this big since Prometheus stole fire and gave it to the humans. Remember how that turned out?"

"Yeah. Zeus bound him to a stake, and now an eagle comes every day and eats his ever-regenerating liver."

"Exactly."

"So, what, Zeus wants to tie me to a stake and let an eagle eat my liver?" I ask.

"No. Well, not yet, anyway," Ares says.

I tilt my head and wait for him to name my punishment. When he remains silent, I roll my hand in the "hurry up and spill it gesture." Finally, he gets to the point.

"You are to defeat the Keres and retrieve your shears yourself, within two months, without any intervention from the gods," he says.

"Zeus doesn't want to intervene?" I ask. "Even though the Keres are killing indiscriminately and the population of Earth is decreasing at an unsustainable rate?"

"Nope. Zeus doesn't care about the humans. They're playthings to him, and this is just another game. If you can't win, I suspect he'll fix this and save the humans at the last possible second so he can look like the hero. After he punishes you, of course. Right now, it's a sporting event for him. It's you versus them."

"Great. Two months. I doubt that's possible, but okay. What happens if I don't win?" I ask, knowing that this is likely to be the worst punishment ever created for a god.

"First, Ker will be given access to the room of lifelines. She will take over your job permanently, to do as she sees fit. She will become the Death Fate and work with your sisters. She'll have to slow down on the indiscriminate killing, of course, but Zeus will give her enough leeway to keep her tribe fed."

"Ker will become part of my family? She'll work with Clotho and Lachesis?" This is almost worse than the thought of her controlling death.

"Zeus thinks it fitting that the victor should have the job. If you can't win, you aren't fit for the work. Ker will be made a legitimate goddess, and the humans will die a lot more often and a lot more painfully." He shrugs as if this is all fine and dandy.

"What happens to Thanatos?" I ask.

"He'll get his fondest wish. He will replace Hades as the King of the Underworld. Zeus isn't happy that Hades took your side and is using this as an excuse to punish him, too."

"Great. So in Zeus' sick mind, the ones responsible for this mess get rewarded while the rest of us get screwed."

"No one ever said he was fair," Ares says.

I know that my sisters will work with Ker if forced, if for no other reason than loyalty to their jobs. But they'll hate every minute of it. The joy in their lives will be snuffed out. This is Zeus' way of punishing them, too. Of course, Lacey deserves it, but still. And Hades? What would my uncle be without his job as ruler of the Underworld? I can't even imagine it.

I sigh. "And he doesn't care that Ker will kill every human in the bloodiest and most violent ways possible? That there will be untold suffering? That Thanatos will screw up the Underworld so badly with his incompetence that the dead will likely end up walking the Earth and terrorizing the living?"

"Why should he?"

"Spoken like a true god," I sarcastically say.

"Hey. I'm just passing on the message here," Ares says.

"A little too gleefully," I mutter. "Okay, what happens to me?" I ask in a louder voice. Zeus has devised a cruel punishment for everyone connected to me. I'm sure mine will be a hundred times worse.

"You will be made mortal. At the end of your life, you will face whatever death Ker devises for you. That's likely to be painful," he adds helpfully.

"That's not too bad. It's actually great," I say, thinking that at least at the end of my life I will be able to see Alex again. If I can stand whatever death Ker devises for me, the rest will be easy. As a mortal, I can get a different job, have something of a normal life, and, at the end of it, be reunited with Alex in the Underworld. Zeus is actually giving me a gift.

"Well, it's not so great when you add this last part," Ares says.

"Leave it to you to leave out the important bits," I say. "Would you just get on with it? I'm tired and my patience with you, Zeus, and pretty much everyone is at its limit."

"Wow, you're stressed. Relax, Little Atropos," he says, putting a hand on my arm.

"Don't call me that," I say, slapping his hand away. "The time for that name is long past." I let him get away with calling me by my old pet name earlier, thinking it was a slip, but twice is too much.

"Just finish explaining my punishment, you big brute," I snap.

"Okay, okay," he says, taking a step back. "The Underworld will be forever barred to you. You will never be able to enter and rest there. Your soul will wander the Earth forever, never finding peace, never seeing your beloved Alex again, and never finding society with humans or gods again. You are guaranteed nothing but endless wandering, loneliness, and no peace or rest. That's an exact quote, by the way," he says, looking smug.

"Well, that does suck," I say, sitting down on one of the rocks bordering the pool.

I'm good with being alone. In fact, I prefer it most of the time. But I've always had the option to seek out my family or the few other gods I like when I want company or need advice. Being alone forever is scary. I know I'll miss Clotho the most, followed by Themis. Missing Lacey is a crapshoot, but after a few thousand years, I'll probably miss even her.

And, of course, Alex. Of course, as long as I am immortal, we'll be separated forever and I know that. The best I can hope for in the normal course of events is to talk Hades into letting me see Alex once or twice once he makes it to the Underworld. It isn't much, but it's something to hope for, at least. If Zeus makes me mortal and condemns my soul to wander forever, I won't even have that shred of hope. Even Asclepius' powder won't help.

Ares sits down next to me and puts his arm over my shoulder. I try to lean away, but he simply tightens his grip, keeping me where I am. I sigh and give up, dropping my head to his shoulder, not out of affection but exhaustion.

"There is one bright spot," Ares says after a few minutes.

"And that is?" I ask, not seeing anything bright about my situation.

"After several hours of arguing from myself, Hades, Persephone, and Aphrodite on your behalf—" he begins.

"Wait," I interrupt him. "Aphrodite said something on my behalf?"

"She did. Shocking, I know, but she did. She is the goddess of love, remember. She took pity on you because your actions were motivated by love."

"But she hates me because of you," I say.

"Oh, she does, you're not wrong. Even though she and I are no longer together, she still hates that you had me first. But, she loves love and that's why she spoke up for you."

"Huh," is all I can say. So he and Aphrodite are no longer together. I wonder what happened there, but I push it to the back of my mind to ponder later. She probably realized what a jerk Ares is and went back to her husband.

"Anyway," he continues, "we argued that you should have at least one champion on your side. After all, the Keres number in the thousands, plus they have Thanatos' strength now. We argued that it would only be fair if you had the help of one god. Zeus reluctantly agreed."

I snort.

"Well, only agreed because he felt it would make it more sporting. There's a lot of betting going on around Olympus right now on the outcome, and the odds were stacked too high on the Keres. He allowed you to have a champion to even the odds somewhat."

"Of course. He certainly didn't do it because he cares one iota about me. Do I get to choose the god I want?" I ask, thinking immediately that I'll take Hades. Not only do we get along well, but as a god of death with considerable powers, he'll be able to control Thanatos while I work on the Keres. Plus, he's got his own motivation for me to succeed.

"Sort of," Ares says. "You can choose only from those who volunteered to help you."

"And who volunteered?" I ask.

"I did."

"And who else?"

"No one else."

"So I choose you or I go it alone?" I ask.

"Pretty much."

"Well, now, this really sucks," I say.

Ares chuckles.

"Don't you dare laugh," I say.

"Wasn't planning on it," he says, suppressing his laughter beneath a cough. I just glare at him.

"Why'd you volunteer? Why no one else?"

"Everyone else hates you right now. They're facing punishment because of you, their jobs are screwed up because of the mess that death has become, or they're pissed that you risked exposing us all. I thought you could use the help. And I feel like I owe you one. For what happened all those centuries

259

ago."

I wave my hand, "It's forgotten."

"If that's so, I'm glad. But if it's true, I wonder why you seem so skittish around me. You keep backing away from me, Little Atropos," he says, pulling me closer.

I try to pull back again, but fail. "Self-preservation, you big jackass," I say.

"Like I said. I owe you something and helping you is all I can give. Atropos, I wronged you horribly all those centuries ago. I got what I deserved, I suppose, when Aphrodite's husband strung us up in that damn net for all the gods to laugh at. Had I stayed with you, none of that would have happened," he says.

"I wouldn't have wanted you to stay with me just so you could avoid a worse fate elsewhere," I say.

"That's not what I meant," he says.

"I know. But it's done and I don't want to talk about it. If I take you up on your offer of help, will you expect me to be your lover? Because I'm pretty much done with love."

"No. I don't want anything in exchange for my help."

I raise my eyebrow in disbelief and wait.

"Well, it will anger Zeus, which is always fun. And he and I have a score to settle."

"Ah. Spoken like the Ares I know," I say.

He's not in this just for me, which is kind of a relief. He volunteered so he can advance his own vendetta against Zeus. I don't really care what that's about, as long as it makes him loyal to me. Maybe he and I can work together, after all.

"I will train you to fight and I will teach you to wage a war that will not only win back your shears and avenge your Alex, but which will never be forgotten in history. And I will ask for nothing in return," he says.

He finally lets me go and I hunch forward on the rock, resting my elbows on my knees. I have to think. I know I can't win alone. Ares might be able to win alone, but even he would have a difficult time against such odds. Alone, I will surely lose.

I slide my eyes toward Ares still sitting beside me. Why

does it have to be him? I told him it was long done and buried between us, but I lied. While I have moved on and loved Alex with everything I had, Ares is still my first love. A girl never forgets the first time she gives her heart away, particularly not when it is returned to her in such a brutal manner.

It doesn't matter that centuries have passed, that wound is still raw. Spending every day with Ares will only continue to chafe it. However, if I want to win this war, save my family and Hades, and remain immortal with even a tiny chance of seeing Alex again someday, I have to use Ares.

I huff out a breath, standing up. Ares rises and stands next to me.

"Okay. I'll take your help," I say through my teeth.

"Don't sound so enthusiastic," he chides.

I stick my hand out. He takes it, and we shake on the bargain.

"We're agreed, then?" he asks.

"We're agreed. You will train me and teach me the ways of war, and we will win back my shears and avenge Alex. And then we will go our separate ways," I add.

"Oh boy. This is going to be fun," Ares says, rubbing his hands together and gleefully pondering the art of war.

We leave the portal and head back to the car, Ares talking non-stop about his plans and me trudging along behind, completely unsure about what I've just let myself in for.

ARES WANTS TO SET OUT ON OUR MISSION IMMEDIATELY, BUT I
want to visit my family one last time. I don't want to disappear
without a word. I want to say goodbye in case I fail and end
up cut off from them forever. Plus, I want to warn them about
what might be in store for them. They deserve a chance to make
contingency plans. Besides, I need to pack.

After arguing for thirty minutes in the car, Ares finally gives
in and says we can go back to my house for the night. I get to
spend one more night in my room. Ares can bunk in the damn
basement, for all I care.

Once that's settled, I can't get him to stop blathering on
about his plans for war. I tune most of it out, wanting to live in
a bubble of denial for just a bit longer, but I tune back in when
he starts discussing an actual battle scenario and my role in it.

"It will be bloody and painful. Especially for you," Ares
muses.

"Why more for me than for you?" I ask.

He stops talking and stares at me. "You really don't know?"

"Know what?" I ask.

"Did you ever ask Zeus why you have to dip your sword in

your own blood to bring it to its full size?"

"No. I just assumed that it was so I could easily conceal it in whatever I was wearing."

"Partly, yes. But Zeus insisted that it be made that way so that you couldn't injure someone without injuring yourself. It was supposed to make you think about the consequences of your actions and to make sure that you only used the sword when there was a good reason. In other words, something so important or life-threatening that injuring yourself was worthwhile."

"Did Zeus think I was going to go around hacking people's heads off for no reason?" I ask.

"Not necessarily. It was a precaution. All the gods who have weapons, except for Zeus' siblings and myself, are under similar restrictions. Ever notice how some gods are only given weapons when they are sent on a specific quest? Or how weapons are only given as gifts after a certain level of trust is reached? And how most of you outside of Olympus don't even have them?"

"I noticed, but I never thought much about it," I confess.

"You only have your sword because Hades stood up to Zeus and made a convincing case as to why you should be armed. He felt that someone dealing with death needed protection. Turns out he was right."

"So what is Zeus protecting against? Against one of us going rogue and killing humans?"

"No. He's protecting himself and the other Olympians. The fewer armed gods and demigods, the fewer threats to his power."

"Well, that's kind of ridiculous," I say. "It's not like we can kill him."

"No, but enough gods working together could capture and bind him. You know that Zeus overthrew Kronos, his own father, and that Kronos overthrew his father, Uranus, before that. Zeus lives in fear that one of his children will do the same to him. Therefore, the limit on weapons."

I start to laugh at the very idea, but then I realize it makes a twisted kind of sense. Maybe Zeus' paranoia is justified, given his family history. "So to wage war on the Keres, I will have to repeatedly cut myself in order to use my sword."

"Yes."

"Well, I could just leave it extended permanently," I say.

"Aside from the attention a claymore-wielding young woman would draw among the humans, your sword won't stay extended forever."

"It won't?"

"No. You've always retracted it yourself to keep it from being noticed or in the way but if you don't retract it, it will retract itself after six hours."

"Well, that sucks," I say.

"It does. It likely would never have been a problem for you, but in a full-blown war campaign that will likely have many long battles, you're going to get awfully tired of slicing yourself open," he says. "Even if you do heal quickly," he adds.

"Can't you loan me some other weapons?" I ask.

"No. Zeus was very clear on that point with regards to helping you. I can help you, and I can fight for you using my own weapons, but I cannot give you anything of mine."

"Zeus sure did think of all the ways to make this as hard as possible for me, didn't he?" I ask bitterly, already wondering how I can steal a few swords. Where do you go to steal a sword, anyway? It's not like they sell them at Walmart.

"I'm still looking for loopholes," Ares says. "It would be helpful if I found a few before we begin this suicide mission."

His comment about suicide reminds me that there is likely a consequence for him, too.

"You didn't tell me what happens to you if we fail," I say. "Do you get off completely free, since you were only added to this game to make it sporting?"

"No, I don't get off free. Do you seriously think Zeus would miss a chance to punish me? If we fail, I will no longer be the god of war. That job will go to Athena. Can you imagine? She's never waged a proper war in her life. Too busy being the peacemaker and protector. She doesn't have the killer instinct," he says.

"That's a shame," I sarcastically mutter.

"I will be made mortal and normal. Weak." A shudder passes through him at the very thought of being reduced to normalcy.

"I will die eventually. Unlike you, though, I'll at least get to go to the Underworld. Zeus said that since I'm his son, he couldn't deny me that right."

"But he could deny it to his daughter," I say.

Ares shrugs. "You know he never makes sense."

"I'm sorry," I say. "You didn't have to get involved in this."

"Don't be. I wouldn't have volunteered if I didn't believe we could win. And if we lose, well, I think it will have been fun to try."

"Fun's not the word that comes to mind," I say.

We are silent for a while, both of us lost in our own thoughts. Finally, Ares speaks.

"You know you can't save him, right?"

"Who?" I ask.

"Alex. You do know that nothing that happens will bring him back. He's lost to you forever."

"I know that. And that's not why I'm doing this."

But if I am honest with myself, there is a part of me that is taking on this suicide mission for exactly that reason. Some part of me believes that I can save Alex. If I just prove myself good enough or strong enough, surely the gods will restore him to me.

"Keep telling yourself that and maybe you'll believe it," Ares says. "I see it on your face. You're harboring some hope that victory will give him back to you."

"Look. I know you're right and I'll adapt to that reality soon. But he's only been dead for two days. For crap's sake, aren't I entitled to a few fantasies?"

"Sure you are. But war is a costly thing. All the killing, the pain, and the suffering will cost you your soul. I'm immune to that because my soul was compromised a long time ago. I have nothing left to lose. But you do.

"It's fine to go into it wanting vengeance because vengeance is something you can attain and, once you have it, you can live

265

with and justify the things you did in war. Wanting vengeance can carry you past the ugliness to victory.

"Wanting to save someone is no reason for entering into war, though. You can't win that battle and the war will only leave you emptier than you are now. So if you're only doing this to save him, to bring him back, go to Zeus and take your punishment now. You'll be better off."

"Wise words from someone like you," I say.

He shrugs. "I've seen it all, and I know which wars are winnable and which are not. You have two wars you can fight here. The war fought for vengeance against the Keres and Thanatos is winnable. The war fought for personal gain or the return of love will bring you nothing but loss, in every way."

"Then I'll fight for vengeance," I say.

"Good girl," Ares says. "As Shakespeare said in Henry the Sixth,

'Oft have I heard that grief softens the mind,
And makes it fearful and degenerate;
Think therefore on revenge and cease to weep.'"

"I didn't know you had a poetic bone in your body," I say.

"Grief has no place in war. Bury it deep and concentrate on revenge."

We reach my house, and I pull into the driveway. Chloe and Mom come running out to meet me. Of Lacey, there is no sign. They stop and glare as Ares unfolds himself from the front seat of the Thunderbird.

"What's he doing here?" Chloe asks.

They look ready to murder Ares. They know our history, of course, and it's gratifying to see that they so readily defend me.

"It's a long story," I say, herding everyone inside.

As Ares and Chloe pass through the front door, Ares bending so he won't conk his head on the lintel, I hang back and pull Mom with me.

"Ares and I leave tomorrow to try to get my shears back and end this business with the Keres and Thanatos."

I give her the quick-and-dirty version of the game Zeus has

laid out for me.

"Is it a good idea to go with him?" Mom asks, looking into the house at Ares, who is looking at our family pictures on the mantel.

"Probably not," I admit. "But he's all I have now; the only one who can help me."

"Do you trust him? He has a tendency to switch sides in battle just for the fun of it, you know. He might sacrifice you for his own gain."

"He might, but I don't think he will. He has a stake in this, too, and I think he'll play fair. But no, I don't really trust him." I sigh. "I have no other choice, though. Thank Zeus for that, would you?" I say.

Mom just reaches out and hugs me. "You go kick their butts from here to the Underworld and back. Just be safe doing it," she pleads.

"I'll try. If I fail, and Zeus carries out his punishment, I'll never see you again and you'll have to live with Ker. I just want to say goodbye and thank you for helping me through the centuries. And to apologize if you get stuck with Ker."

"Don't even talk like that," Mom says. "You'll be back before you know it."

"Maybe. But I just wanted you to know that I love you. I know I don't say it often, but Alex opened that part of me again, and I want you to know it."

"I know it. And I love you, too," she says.

We stand there on the sidewalk, nothing left to say. Mom has tears in her eyes, and I hate that I've put them there. She reaches for me again and we embrace until we hear Ares yelling from inside.

"Little Atropos, your sister baked a cake and I want to eat. Get your butt in here."

Mom and I break apart, laughing.

"It's going to be a long journey," I say. "With him, at least, it won't be dull."

"Well, then, let's go inside and eat that cake and get you

packed. The sooner you go, the sooner you can return," Mom says.

We walk inside, arm in arm. My family will help me get ready for this battle, and they'll be here if I return. If I don't return, well, I can only hope they'll find some happiness in life and maybe miss me a little. Knowing my mother, she'll make it her mission to make Zeus' life miserable for eternity. That thought makes me smile.

When we walk into the kitchen, Ares extends his hand to me and I take it, joining my other hand with Mom's as he leads us to the table. We eat and talk for hours, everyone offering opinions and ideas on how best to defeat the Keres.

It's well after midnight when Mom and Chloe decide it is time to turn in. Before she leaves, I tug Chloe aside.

"Where's Lacey?"

She shrugs. "Don't know. She took off right after you left for Alex's house and hasn't come back since."

There's something odd about that. Lacey doesn't just "take off," and I can't see her wanting to miss all the drama circulating through the house. If nothing else, she'd enjoy being here to lap up my failure. I don't have time to figure out her quirks, though.

"Should I take the couch, or would you rather I sleep outside?" Ares asks after Chloe's gone upstairs.

"Neither. I don't want long, drawn-out goodbyes in the morning. I've said all I need to say. Let's just go," I say.

"Are you sure?"

"Very. Just let me throw some things together. We'll go tonight."

"Okay. I'll wait outside."

Running upstairs, I pack as quickly as possible, taking only the essentials. I double check that the necklace Alex gave me is fastened around my neck, and I throw the only picture I have of him into my bag.

I took it the day after we brought Maggie home, during Alex's first visit to my workroom. He was sitting on the stool by the door and he'd smiled for me, but beneath the smile was awe

268

and wonder at my room and my job. I realize now that it was one of the last times I really saw him smile before his illness took that spark away.

Zipping the bag shut, I drag it downstairs to the basement. I want to check my workroom to see if there's anything there that might help me. When I open the door to the room of lifelines, I'm shocked by the change. Instead of the glittery, soft lifelines that shimmered so brightly from my racks, I see only rusty, stiff, jagged lines. They look more like old coat hangers that have been unfolded and left to hang out in the weather for decades.

People are dying in unnatural ways and at unnatural times, and their lines aren't being disposed of properly. It doesn't mean much outside of this room, but to me, it is a horrible sight to see. It only illustrates just how far out of control death has become.

I don't find anything in my work area that will help me, so I head back upstairs. At the front door, I pause long enough to look around my house one last time. I know now what Alex felt when I carried him out of his room on his last night. To think or to know that you'll never return to your home is to feel scared, lost, and sad all at the same time. This is just one of many houses I've shared with my family, but the sense of loss is as strong as if it were the only one.

Ares is waiting for me on the front porch, and I hand my bag to him. We climb into the Thunderbird. I crank the engine and back down the driveway.

"Which way?" I ask as I pull out on to the main road.

"We'll head for my place on Mount Washington, first, so I can gather what we need. We'll take a couple of days there to plan."

He glances over at me as I drive.

"You okay?" he asks.

"Not really, but I'll get it together before we have to fight. I won't fall apart on you in battle, if that's what you're asking."

"Good. You know, I'm not a complete asshole. I'll do whatever I can to help you win this war."

"Thanks. That means a lot."

269

Surprisingly, it does mean a lot. I still hate him for what he did to me, but I can see a hint of greater maturity in him. He is no longer the man of my dreams but, as he said, neither is he a complete asshole, either. He's a man with his own motivations, but also a desire to help me. To make amends. I begin to think that we might be able to pull off this crazy mission, after all. And if we fail? At least I won't fail alone.

About the Author

JENNIFER DERRICK BECAME A WRITER AT THE AGE OF SIX WHEN her parents bought her a child's typewriter for Christmas and agreed to pay her a penny per page for any stories she churned out. When she got older, Jennifer realized that she needed to make (much) more money from her writing so she first turned to the corporate world (where she learned that she is spectacularly unsuited to cubicle life) and ultimately to freelancing where she now writes everything from technical manuals to articles on personal finance and European-style board games. Her writing career came full circle when Clean Teen Publishing published Broken Fate, her first novel. By her calculations, her parents owe her about $3.00 for the book.

She lives in North Carolina and, when not writing, can often be found reading anything she can get her hands on, playing board games, watching sports, camping, running marathons, and playing with her dog.

Acknowledgements

The biggest thank you goes to my family. You all never fail to support whatever strange endeavors I pursue. Jimmy, thank you for never giving up on me and for telling me that I could do it, no matter how many times I swore I couldn't. Mom and Dad, thank you for raising me to be a reader and a lover of stories. You never batted an eye at whatever weird stuff I carted home from the library and you launched my writing career with a kiddie typewriter and a promise to pay a penny per page for my stories. (I'll collect my $2.80 for this one soon.) I only hope my stories have improved over the years.

I'd also like to thank the fabulous folks at Clean Teen Publishing. Thank you for opening your door to me and making me feel welcome from day one. You took the ugly little file that lived on my computer and turned it into a swan. Thank you especially to Melanie Newton for seeing my pitch and getting this crazy hamster ball rolling, Cynthia Shepp for a thorough education in editing, and Marya Heiman for a gorgeous cover. Most of all, thank you all for making this process fun.

I also owe a big thank you to my friends at iSlaytheDragon. com. You pushed/shamed me into getting on Twitter, even though I didn't want to be there. But now you get to say, "I told you so," because it was my participation in #Pit2Pub that led to Broken Fate's publication. I owe this one to you guys.

CPSIA information can be obtained at www.ICGtesting.com
Printed in the USA
LVOW10s1131200516

489198LV00002B/15/P

9 781634 221658